Copyright © 2023 by Claire O'Connor

All rights reserved.

This book is a work of fiction. Should a part of this book resemble any real life stories or characters, please note it is completely coincidental.

No portion of this book may be reproduced in any form without written permission from the author, except as permitted.

For Pen,
Your encouragement and cheerleading never cease to amaze me,
Thank you.

Contents

1. Chapter One ... 1
THREE MONTHS EARLIER ... 8
2. Chapter Two ... 9
THREE MONTHS LATER ... 12
3. Chapter Three ... 13
4. Chapter Four ... 18
5. Chapter Five ... 21
6. Chapter Six ... 26
7. Chapter Seven ... 30
8. Chapter Eight ... 35
9. Chapter Nine ... 39
10. Chapter Ten ... 42
11. Chapter Eleven ... 48
12. Chapter Twelve ... 57

13. Chapter Thirteen	59
14. Chapter Fourteen	62
15. Chapter Fifteen	69
16. Chapter Sixteen	74
17. Chapter Seventeen	81
18. Chapter Eighteen	86
19. Chapter Nineteen	96
20. Chapter Twenty	105
21. Chapter Twenty One	108
22. Chapter Twenty Two	113
23. Chapter Twenty Three	117
24. Chapter Twenty Four	121
25. Chapter Twenty Five	123
26. Chapter Twenty Six	127
27. Chapter Twenty Seven	136
28. Chapter Twenty Eight	141
29. Chapter Twenty Nine	146
30. Chapter Thirty	150
31. Chapter Thirty One	154
32. Chapter Thirty Two	159
33. Chapter Thirty Three	163
34. Chapter Thirty Four	169
35. Chapter Thirty Five	176
36. Chapter Thirty Six	181

37. Chapter Thirty Seven — 187
38. Chapter Thirty Eight — 195
39. Chapter Thirty Nine — 201
40. Chapter Forty — 204
41. Chapter Forty One — 209
42. Chapter Forty Two — 211
43. Chapter Forty Three — 214
44. Chapter Forty Four — 217
45. Chapter Forty Five — 221
46. Chapter Forty Six — 223
47. Chapter Forty Seven — 229
48. Chapter Forty Eight — 236
49. Chapter Forty Nine — 238
50. Chapter Fifty — 248
51. Chapter Fifty One — 254
52. Chapter Fifty Two — 258
53. Chapter Fifty Three — 265
54. Chapter Fifty Four — 271
55. Chapter Fifty Five — 274
56. Chapter Fifty Six — 278
57. Chapter Fifty Seven — 282
58. Chapter Fifty Eight — 285
59. Chapter Fifty Nine — 293
60. Chapter Sixty — 295

| About the author | 299 |
| Also by | 301 |

Chapter One

She didn't twant to stab him but what was the alternative? Despite the support of those around her, she managed to create chaos, ultimately impacting someone's life. They warned her. The strength and independence she believed she had was nothing more than fear and stubbornness. Unfortunately, she wasn't the only one that reaped the repercussions.

It was one of those bright days at the end of Summer when the birds chirped, and the spirits were high. Keziah walked through the park towards the bus stop. The sound of the fountain trickling and the children laughing at the squirrels scuffling around made her smile. Her first days here in the park, taking the plunge and leaving the flat alone had been monumental. She learned to relax again in this park, if not reading, she jogged or just sat by the fountain, thinking. This place had been a sanctuary for her. They were good days even though it didn't feel like it at the time. Who could have guessed what would happen next. Finding a seat on the bus, she checked she had everything in place. The note to pass on, hopefully to Mother Abi, was rolled up in her purse inside some cash. Her wire had been fitted earlier, and her phone was in her shopping bag with her list.

The bus pulled in, groaning before it came to a slow stop. Keziah hopped off and began the walk towards the monthly market. It occupied a massive walled wasteland of a demolished factory. This neighbourhood was full of 'hipsters', as Ish called them, ready to buy quality produce. If only they knew the truth about these strange looking folks with long skirts and scarves, and what they were supporting by spending their money on the stall of The Genus.

Growing up, she'd never been allowed to go. Mostly, the Bearers went because the Carers were much busier with their duties. Back then she thought she'd be chosen as a Carer, like Mother Abi, and certainly not a Bearer to *his* children. A knot formed in her stomach at seeing some of the people from her past. She didn't know who'd be there, but would they even give her the time of day? The men who escorted them usually hovered around, patrolling. If they spotted her they'd attempt to stop any communication, but as agreed with the detectives, she would try to talk to one of them in this case, just to plant the seed she was around and trying to make contact.

Once inside the gates Keziah scanned the place. They were nowhere in sight, so she had time to browse around casually. On her right, cured meats hung on large metal hooks beside ribbons of dried chillies. Rounds of bright yellow cheeses sat proudly on stalls alongside bulbous loaves, homemade jams and preserves. It reminded her of the amazing apple compote Mother Abi used to make and probably still did. To her left were the clothes and craft stalls. She'd make her way around from this side and hopefully spot them from a distance. Ambling through the stalls, she stopped to watch a couple of elderly ladies crochet lace items. Another sat contentedly knitting scarves she sold on the stall. Mother Abi taught her how to sew and knit when she was very young, and she'd taken to it like a duck to water, that and baking. Keziah missed the slower pace of life in The Genus. And through her therapy, she realised it was fine to admit it. It could never compensate the abuse and humiliation she suffered on a daily basis on the other side of the wall. Maybe she should start doing those things she missed out here? Why not? She was healing, going in the right direction, and here she was going back in.

She could run now and cancel the whole thing. Ish would be happy, and probably Yvonne too. The detectives would understand. They've said all along she could opt out any time. Fear was late arriving, and it slapped Keziah hard across the face. She ran to the toilet in the centre of the marketplace and threw up. As she stood up against the dirty old tiles of the factory toilets, her only thought was of Zadie. In all this madness, if she could somehow, manage to get Zadie's daughter out then everything would be worth it. Of course, the detectives wouldn't approve. The plan, repeated time and time again, rattled off word for word in her mind at this stage. Get in, get data, and get out. But, if she could help some members escape, surely it would be even better?

Keziah bent over the rusty old sink and splashed cold water all over her face, rubbing it into the back of her neck. Just as she began to dry off with a wad of paper towels, she heard someone come in. Her face still dripping, she looked up to see Charity glaring at her from the entrance.

"Charity! How are you?"

The young woman's face turned into a dark angry scowl. "I have nothing to say to you," she hissed.

Keziah heard the emotion in her voice and thought it best not to contradict her.

"Everything got messed up Charity. It wasn't meant to happen the way it did."

Charity looked her up and down. 'Why are you here?"

Keziah held up her shopping bag with a grin. "I'm here to get some bread and cheese."

"I don't want to see you! Just...just go away."

She rushed past her into a booth. Keziah jumped with the slam of the door. The sound of sobbing came from the cubicle.

"I'm so sorry for leaving you. It all happened so quickly. He was going to..."

Stopping to remind herself she was to make everyone believe she sought repentance, she redirected her approach. "I'm so sorry for everything."

"What are you really doing here?"

"I wanted to see you all, from afar. I miss you all: Mother and you and the other girls."

"Why didn't you come back when Father gave you a chance? You were shown the light again and you refused it." She spoke quietly between sobs. "I don't think you should be here, Keziah."

Keziah didn't want to ruin this chance so had to think on her feet. "Who is here with your today? Is Mother here?"

"Yes, and she will follow me if I don't get back soon."

"Are you a mother now?"

Silence.

"Do you have any of the delicious apple compote on the stall today?"

The door opened. Charity's face was softer now, but tear stained, full of caution and fear.

She put her hands out onto her Charity's shoulders. "I'm so sorry about how things happened; with you and the plan we had, and with Abe."

"Keziah, you're going to get me in trouble, again."

"Do you think Mother Abi would sell me some of your compote?" She was trying to make her laugh in the childish way she used to but was instead met by a harder and darker exterior.

"I can't account for what Mother would say or do. Now I have to go." She stormed out and Keziah watched as she bumped into Mother Abi. They spoke for a moment and walked away together. From Keziah's vantage point, it didn't look like Charity had revealed her presence. She stood against the sink wondering how best to approach things when she heard the crackle in her ear.

"Keziah, you're doing great. Go back out and continue to browse. Locate their stall."

"Okay, Jim."

At the very least she would get her bread and cheese and come back next month. Continuing around until the end of the clothes and craft section, she stopped and looked at the start of the food section of the circular market. After buying a large crusty bloomer and some unpasteurized cheese she spotted the Genus stall just two stalls up, so stopped and pretended to scan a stall selling craft beers and wines.

"Would you like to try some dear?,'" called an old red-faced gentlemen as he handed her a plastic cup of cider.

She smiled. "Why not?"

Dutch courage, they called it. She necked the little cup as she watched the women fuss around the stall and restock the bread from their van behind. One of the men stood studying every move the women made. This was going to be tough.

A younger woman smiled politely as she exchanged some bread for money with an elderly lady. Mother Abi stood between the stall and the van overseeing all customer transactions. Strands of grey hair escaped her head scarf and the lines around her eyes were deeper. Keziah's heart skipped a beat. This woman cared for her since she was and infant. She changed her nappies when she was a baby. She nurtured and nourished her until the day she left. Her eyes with tears, and even though she tried to swallow them back, she cried, as she watched her aging mother.

Mother Abi's scanning eyes finally reached her, and they stared at each other. The woman's face turned from anger to joy. Keziah knew her emotional outbreak put her in a weak position before this mission even started, and it unsettled her. She wiped her tears and raised her eyebrows as if she was asking for an invitation over. Mother Abi smiled in response and so she began to amble towards her.

As she got near enough to be heard, she held up her shopping bag and smiled.

"I was just out getting a few things when I remembered your delicious apple compote. I had a sudden urge to see if you were here."

Mother Abi pursed her lips and put up her hand as if to tell her to come no further. "Child, we cannot speak to you. You must go away."

Keziah took a deep breath in. "I understand. I know how much I hurt you. I'm sorry Mother."

"I am not your mother now. You chose a different life, Keziah. Please go, before one of the men see you."

"Okay, but can I at least buy the compote?" Keziah held out the money.

Mother Abi went to the stall and took two compotes from the pile. She looked sideways to check for the men guarding, and then walked quickly towards her.

"Here, take these. Please don't come back." She touched Keziah's chin softly. "It's not safe for you here."

Keziah swallowed hard and handed her the money, but Mother Abi shook her head and pushed her hand away.

Keziah glared at her and then the money. "Take the money – there's a note."

Mother Abi took the paper with shaking hands, and then turned on her heel. Once back at the stall she immediately got involved with a customer and began giving orders to the younger women. Charity stood at the edge of the stall watching it all.

Keziah lingered for a moment watching her mother, just a moment longer. She walked straight out of the market not stopping until she reached the bus stop. Tears streamed down her face as she thought about what might happen next. It was the first time she was genuinely frightened of what she had committed to. If this was how she behaved after one meeting, how would she cope with it all? She couldn't go back now. Not that the detectives would mind too much, but everyone else had become invested in this upon her insistence.

THREE MONTHS EARLIER

Chapter Two

Ish paced the floor, sighing as he moved. Zadie sat quietly in the armchair, with baby Rachel in her arms, staring into space. Yvonne, who was sitting in the armchair in the corner, cleared her throat and shifted a little. Everyone turned to her, knowing she would have some sensible input.

"It's a tough call. I'm worried for you Keziah. I know you want to help but you've been through so much, I'm just not sure it's the right time."

"It was ten months ago. You know how far I've come since then. I've been working very hard, and you even said the detective said I would be trained as if I were a professional, and I'll have a way out at all times."

Ish stopped pacing and stood in front of the old mantel staring at Keziah. "You're being naïve, Kez. If any of them, and I mean ANY of them, get a whiff of something suspicious, you're done for. You know what Sy is capable of. Consider the very worst that can happen because it can happen very easily. He's even crazier than before."

Zadie stood up. They waited for her to say something, but she just grabbed the baby bag and walked towards her bedroom.

Ish sighed. "And how do you think all of this affects Zadie? She's getting her hopes up on getting Laura out of there."

"If I go in there we might get the whole thing disbanded. We might be able to free everyone and get Sy imprisoned. I'm sorry. I don't think I can say no." Keziah looked over at Yvonne. "I'm going to call the detective and tell him I'm doing it."

Ish sat down on the sofa and looked up at Keziah. "This isn't going to end well."

"Ish, I agree with you," Yvonne sat back and folded her arms. "I understand this is an opportunity to stop Sy in his tracks, but it is dangerous. There might be some serious repercussions. From what the detective told me, Sy is becoming more erratic." Her eyes met Keziah's and she held her look.

"Is it not more of a reason for me to do it?"

"Keziah, you don't need to be a hero, you know," yelled Ish. He shook his head and crossed his arms.

"You think I'm looking for praise here, Ish? Look, let me go and talk to them about it. Let me understand what they want me to do. You can come if you like."

"This seems like a sensible approach. Ish?," queried Yvonne.

"I'm not sure I want to know the details."

"Sy deserves to be taken down. If the plan is simple and quick, I'd be so willing to help. Think of all the misery and trauma he caused us all."

"I mean, I just hope you're not doing it for the wrong reasons." Ish looked at her.

"What do you mean? What wrong reasons?"

"Well, guilt for starters, about Abe."

Keziah sucked her breath in. She looked over to Yvonne. "How is he?"

"He's pretty much the same, darlin'. I visited him last week. He recognised me. He's doing some intensive therapy and is very slightly more mobile but..."

"He or Sy could have killed you." Ish spoke firmly.

"Ish, it's not guilt! But think about how Sy manipulated Abe with false promises."

"He was vulnerable," agreed Yvonne.

"It doesn't matter. This is too dangerous. What was the point of ever getting out of there if you're willing to risk it all for – for something possibly worse."

THREE MONTHS LATER

Chapter Three

His curly grey hair and bulbous nose added a softness to his face. She was welcomed with a warm smile and a firm handshake.

"Keziah. I'm Detective Power. You can call me Frank, and this is my partner Detective Reagan, Amanda."

"Hello Keziah," smiled Amanda. "Will we find somewhere a bit more private to talk?" she asked the group.

They headed to a meeting room with a glass wall and executive chairs arranged around a large oval table. Detective Frank pulled the blinds closed.

He threw his file on the table and sat down across from her. "Look, there is a lot to this. I'm going to start at the beginning. Sy has been on our radar since well before he joined The Genus." He slid the file over towards Keziah.

She looked at Yvonne and picked it up.

"Fraud, domestic violence, tax crimes and other bits and pieces," he continued. "We suspect he was involved with a well-known gang called the Arma Bloods, in more recent times, moving cocaine at one point too. We don't have proof of that. It might have finished up."

"We knew about most of these, didn't we Keziah?" asked Yvonne. "But drug trafficking – this guy really has his finger in all the pies."

Keziah flicked through the file, stopping every now and then to look at photos of Sy when he was much younger. He looked different. Human.

"So, what exactly is it you can arrest him for right now?" asked Keziah.

"Well, we could try to use all of your statements, which could lead to multiple charges. But we don't want to go to a judge with just this. We have reports of him buying arms and selling them. We've also had one report about him being involved in some other organised crimes associated with a well- known gang in this city. But at this point, we have no evidence."

"The other thing we need to get on top of," said Amanda, "is, as you know, guardianship and DNA tests. Ideally, we'd like a judge to give us permission to go in there and test everyone. He is knowingly creating families with related couples, but we don't know to what extent. He is not registering births or deaths. That alone is highly illegal. We have no idea how many children are being born per year or many he is fathering. His crimes are running across almost all government departments."

"Ironically, he was quick to try to claim guardianship of Abe once he got wind of what happened," said Yvonne.

Detective Frank continued "We'd like someone on the inside who can access his office, files, computer, that kind of thing, or even just talk to people who know more. We'd like to know more about his coming and goings, any changes, you know, more information on what his daily activities look like. We're pretty sure he is using The Genus as a cover. Intel tells us his behaviour is becoming more and more erratic."

"And we don't want to get him seven years for kidnapping, if we can get thirty years for much more," added Amanda.

"What intel? Where did you get information? Charity?" Keziah couldn't imagine anyone else talking to the police and betraying Father Sy.

Frank smiled. "No, no. Not Charity. We've had one of -eh- his men working undercover for us for a while."

"Really?" Keziah was quite shocked at the idea of one of his guards going behind his back. "Which one?"

"It's better you don't know for now, but should you decide to proceed, he'll look out for you as much as he can."

"Frank," started Yvonne, "We're all a little concerned for Keziah's safety".

"Of course. This is a risky mission. There will be months of preparation both mentally and physically. It will need dedication."

He looked at Keziah. "If you go back in, the risk of some kind punishment is high. He may even try to marry you again."

"What if...," she started.

He interrupted. "Before we even go there let me tell you, we will have things in place to get you out very quickly should you need help."

Keziah nodded. Yvonne sighed and put her head down on the table.

"What I would suggest for now, if you're willing to proceed further, we start with an induction, then some training, knowing you can opt out any time."

She nodded again. "Makes sense. What exactly will the training involve?"

Detective Frank looked at Amanda. "Over to you."

"So, we'll start with some security and crime training, just to gain a base knowledge of what we can and cannot do. You'll have a personal trainer, you'll learn self-defence, and how to use undercover technology – a whole host of skills. We won't send you in until we think you're ready."

Yvonne nodded. "How long do you think it will take?"

"Anywhere from 1-3 months." said Detective Frank.

"I know you have worked in this area for a long time Frank, but may I ask, why Keziah? Why not ask Ish or one of the others who've been out longer and maybe a little, well, less vulnerable. As you know she has been through a lot and..."

Detective Frank put his hand up. "Keziah's vulnerabilities and length of time out here will just add to her authenticity. Her request to get back in, after everything happened, will be much more believable."

"It's a good time, and a perfect opportunity," said Amanda.

"Only because he'll be seething she escaped rather than marry him, and she managed to escape him a second time," persisted Yvonne.

"Ok. I'm going to do it." Keziah placed both her palms down on the table and looked at Yvonne.

"You don't need to make any decisions now, honey."

"No, Yvonne's right," said Detective Frank, "but the sooner we get going, the better. We know he's getting more erratic by the day. His rules are becoming even stricter, as are his punishments." He looked at Yvonne while Amanda spoke.

"Look, as we said, there's every opportunity to bow out right up till the end of the training, plus we'll be ready to pounce from outside if things go sideways." Amanda spoke to Yvonne and then looked at Keziah. "What do you say, how about just starting with the induction and we'll assess as we go?"

"Your studies, Keziah," sighed Yvonne

"Yvonne, I can defer my degree for a year. It's no problem."

They walked to the car in silence, both digesting what had been proposed. She appreciated Yvonne's care so much. She didn't push her at all.

As she dropped her home she gave her a tight hug. "Sleep on it, honey. We'll talk tomorrow."

Chapter Four

Mother Abi tensed at the familiar crackling of the gravel under the tyres of the van as it rolled up the stony path home. What a day, and what was she to do with the rolled-up note hid in the cuff of her sleeve. hat was to be done now? She suspected Charity caught something but did not want to ask her outright. Maybe she could take her directly under her wing so they could discuss Keziah together, calmly, and decide whether to react at all? But Charity did not have a great track record for keeping secrets. Keziah should not return home. Father Sy had tightened the ship, and they all suffered greatly for the sins of both Keziah and Abe. She discerned a much less pure approach in Father Sy's actions as of late. Dare she say it – a sadistic side she hadn't seen before. Where was she letting her mind go? Why couldn't she focus on The Goddess, who worked through Father Sy? He helped her to live a pure life.

The women waited in silence for one of the guards to slide the door open. They knew better to get up and try to disembark themselves. They were once known as wardens or stewards, and were there to help, not control. As they all began to pour out of the van with their baskets and left-over stock of the day, ready to store for the next market, she observed Charity hang back and let others out before her. Mother Abi was always the last to leave, as she liked to make sure everyone was out, and no one had forgotten anything. She turned and looked directly into the young women's eyes. Charity sat in her seat and looked back at her.

"Charity? What is it?"

"Keziah."

"She is lost to us. Forget her."

"Mother Abi, I know."

"Get to the dining hall this instant."

Charity raised her eyes and sighed. She got up slowly just as one of the men came to find out what the delay was. Mother Abi clucked and fussed in her usual motherly manner to avoid raising any concern.

"That's it Charity. Let us make our way to have supper."

She strolled up the rounding path to the main hall, with the girl walking slowly in front of her.

She looked around to make sure there was no one in hearing distance. "Charity, we must not let today's encounter bring up dark emotions. We should think no more of it."

"You hid something, Mother. Keziah gave you a note, didn't she?"

She flushed and as the panic rose inside. Charity's menacing tone unsettled her.

"It is no concern of yours. I will discuss it with Father Sy directly. Now, you watch your tone, or I will have one of the wardens take you to The Fulcrum for extra prayer. Do you understand?"

Charity turned on her heel and glared at her elder. She clenched her jaw as she nodded slowly.

"Yes, Mother Abi."

"Good. Now let us hurry. It has been a long day."

Mother watched her walk off sulkily. Now she had no choice but to tell Father about the note. While she wanted to keep Keziah safe, she must prioritise herself and their family first. She dreaded it, but she would request a visit with Father Sy this evening. Although always harsh in his service of the Goddess, since he spent time outside trying to get Keziah and Abe back, he was more volatile. A man like that, with such power, to fail so badly surely took its toll. She hadn't even read the note yet. It was dark now. The light over the door of the dining hall above on the hill lit the way down the path. Mother Abi braced herself for what was to come. It will be the will of Gena, she told herself.

Chapter Five

Things were strained in the flat. Zadie was not herself and Ish persisted in vocalising his frustrations with Keziah. Eli and Dorcus, when home at all, spent a lot of time in their rooms or with headphones on.

"Ish thinks I'm getting Zadie's hopes up," she told Yvonne at their weekly session.

"Come on now, you can see how it might upset her. You're going back in there, where her baby is, where her parents are."

"Exactly! I don't understand why everyone isn't as pumped as I am about this".

"They're scared."

"Eli and Dorcus avoid talking to me at all these days, unless it's small talk."

"Honey, they escaped The Genus. This business is bringing up old wounds. And they're worried about you too."

"I just feel like they're all missing the bigger picture here. The opportunity…no, the privilege, of being able to contribute to getting

Sy jailed is, well, it's simply great to think we can get rid of him once and for all."

"I do understand, but I think you're looking at things with rose-tinted glasses right now. Sure, it's great you can help, but you need to think about what it entails."

"I do. I know. And I am. Plus, it will be covered repeatedly in the training." Keziah threw her hands in the air and sat back in frustration. "Anyway, the date is set for the training to begin on Monday, so we'll all know more before too long."

"I'd like to remind you can do all the training, and still change your mind."

"Got it. Hey, didn't you go before the board last week? I completely forgot. I'm so sorry."

"It's not your job to remember these things. Anyway, it went okay. Thankfully, my history spoke for itself. I'll have a new direct manager though, and someone will be collaborating with me so I can put all my time into my cases. Every cloud has a silver lining."

Keziah leaned over and kissed her on the cheek. "Thank you for everything. I don't know what I'd have done without you during this time."

"You'd be doing as well as you're doing now. In fairness, I could have done better."

"Rubbish! Anyway, shall we go to the Lebanese restaurant to celebrate our last official appointment together?"

Yvonne grinned. "Sounds like a great idea." She began to pick up her papers and tidy up before leaving when she stopped in her tracks and turned around to her. "Keziah, you know I'm still here, right? We can still meet up weekly or every other week for a coffee and a chat?"

Keziah took Yvonne's hand and smiled. "I'd like that."

Next week she'd meet the personal trainer. It could be interesting. She could do with getting fitter, and learning self-defence appealed to her so much. She inhaled sharply, as she thought about Sy. The mere idea of facing him again made her cringe, so she shifted her focus to Mother Abi instead. At the very least Keziah was grateful to reunite and spend more time with her.

After work she headed home despite Lila's insisting on going out. Keziah wanted to suggest a pizza and movie to anyone at home this evening. She missed those evenings, and she guessed the others did too.

Zadie looked up and smiled as she sat on the big armchair by the window, feeding Rachel.

"Hey, I hope I'm not disturbing you. Will I put the kettle on?"

"Yes please. I'd love a tea."

Keziah brought the tea over, sat it on the table beside her, and sat herself back on the sofa.

"How are you doing?" asked Zadie.

"Honestly I feel good, but I don't like the atmosphere all this is causing around here."

"You know Ish. He's just being protective."

"It's not just that. The others are avoiding me, and you don't seem to be yourself at all."

"Well, you know, Rachel is teething already and I'm thinking about finishing the breastfeeding. I'm tired all the time. Being a mother is exhausting."

"It sounds tough. I'm sorry." Keziah took a sip of her coffee.

"Yvonne reckons I might have a touch of postpartum depression," she continued, "so we're looking into it." She forced a smile. "I just think I'm tired."

"Fancy a pizza and movie tonight?"

"Yes, if I can stay awake," she laughed.

"I'll try to get the others on board."

Zadie finished feeding Rachel and gently placed her in the bouncer at her feet. She was so careful and attentive.

"Listen, Zadie, I wanted to talk to you about Laura."

Zadie looked into her eyes, but Keziah couldn't read her expression.

"I don't want to put any pressure on you to do anything in there."

"No, but we should at least have a chat about it. Chances are my assignment will have nothing to do with caring for any children. I don't even know if I will see her. I have no idea what to expect in terms of day to day life in there."

"What do you want to talk about?"

"If I do see her, or your parents or –

"Then what?"

Keziah sighed and dropped her head. "Then I don't know."

"Exactly."

"I could talk to your parents, or bring a note to them?"

"Will the detectives let you do that?" Zadie's eyes widened.

"I don't know, but maybe they don't need to know about it."

"Let me think on it."

"Sure. I appreciate this is heavy stuff. I just think if I have the opportunity to talk with your family, I should take it."

Eli barged through the door and let his backpack fall from his arms to the floor with a thud. He walked to the fridge, took out a carton of orange juice and glugged it down. When finished, he threw it in the bin, burped and looked over at them.

"Hi!"

"Charming as always Eli," chided Zadie

"Eli, fancy a pizza and a movie tonight," asked Keziah.

"If it's not some sappy family drama, I'm in."

"How about romance then?" Keziah winked at Zadie.

"Definitely not." He grinned and made his way back down the corridor to his room.

Chapter Six

As she walked to work the following morning, Keziah thought about how to tell Lila she'd be away for a while. She smiled to herself as she thought about how working at the library had changed her life so much. Somehow, it made her feel part of this world. The staff welcomed her with open arms and knowing her past encouraged her in everything else she attempted to do. Lila became such a close friend.

"....So, then we just decided it was over. We've both had enough. It was amicable."

"Oh Lila, I'm so sorry. Even if it's amicable it's still sad."

Keziah grabbed her friend's hand across the table. Despite the sad news, Keziah was grateful for the distraction of other people's lives instead of her own.

"Ten minutes left on break. Do you want another coffee?"

"I've already had three today, Keziah! Oh, go on then."

They sat in the coffee shop on the ground floor of the city library, where they both worked. Just as Keziah stood up, she spotted a guy walking through the main entrance and straight to reception. It was the guy she used to watch from the window, the one who lived in a flat across the garden!.

"Who is it? You've gone puce."

"No, I haven't"

"Oooh, who's he? Nice hair!"

"He lives across the way from me."

"What's his name?"

"I have no idea. He's just a neighbour."

He stood chatting to Shane, one of the full-time receptionists. As he headed towards the stairs, he glanced sideways. They locked eyes and he smiled automatically. She smiled and waved, and suddenly feeling awkward and confused, she sat back down.

"Well, he knows you well enough to wave."

"Lila! Leave it."

"Okay, okay," she giggled.

Keziah got back up and went for the coffees. The reception area was quiet, and she heard Lila shouting over to Shane.

"Hey Shane! Who's that guy?

Shane grinned. "Who wants to know?"

"He's Keziah's neighbour."

"Oh right." He looked over at Keziah. "Joe, an old college friend. He's just started a master's, so I guess you'll see more of him around here."

"Oooh, Keziah. Opportunity ks."

Keziah shook her head in frustration as she sat back down with a smouldering face.

", please. The last thing I want is a relationship."

"He's a bit of a lady's man, I believe. You're probably right, Kez!" Shane called over with a grin.

He looked up and started to laugh. ", Joe?" Looking over at Keziah, he slapped his hand off the desk and laughed. "He's hanging off the mezzanine listening to everything and says to tell you I'm wrong, and he's not a lady's man."

The heat rose from her neck to her face. Keziah didn't appreciate this kind of thing at all. Lila was an open person, out there dating and making new friends all the time. She liked her personal privacy, and it annoyed her when Lila teased her like this.

"Never mind Lila! She'd do anything to embarrass me," she called over to Shane, hoping Joe could hear her.

As they walked back up the stairs, Keziah decided it was a good time to break the news to her.

"I might be taking some time off. I've got a chance to go to a kind of camp, you know, for ex cult members."

"That sounds good. What will you do there?"

"Ah it'll be mostly sharing, team activities, some counselling, dealing with trauma –you know the kind of thing."

Lila cocked her lip. "Doesn't sound like too much fun to me. Tell me there'll be guys there at least."

"I suppose," laughed Keziah, "but it's for up to three months."

"What?" Lila stopped in her tracks and stared at Keziah. "Why so long? I'm going to be so bored here without you."

"Oh, you'll be fine. I will look forward to hearing about your escapades when I return." Keziah put her arm around her friend as they walked.

"Well, we can chat, right?"

"Actually, no. It's quite an extreme kind of debriefing thing. No phones. I'll be in contact with Yvonne only."

"Kez, why in hell would you do this to yourself?"

"It will be good for me."

"Hmmm. When are you going?"

"In a few weeks."

Lila staggered back dramatically in shock. "I'll miss you."

They arrived to their workstations and put their bags under the desk.

"Me too."

Chapter Seven

Amanda was at reception fiddling with some papers when Keziah arrived at the foyer of the police station. She looked up with a smile and waved for her to take a seat. Keziah sat and watched the trees blowing in the wind out the window. This was it. She was doing it. She was starting training.

As she followed Amanda down the narrow corridor to her office, she passed a huge bucket on wheels with a mop sitting in it. The air smelled of something rotten along with pine-scented disinfectant.

"Sorry, one of our *guests* had a little accident."

Keziah grimaced and walked around the bucket leaving as much space as she could between it and her.

The place was old fashioned, with small high windows, giving little light.

"Please, take a seat and excuse the mess," said Amanda as she re-arranged files into one pile before pushing them aside. Once finished, she looked up and smiled.

"We're so glad to have you on board."

Keziah smiled and nodded. "Me too."

"I want you to know you can ask questions about anything at any time, and as Detective Power and I told you at our last meeting, you can change your mind at any time. Okay?"

"Yes. I understand." Keziah rung her hands.

"Great! Today we'll run through a few basics. Your personal trainer is around too, so you can say hello. He does circuit training classes for the staff a few times a week."

He.

As she walked back down the corridor, past the reception and on to the other side of the building, she blushed at the thoughts of training with a man. She hadn't considered it a possibility.

Amanda continued talking as she walked, her square heels clunking against the cold tiles. "He doesn't know anything about you going undercover. He only knows you have a mission you need to be fit for." She pushed the heavy door open with her back and held it with her body as Keziah entered.

"Keziah, meet Joe Roche."

His grin sent her into a tailspin and Keziah couldn't contain her embarrassment. It was the guy from the window, the one who recognised her from the library the other day. Joe. She wished the ground would swallow her up. No words would come. He sensed the awkwardness and walked forward with a warm smile and his hand out which she received politely with her sweaty palms.

"Keziah. I've seen you around. Wasn't that you at the library the other day?"

"Yes, I was with my friend having coffee. I work there. You're a friend of Shane's, right?" Grateful she managed to get some words out without sounding stupid, she began to relax.

"Yeah. Shane and I go back a bit."

"He said you were starting a master's?"

"Yep! I start this autumn. A Masters in. I think I must be mad."

"Well, isn't it a small world," chirped Amanda, "and yes, you are mad Joe. You need to stay here and keep us all fit."

"Eh, I haven't seen you at circuit training in a while."

She smacked him jokingly around the shoulders. "Cheeky!"

Keziah watched them tease and joke with each other, with a wide grin stuck on her face, still mortified about the whole situation. She used to watch him with binoculars through the window. She watched him with the girls he brought home. Her face became hotter and redder the more she thought about it.

He looked over at her. "So, we're going to be doing some training, I understand."

"Yes, you have your work cut out for you," she snickered.

. "I'll have you in ship-shape in no time."

Keziah flushed again. *Get me out of here.*

"So, what time are you in at tomorrow Joe? We want to get Keziah started straight away."

"Okay, eager beaver!" he laughed, "Keziah, does noon suit you tomorrow?"

"Yes, perfect."

They said their goodbyes before Amanda led the way further down the corridor. She looked over her shoulder with a cheeky grin.

"He's a looker, isn't he?"

"Yes, I suppose."

Amanda knocked and then opened the heavy double doors leading to a low-lit room. She switched the light on to reveal two men sitting in front of a group of screens.

"Here she is," joked a stout balding man holding a massive sandwich, slouched in his chair.

"Jeez! You're like two vampires in here." Keziah, this is Jim. Jim is our head technical undercover guy. The other one over there is Simon."

Simon waved and smiled.

Jim put his lunch down and swung around on his chair to shake her hand. "Hey Keziah. We'll be working together a bit. You'll mostly hear our voices, or Frank's, when you're wearing a wire."

"Right." She nodded seriously.

They showed her around and talked about what they would be able to hear, and how they use bugs, hidden cameras, wires, and all sorts of other devices. When done, they said their goodbyes and returned to Amanda's office.

"Okay, we have to get a lot of boring stuff out of the way first. We have to do the data protection and health and safety stuff." She raised her eyes to heaven and tutted like it was something she shouldn't have to do, but Keziah was determined to get the first part of this thing over and done with as soon as possible.

"Grab a chair there and come over to me. You'll be doing it here at my desk."

She obeyed and sat down beside her.

"Now, this is wordy, and you can't go back to check once you finish. At the end, there's a quiz. So, see where they have underlined and highlighted some facts? Yeah? I were you I'd take note of those because they will likely show up in the quiz. It's multiple choice, so not rocket science but it does take some people a few attempts."

She handed Keziah a hardback notebook and a pen. "Here, you'll need this. Bring it every day."

Amanda stood up and Keziah moved into her seat.

"I'm off for the rest of the day. You can take as long as you want here, and if you need help with anything, talk to Doreen at reception. Okay?"

"Yep. I'll get going on the first one."

"Great. You're doing great. Tomorrow we'll talk some more." She smiled and waved before leaving the room.

Keziah scooched further over to the desk to make herself comfortable. She'd get one of these quizzes done today. They were like the beginner computer courses she did in the library.

On the way out, Joe entered the reception area from the other side. He smiled and waved over at her not realising they were both exiting the main door.

"Joe! What should I wear tomorrow? Will my running clothes do?"

"You run?" He raised his eyebrows and grinned. "I'll go a bit harder on you then."

She laughed. "I *try* to run."

"We'll have you as fit as fiddle in no time."

They stood outside the main entrance to the building in silence for a few seconds.

"Looking forward to seeing you tomorrow, Keziah." He waved and turned to walk away.

"Me too! Bye," she called after him. He turned and smiled.

Why did she say, 'me too'? Cringe. She didn't know how to talk to men who weren't family or friends. Marching off she put her hand over her scorching red face, reliving her words. Her awkwardness didn't seem to faze him though, thankfully.

Chapter Eight

so intensely Mother Abi almost wondered if he could see right through her, see all of her sins, all of her fears and thoughts. His silence unnerved her. Father Sy sat on a huge armchair he had specially made and shipped into The Genus. It was finished in luxury black leather, with high quality upholstery and an extra tall back, fitting a king.

She jumped when he finally moved. He held his hand up, crunching Keziah's note and throwing it on the floor.

He spoke through clenched teeth. "Mother Abi, what do you think this whore, this evil, selfish whore, wants from us?'

This conversation had played out in her head again and again, and she replied immediately. "I do not know, Father. I told her to go away, and she said she missed us and she was sorry."

"Sorry is it?" He roared.

Mother Abi flinched. "Father, I did not know whether to accept the note or not."

"You did well to take the note for me to see. We can prepare. This degenerate denied the Goddess. She has all but killed my son and her brother. She was never quite right, was she?"

He stood up and walked slowly towards the woman, who knelt with her head down.

"She was an obedient and faithful child, Father."

"You thought so, didn't you? But when it came time for her to demonstrate her obedience and faith, she didn't, did she?"

"No, Father." Mother Abi watched from under her brow as he bent over to pick the note up. The sweat glistened on his forehead, and he panted as he stood upright.

"You will engage. You will reply and you will lure her back to face her rightful punishment."

This was exactly what she hoped he wouldn't say. She raised her head slowly and swallowed her tears as she listened to his instructions.

The following morning, Mother Abi sat on the porch shelling peas, watching the younger children play in the yard. She'd seen so many of them up into adulthood, to marriage or into training as a Carer. So many little ones, all with different personalities, all with different strengths and weaknesses. Oliver tumbled over a chicken who squawked mercilessly. The other kids laughed and teased him as he lay on the powdery dirt, crying at his grazed knee. Silvia, only months older, walked over to him with a smile on her face and offered him her hand. How similar their bond was to that of Keziah and Abe when they were the same age.

She cleared her throat. Sentimentality had no place in her heart right now. Even though she guided both of them, Keziah and Abe, into the hands of Gena, they defied her. She never truly understood why they, in particular, those two soft hearted children, decided to run. If anything, she thought they would do well in The Genus, making decent lives for themselves under the leadership of Father Sy.

She sighed at the thought of him. He had changed so much and lately she had found herself doubting his motives. It took her months to even admit to herself she worried for the safety of the children, and indeed the whole community. He had always been a zero-tolerance leader, and she always believed he was right – until Abe – until Keziah hurt Abe. It shocked her to the core. She wasn't their birth mother, but she *was* their mother. Tracking the Bearers' children was nigh on impossible, and she had given up years before. Years and years she spent nurturing and teaching them, preparing them for adulthood. Now one was completely debilitated, doomed to life of debilitation. The other, well, the other was a mystery. It was hard to say what Keziah was up to, or what she thought she was doing coming back in, but Mother Abi wished she would stay away.

Since the day Keziah escaped, she'd had a niggling pressure to confront her own doubts on Sy's practices for matching and mating. She was often brought back to the ugly night when Keziah bolted. The girl was scared – no, petrified. And she, her mother, forced her into it. Outside The Genus it wasn't allowed, the matchmaking. She barely remembered outside. She was only seven years old when her mother brought her to meet Mother Sarah and Father Ray.

Mother Sarah and Father Jim. Those were happy days. They took in wayward women like her mother, and taught them how to live wholesomely through love, trust and duty, not through shame and punishment. Everyone wept the day Father Ray died. Mother Sarah was never the same again. Mother Abi's own mother changed too, and she did not take to Father Sy, who appeared suddenly to take over from his Aunt. Within days, Father Sy had declared himself the messenger of the Goddess and demanded they all pledge their allegiance and honour to him as the new leader of The Genus.

Mother Abi shook herself to get on with things at hand. She got up and gathered the pea shells to put them on the compost heap around the side of the house. As she emptied the basin into the bin, she felt a presence behind her. Charity stood in silence watching her. She snorted at Mother Abi's shock and shook her head.

"Mother Abi, what has you so jumpy these days?"

Mother continued to empty the basin and walked back around the house, passing Charity without looking at her.

"Whatever are you talking about? And why aren't you tending the hens instead of creeping around startling people?"

Charity laughed again. Mother Abi did not want her to feel her uneasiness. She walked into the kitchen and closed the door. For a brief moment, she felt panic like she had never known before. Her hands tightly held the side of the counter as she breathed slowly until she felt better. Opening her eyes, she looked out the window. The day was turning to evening. She watched Charity march to the bottom of the yard where the hens were, scolding the children as they gathered around to watch her feed them.

Chapter Nine

The sessions with Joe were going well. She had fun working out with him. He really knew his stuff too. They did resistance training in the gym at the station, once per week and then they arranged running at the local track once or twice per week. She'd lost loads of weight and finally started to feel comfortable in her leggings and sports vests.

She laughed a lot with him. He was really charming and had a great sense of humour. Every time she remembered how she used to look at him across the way in the window, she cringed. One day he caught her looking over and waved. She'd been so embarrassed she got tangled in the wire of the lamp and fell, dragging herself to the bed under the window so he wouldn't see her. Sometimes in the gym, he got very close, to show her how to move or hold her in place while she lifted. Every time he touched her, her pulse soared, she was sure. It was a good job she wasn't wearing one of those gym monitors or it would explode.

After their workouts they sat down with a drink and their towels and chatted. They talked about all sorts of things and sometimes he looked at her in amusement, like he couldn't quite figure her out.

"So, I take it you're off on some mission they can't tell me about?"

"I can't."

"It's okay. I understand. I'm a police officer too, you know. Well, ex. I retired last year."

"I didn't realise. How come?"

"It just wasn't for me. It took ages to get promoted from traffic, and then they put me on the beat in a bad area. To be honest, it just wasn't enjoyable or fulfilling."

"So, you stayed on as a trainer."

"For now. Physical fitness was my favourite part of training at the academy, so it made sense to stay on until I decided what to do next."

"I'm glad you did," she smiled and blushed and tried to change the subject quickly. "You are so young to be on your second career and working towards your third in law."

He smiled knowingly. She could sense he knew she liked him. God knows what Lila told Shane in order to set them up.

"And what about you Miss Keziah. You're a bit of an enigma, are you not?"

"Not really. I just, kind of, changed lives and moved to the City last year."

"And you live across the garden from me."

"Yeah. I live with a group of friends in a flat."

He looked into her eyes. She looked back, readily. His hair was shorter now, but soft curls still fell down around his big brown eyes.

"Hey, maybe sometime we could, you know – I mean – I probably shouldn't be asking you but I'm moving on out of the police..."

"What?". Keziah searched his face.

"Maybe we could go out on a date sometime – just for a coffee or whatever." It was the first time she's seen him blush and her cheeks matched his quickly.

"Oh right." She smiled and looked into his eyes. "I'd like that."

Amanda walked in and they both jumped up quickly.

She stood looking at them for a moment with a smirk before she spoke. "Keziah, Jim wants to run through a couple of things with you in the morning, okay?"

"Sure, yeah. Thanks."

"Hey Amanda, fancy a run?" Joe laughed out loud at her expression.

"Sod off, Joe, do I look like I'm dressed for a run, eh? I'm too busy!"

"Excuses, excuses!"

Keziah got on with packing her bag with her gear and headed to the showers.

"Two more sessions left, Keziah," he called after her, "unless you want to fit in a run around the neighbourhood next week sometime?"

"Definitely." *Too eager.* "Sounds like a good idea. I need all the help I can get." She laughed her embarrassment off and pulled her hoody over her head. *Cringe.*

"Hey, maybe we can get a drink or a pizza afterwards? I mean if you have time. I know you're busy." He looked down awkwardly.

She smiled. Inside fireworks were going off, balloons were soaring high, and butterflies swirled around her stomach. "Great idea!"

Chapter Ten

Keziah threw her phone and charger to the top of the pile for her rucksack. She had her headphones, a book, a notebook, a sweater, a drinking cup, and a scarf, but her belongings might be taken as soon as she arrived. Phones weren't allowed but anything incriminating had been deleted anyway. All three of the devices were in her pocket. She had two bugs which she'd try to plant as early as she could: one on the bus for starters. Detective Frank suggested she try to put one on the van with the produce, or the crates holding the breads or conserves if the opportunity arose. They were trackers with mics – impressive little devices. A more sophisticated wire hid in the lining of her rucksack. It might pick up some interesting conversation too.

A knock on the door made her jump. Zadie walked in, sat on the bed beside her and handed her a cup of coffee. They sat in silence for a minute before she put her arm around her.

"How are you feeling?"

"I'm shitting myself, to put it honestly."

"I would be too, but remember, you have the chance to blow this thing apart Keziah."

"I'll do my best."

Zadie tussled her hair, smiled and walked out of the room chirpily. Keziah fixed her hair in the mirror. Soon she'd have to wear a scarf again.

They were all in the kitchen, including Yvonne who planned on driving her to the market. Helium balloons with 'We'll Miss You' bobbed around the pastries set out on the table below. They all stopped talking as she entered the room. Ish looked down quickly with his jaw set. The joyful send-off was a little inappropriate and she guessed he felt the same. Yvonne stood with her usual wide grin.

"Keziah, we're going to miss you!"

Everyone chimed in and the ruckus even brought a smile to Ish's face. She wasn't much in the mood for celebrating but smiled, nonetheless.

"The balloons say so but I'm not sure you'll really miss me," she joked.

"Come, sit down, we have cakes and pastries!"

"I'll have a cake, but no speeches."

Yvonne drove in silence, and as they approached the street where the market was held she started to breathe heavily.

"Everything is going to be ," she said as if she needed to tell herself.

They parked around the corner of the market entrance. Yvonne removed her seatbelt and turned to Keziah. She took her hand and looked into her eyes. "You don't have to do this."

"I know."

"You don't have to do this *today*."

"I want to. You know this already. You said yourself, it's going to be okay, Yvonne."

"You can back out anytime." The tears arrived and she brushed them away quickly.

Keziah didn't want to draw this goodbye out so gave her a huge hug and got ready to leave. "I love you Yvonne. Thanks for everything."

Inhaling sharply, she jumped out of the car. Keziah stood on the pavement fixing her rucksack and then bent down to the passenger seat window and waved.

"Get out of here," Yvonne called through the window. Keziah could see the tears sliding down her face as she waved her away.

She checked the wire by tapping it twice as she walked through the gates of the market. It was mere seconds before she heard "Jim here. ."

Headed directly to the stall where she had the little cup of cider the previous day, Keziah stood at a distance. Pretending to admire the little wooden ladles, she glanced sideways to see who was at The Genus stall today. She needed to see Mother Abi, or at least Charity. Their stall was buzzing with people looking at their cheeses and breads and trying samples. All of the women on the stall were engaged with customers. Keziah scanned the tables under the tarpaulin for a familiar face. Sure enough, there standing at the top watching over all the girls, was Mother Abi. Her heavy green dress fell past her ankles, and she wore black closed lace-up shoes. Keziah wondered how she coped in the summer heat. She couldn't remember how she'd done it herself. Charity was talking to a man with a loaf in his hand. She swayed and giggled as they spoke. How on earth did she get away with such obvious flirting under the nose of Mother and the men supervising.

"Excuse me love, fancy a freebie?"

She looked up to see the same man who had given her the cider the previous time.

She instantly smiled and waved her hand. "Not today but thank you."

When she looked back again, Mother Abi was walking towards her with a face that screamed *I don't want to see you*. Charity was coyly watching from a distance.

"Keziah, what on earth are you doing here again? I told you it's not safe."

She was flushed and agitated, but Keziah could tell she had her best interests at heart. A sudden sadness washed over her. She was about to trick Mother Abi – lie, cheat, and possibly incriminate her in a police investigation.

"Mother Abi, I wanted to see you again. I - I wanted to talk and maybe I don't know – look can we talk?"

The woman sighed, obviously drained. She took her elbow and pushed her in the direction of the toilets. Keziah reminded herself Sy had most likely already put plan in place.

Inside Mother took both of her arms and gently stood her against the wall. "I will tell you this once more, Keziah. I do not believe you are safe here. I do not want you to come here again. If you do not comply with my wishes, I cannot control what happens next." She paused and took a deep breath before continuing, never taking her eyes off Keziah. "Do you understand what I am trying to tell you?"

Keziah nodded with pursed lips. "I understand. But I've made a mistake. I don't belong out here."

Mother Abi shook her head and put her hands over her eyes. "No, no, no." Her pitch was getting higher. "How on earth can you decide this, after so many months? After everything that happened. How?" She slapped her hand off her hip and turned her back on Keziah as if trying to compose herself.

"Mother, thank you for the warning, I understand, really I do – but I have to do this."

It was unlikely Mother would understand why she really wanted back in, but in case she guessed, she wanted to be as honest as possible upfront.

Mother Abi looked at her suspiciously. "Why do you have to do this? You have your own community out here."

Keziah took a deep breath in. "I need to come home."

"Need? What do you mean?"

"I mean I want to come home. I want redemption." She dropped her head. "I'm sorry."

"Keziah, I am not sure what will happen to you." Mother placed her arm gently on her shoulder and pulled her chin up to look into her eyes.

"I understand, Mother."

"You understand, but you do not heed."

"Mother, thank you for the warning. I understand, really I do, but I have to do this."

A crackling hiss brought her back to earth. "Keziah, Probe her. What will happen if you go back in?"

"Will Father Sy forgive me?'

"What do you think? You ran away from the chance to marry the blessed father, to bear his children, to have great standing. You have rejected him therefore, you rejected us all." Her tone changed, like she was reeling off a script.

Keziah felt a hot stinging in her eyes. "I never rejected you Mother, I promise."

Mother Abi's face softened.

"'ill he hurt me? Will he try again to...?"

"I don't know. Who knows? Punishments are, well, different now, harder since everything happened with you and Abe…"

"I had no choice. Abe kidnapped me and was beating me and I…"

Upon seeing Charity, Mother put her hand up and raised her chin. "I do not want to know the details of your sordid life out here. This is not the way I raised you."

"Yes, Mother," Keziah answered obediently.

She raised her head and spotted Charity watching them. She wanted to catch it on her wire, so she spoke loud and cheerfully.

"Hello Charity! It's lovely to see you again."

Mother Abi turned around and clenched her jaw She put her head down and whispered quickly. "I have no choice now."

Keziah's heart began to pound. It was happening. Mother warned her things would not be pretty and she confirmed she understood. Charity's presence unnerved her Mother, as if she had some kind of hold over her.

"Thank you, Mother."

The crackle came over the radio again. "Frank here, Keziah. Well done. Keep your cool and see what happens next."

The thumping in her chest and throat was taking over her body. She ran into the cubicle and sat down on the toilet lowering her head between her legs.

"Keziah, come to the stall when you are done."

Mother Abi said something to Charity, and they left. The dizziness set in, and Keziah swallowed hard, but it didn't stop her mouth from watering.

Detective Frank's voice through came again. "Remember, keep the wire on for as long as you can, but don't take risks. If you get into the van with the bag, it'll be good enough."

She stood up, and quickly bent over the toilet to vomit.

Chapter Eleven

The van rolled up the stony path as the light turned to dusk. Keziah said very little on the way, despite Charity's constant chatter and questions.

"Why are you back? Did you really maim Abe? Sy is going to punish you, but I suppose you already know."

For the whole forty-minute journey to The Genus compound she chattered insensitively despite Keziah's obvious reluctance to answer.

"Charity, please stop this chitter chatter. This is a time of reflection for Keziah, not a time to gossip."

Keziah sensed a real issue between Mother Abi and Charity but could not imagine what it might be. Charity was a changed person; darker, and definitely more sarcastic. Mother Abi reacted strangely when she spotted her earlier, like she had been caught doing something she shouldn't. Does Charity know she was warning her away?

Father Sy gave Mother strict instructions on how she would have to have to go through a purifying ritual before being allowed back inside. Mother Abi explained calmly how she would help her strip, wash and change into more suitable clothes. Keziah panicked momentarily as she remembered the wire was still on her person, but Jim trained her on how to scrunch it up quickly so when she dropped it no one would notice. She just had to find the right moment to take it off, and then a place to dispose of it. As the bus pulled up beside the storeroom, Mother Abi stood up and announced to the group they should all go ahead. She and Keziah would stock and lock, as they called it.

Charity snarled bitterly, annoyed she would miss out on any information. "I usually do it with you. I see your favourite is back."

"Less of your insolence please, Charity."

Since when was anyone allowed to be disrespectful without consequence? Keziah looked at Charity in disbelief.

Once in the storeroom, Mother Abi explained where to store the various produce. She spoke loudly so the guard outside with the key would not pay attention.

Between orders, she asked urgently. "Why are you fiddling with clothes? Do you have something under there you need to dispose of?"

As Keziah began to untangle herself from the wires, Mother put her hand to her mouth in shock.

"Where do these cheese knives go Mother?" she asked loudly as she rolled the cables up into a tiny ball, just like Jim had demonstrated. She handed it to her elder. Abi stared in disbelief and shook her head as she put the little ball of wire in her dress pocket and responded in kind.

"Just here. Hurry up now. The poor guard must be hungry and waiting for his dinner."

The guard locked the door and walked ahead of them as they climbed the hill together in silence. Charity lingered, walking slowly in front of them. When there was enough distance from both, Mother Abi touched Keziah's arm to stop her for a moment.

"You must be cautious of Charity."

"She is behaving very oddly. What happened to her?"

"I'll talk to you some other time about it, but she has been loitering and spying since the first day you appeared at the market. Something is not right with her these days."

"After I wash what will happen to me?"

Mother Abi looked straight ahead as she walked by Keziah's side. "Only the Goddess can decide that."

"Will there be punishment?"

"I expect you will have to repent, yes."

"Will I see Father Sy tonight?"

"I expect so."

"I'm scared."

"You chose to come back."

Keziah stopped walking. She looked up the hill to the lit dining hall. Charity stood at the door watching.

"Mother, why did you help me with the wire?"

"Come, you must be hungry. Let's eat before the cleansing."

"Do I have to go in there and eat with everyone? Right now?"

"Yes."

At the door, Charity's curled lip said it all. "Are you ready for this?" she asked with a spurious smile.

Keziah wasn't ready. Of course, she wasn't. She had no idea what she was walking into. She turned around to Mother Abi who looked into her eyes sadly.

"You cannot run away this time Keziah," she said quietly as she looked down.

"Is he in there?"

Charity and Mother Abi nodded their heads in unison, Charity with much more enthusiasm. A hot tear roll down her cheek. Mother

Abi took her by the hand and walked through the door into the hall to face a glass double-door to the dining hall. She looked in to the top of the room and sure enough, there he was at the top on the platform, sitting like some kind of slovenly King on a large chair. He stared directly down through the doors into her eyes and smiled, and as he stood up he began to clap slowly. There was a hush in the room as everyone followed his gaze: the women and girls sat to the left and the men and boys to the right, with tables and benches running from the top of the hall to the bottom. The scraping of the benches started and got louder as everyone realised what was happening and stood up to join his clapping. It was deafening. Charity opened the doors and ran to take her place in the clapping crowd. Keziah watched as she chatted to her group with a grin.

"Look up to him, Keziah."

As she did so, he beckoned her to come forward. She walked through the doors and began the march through the hall. As she reached halfway he roared. She jumped, and looked back at Mother Abi whose stern face told her to move forward.

'Heathen, Murderer, Traitor, Whore, Repent!'

The clapping came harder, louder, and faster, and her whole body shook. Would she even make it to the top of the hall? The gentle push of her mother behind her pushed her on. A guard ran ahead and put a mat on the floor in front of the platform where Sy was standing. He looked down at her, still grinning facetiously, and pointed to the mat. She heard her mother whisper 'kneel' so she let her body drop to her knees onto the mat and hung her head.

She went somewhere else, to a different space, and came to feeling something wet the back of her neck. She looked up to find some of the men circling her. They walked around her leaning in, whispering and spitting.

"Bitch"

"Whore"

"Murderer"

"Whip Her"

Mother Abi over to the side of her, implored Sy to order the men away. "Father, please. She will faint. She needs to eat and wash."

There was silence and the men retreated. She breathed a sigh of relief but didn't dare to look up.

"Look who has come back to us, back to the Goddess, with her ungodly tail between her legs." He paced the stage above her. The silence was stifling as everyone waited in anticipation.

"Look at the one we once knew as Keziah. The one who denied the orders of the Goddess. The one who ran away to the outsiders, to the impure and base world of degenerates."

The room hung onto his every word as they waited for more.

"Keziah decided The Genus was not good enough for her. She plotted with the other *dishonourables* and climbed over the wall into a foul world. She *chose* to go. She *chose* to turn her back on The Genus, on The Goddess, and on *you*!"

An alarming roar travelled up into the high ceilings of the hall. Keziah looked up and around, wide eyed. Angry dark faces of people surrounded her. Mother Abi mouthed the words 'Hang your head', and Keziah immediately did so. She must not say or do anything to provoke the situation.

"And then, when an ex-communicated member declared his repentance and wanted to bring them both back inside, back to the Goddess and to us, what did she do? Guess what she did? She *stabbed* him! She stabbed him so badly he might never talk or walk again."

The hall vibrated with the noise: roars, hissing, and banging on the tables. Keziah didn't doubt they would tear her apart if they were let.

"There he is, in one of those institutions, alone, without any of us to guide him or help him back into the arms of Gena, as he wants."

As he clomped around the wooden platform she heard his erratic heavy breathing.

"What should we do with this dark angel?" he continued, "How shall she repent for her betrayal of the Goddess, to Abe, to all of you?"

"Beat her." came a voice out of the silence.

"Whip her."

"Lock her up."

Then she heard her mother's voice.

"She has come back of her own free will, Father. To return took courage. She is with us by the will of Gena. She has seen the error of her ways."

The room went quiet again, and Mother continued. "Perhaps we should let her eat and have a wash while you decide what should happen next."

"The Goddess has brought her back to us."

Another female voice came, and then another. The women were taking heed of what Mother Abi said.

"Praise Gena."

"Let her eat."

"It's the will of Gena."

Just as Keziah started to have a little bit of hope, another familiar voice shouted clearly. "Whip her."

Keziah immediately recognised Charity's voice. What a spiteful thing to do, just as things were calming down too.

"You will be known as *Unclean* until you have repented," announced Sy, as if he wanted to interrupt the women's turn in mood.

Keziah didn't budge.

"Look at me when I speak to you, Unclean!" he shouted, showing his teeth.

She quickly raised her head and looked into his eyes. She was both terrified and seething with rage. He was much bigger than before, and almost looked like a different person as he stood there bloated and sweating venom, with pleasure on his face.

"You will have your trial." He nodded and looked out at his people. "No one can say The Genus are unfair, or people are treated unfairly here. She will get her trial."

He looked back down on her as he continued. "Until then, you must seek permission from your Carer or Section head to speak with her, now known as Unclean."

He looked over at Mother Abi. "Take her away."

Mother scuttled over and helped Keziah up by lifting her from under her armpits, whispering into her ear to stay calm and follow her. Keziah rose slowly, her legs like rubber. She focused on her mother's arm as she guided her through the crowd to the end of the hall. A small table had been set for her, with her back to everyone else. Sitting down, the smell of the boiled vegetables rose to meet her and she instantly wretched.

"Be strong Keziah. It will all be over in a day or two," whispered her mother.

The next morning Keziah woke at dawn and lay in the bed made up for her in the room next to Mother Abi's. She remembered this room. It used to be for any poorly children who needed special attention during the night. These buildings, each managed by a head Carer, essentially housed nurseries, laundry, and kitchens for preparing of food, canning, fermenting and the likes. Each of the four senior mothers managed such a household. Father Sy put her under Mother Abi's care, thankfully.

Her mind ran over the day before from start to finish. It was hard to believe yesterday morning she woke in the big flat in the centre of Old Town with her friends – her family. Yvonne and Ish must be wondering how it's all going. They will be worried once the detective explains she ditched the wire. The nearest wire was about three kilometres away, and she was being watched like a hawk.

Glancing over towards the wooden drawers, she couldn't believe her eyes: her rucksack sat on the floor. Mother Abi must have brought it in there secretly. She jumped up from the bed and pulled it up, reaching into the little pocket and pressed a button.

"Can anyone hear me?," she whispered.

"Keziah, It's Simon here. Great to see you still have the rucksack. All okay?"

It was too early for her to complain. It wasn't like she didn't know what she faced when she came in.

"All's okay. The wire is gone. Staying with Mother Abi but I will face a trial."

"Try to keep the rucksack out of sight so you can use it for reporting in whenever you can."

"I'll try. Only Mother Abi knows I have it, I think. I'll hide it."

Simon signed out and a panic rose within her. They had no idea what she had already been through the day before.

After the events in the dining hall the evening before, she was brought to the shower house. Some of the women tried to get in but Mother closed the door and locked it. She was protecting her even though she knew about the wire. Surely she realised she was working for the police to get at Sy? This meant Mother Abi might have come to terms with how messed up everything was. Maybe her mother wanted Sy's demise too. In training, the detectives advised to 'start low and slow'. Keziah resolved not to ask too many questions until things had settled.

They would know now too, that Mother Abi was somehow in on the plan. Or at least she helped her. This was a turn of luck in terms of security. If she could just get through the trial safely, she'd be able to blend in a little more, and maybe get talking to more people.

The light through the curtains grew stronger. Keziah leaned over and looked out the little window beside her. It was like being transported back in time. The sun was shining, and Mother Abi was at the clothesline at the end of the yard with some younger women. Cheerful sounds echoed all around. In front of the adjacent barn, chickens ran around freely scratching the dry earth, and little children chased them; shouting and laughing as they went. She did the same at age. She looked down at the barn. It came up in her debriefing with Yvonne more than once. It was there she first understood a different side to her Father, the day he humiliated her about being too old for her clothes. Puberty had been very hard in here.

The main things for the moment were being assigned to Mother. With her being somewhat complicit, she felt secure. She still had a form of contact with the detectives too. The thought of the punishment weighed heavily, though. She tried not to imagine it but her mind could not help go to dark places, it would be naïve not to anticipate some kind of violence. In fact, she thought she would have faced such a punishment already.

Chapter Twelve

The phone shrilled. Yvonne jumped and held her chest as she exhaled.

"Detective Power. Finally. Is there news?" She listened intently and then smacked her lips. "Okay, thanks for updating me."

She stood against the wall holding the handset for a moment. The update was there was no update. Keziah of the wire safely with Mother Abi, and still had her rucksack, but there was no other news. Mother Abi was helping her. What a relief! But she hadn't made it to the next pack yet. Keziah knew to tread carefully and keep her head down in the first days - even weeks, but it didn't make Yvonne feel any better about it. She regretted it from the very first day she brought the proposal to her.

Keziah was never a straightforward case. In all her years of social working and counselling, she'd never been so emotionally involved. Yvonne had never broken the rules for anyone else, but with Keziah, she compromised herself professionally on more than one occasion. She held herself responsible for what happened with Abe. Poor Abe was seriously ill, and unlikely to regain full health. She was due a visit soon. And then Keziah, severely traumatised, ventured back in the cult to try to prove she was worthy of being on this side of wall. What a mess. She just hoped she got out in time.

Chapter Thirteen

Keziah wasn't allowed to leave Mother Abi's side. She couldn't do any tasks involving speaking with others. It felt like she'd been there weeks when it was only two days. Surely it was a tactic. Sy was tormenting her by making her wait.

They sat on the porch in the evenings when there was no one around, usually embroidering.

"You've not lost your touch with the needle."

Keziah smiled. "I've missed it."

"Can't you do embroidery over the wall?"

Keziah looked at her mother's wide-eyed expression of innocence and was reminded this woman had not been in normal society since she was a small child. She had no idea of what it was like, only what Sy told her.

"Yes, you can. There are clubs and groups where people can go to sit together and share their work."

Mother Abi nodded and smiled in satisfaction.

"But we don't tend to do it at home. We don't even darn clothes so much."

"What? But how do you repair them?"

"If you really like them you could bring it to an alteration shop, but people buy brand new clothes all the time. Old clothes go to the refuse or maybe to a charity."

Mother Abi shook her head in disbelief and Keziah chuckled.

"It's different but it's not necessarily bad. Just freer I suppose."

Mother Abi didn't look up this time and Keziah realised quickly she should not have gone there.

"Freer indeed. Look where your free world has got you, Keziah."

She deserved those word. Her mother did not know what had happened with her and Abe. She wanted to explain Abe left her no choice, but it wasn't time. She must focus on the point of her being here. She must gain trust.

"Mother, do you know when Father Sy will try me?"

Her face tightened but she still didn't look up. "Soon, I expect he will set a time tomorrow."

"Will he hurt me?"

She looked up directly into Keziah's eyes. Her lips began to quiver. The words tumbled out quickly. "I loved you like my own. You never left my side." Mother gasped and held her hand to her mouth as if she could not bare to release her feelings.

"You are my mother. I missed you so much." Keziah's voice broke.

"I thought he would make you a Carer like me. You were so nurturing and great with the younger children," she continued in a low mournful voice, as she wiped the tears away with the back of her hand.

"I am sorry, Mother. But I could not let –"

"Hush now, please. We need to get you over this trial and then we will discuss what is next for you." She nodded knowingly and Keziah reciprocated.

Seeing Keziah remove the wire perhaps revealed to Mother there was a bigger reason for her being inside again. Hopefully, over time they could speak more frankly about her mission, and about Abe. For now, she would take everything slowly, hour by hour, day by day.

Chapter Fourteen

A gentle knock on the door interrupted her already restless sleep. As she sat up, Mother Abi entered and sat on the bed.

She looked at her anxiously. "The trial is today."

Keziah's stomach churned as she tried to wake herself up enough to respond.

"What time?"

"After breakfast."

Keziah pursed her lips and searched her mother's face for some guidance.

"It will take place in the dining hall. You will be asked questions by various members of the community. I am one."

"What kind of questions? Who else will ask me?"

Mother Abi cleared her throat and scooted up on the bed closer to Keziah, taking her hand.

"Father Sy, one of the guards, Charity, and me."

"Charity? Why on earth should she get a chance to try me?"

"I asked for a fairer group. I asked Father Sy for more women."

"Yes, but Charity?"

"Charity has been getting closer to Father recently. I've seen her visit his quarters in the evening, more than once."

"In the evenings? You mean...?"

"I don't know what I mean. I know nothing about it."

Keziah blew her anxiety out through her mouth as she tried to imagine what kind of questions Charity would ask.

"We need to make a plan." Mother breathed in. "I should have done this before. You need to tell me your story as quickly as you can, and we will make one together."

An hour later they were folding clothes in the laundry room practicing important points. Surmising what the others might ask and how she should respond.

After breakfast, they silently made their way to the dining hall, where the community were finishing up, and moving furniture in preparation. Keziah gasped. A square dock sat up on a height in the centre of the room for her. She was doing this for Abe, for Zadie's little girl, for all the escapees, and for those who never got away, like Charity. She was doing it to help bring this psychopath down. Keziah brought herself back to the calming smile of Yvonne and thought about everything she did for her. Yvonne empowered her. Ish, her brother, got her out in the first place, and protected her every day since.

Mother Abi advised Keziah not to show any kind of rebellious attitude. She must remain humble and show remorse. What she felt on the inside should not be seen from the outside. It was good advice, advice she heard from the detectives. She stood at the door waiting for instructions. A guard came and took her by the arm, then roughly walked her to the podium. She surveyed the hall and watched the excited audience work together to make space and take their place for some thrilling action. On the platform in front of her sat Sy. To his right, a senior male guard, and to the other side was Mother Abi who was just taking her seat. Charity was on the end.

Sy stared at her with his infamous twisted smile. He licked his lips and smiled. She clearly could see he was even more insane – more unstable. He sweated through his white starched shirt and the constant wheeze was unsettling. The furniture removed, everyone sat on mats on the floor looking up at her. She closed her eyes and swallowed hard as she heard him order to begin.

The guard stood up and called out from a piece of paper in his hand: "*Unclean*, formerly known as Keziah, is on trial today. The charges are as follows.

Profanity.

Blasphemy.

Unholy acts such as fornication.

Violence to a fellow member of The Genus."

Ex-member

The crowd gasped which reminded Keziah they no idea what happened with Abe.

The guard continued: "*Unclean*, after showing an interest in returning to her community and leaders and the Goddess, has been given a chance to explain her actions and undergo a suitable punishment. Each of us here on the panel, guided by Father Sy, will interrogate *Unclean*. After the trial she will continue to be under the care of Mother Abi until punishment is decided and executed."

Executed.

Anything could happen to her now. She breathed calmly and kept her glance downwards.

Sy proceeded to tell the story of a demonic young woman who ran from Gena's gifts, who denied her community their rights, who then stabbed a young man who worked hard at turning his life around and who was trying to repent. The gasps and bays were intermittent and usually hushed by seniors. Mother Abi intervened where possible, in a very polite and submissive tone, to correct some facts.

How brave her mother was. When question time came around, the tension in the hall was palpable, a collective atmosphere of anticipation. Small children were hushed or removed from the hall altogether. The women just below, surrounding the box. Showed horror and disgust. One woman, whom she recognised but couldn't put a name to, constantly tutted and shook her head.

The senior guard was first. He ordered her to face each member of the panel by looking at them directly when listening and speaking. She remembered him. He was a fat cat, one of Sy's cronies, who ate almost as well as Sy did. She slowly raised her head and looked at him directly, and as plain as she could.

"Do you admit you have done wrong?"

"Yes, sir."

His mundane questions were easy to answer. Next was Charity. Keziah could see the anxiety in her face and for a moment was unsure just whose side she was on. Perhaps she didn't know herself.

"Isn't it true you planned to leave The Genus for some months?"

"Yes."

Disappointed with Keziah's candid answer, she twisted her mouth as she read something in front of her. "And weren't the ex-communicated in touch with you, and helping you to plan your exit months before?

"Yes."

Charity clenched her jaw. "Didn't you try to get me to run with you, over the wall?"

"No."

There was movement in the hall, shifting and whispers.

"Come now, did you not approach me and tell me we could leave together?"

How low could she go? Yes, she was very hurt. Yes, she needed to protect herself, but this was horrid. She wanted to avoid telling everyone how Charity was involved, meeting Ish at the market, and passing notes. Didn't she understand she was putting Keziah in a hopeless position? It was baffling.

"Charity, you wanted to leave with me. You were in touch with Ish before me."

There was outcry across the hall and Keziah immediately regretted challenging her. Keziah looked at Mother Abi who stared back disapprovingly.

"Sorry, yes. I told you we could leave together."

"Yes, you did. But what happened instead?"

"Things turned out differently. I left earlier."

Sy interrupted, speaking for the first time.

"So, *Unclean* decided to desert the Goddess, and somehow contact the infidels over the wall. The ones who turned their back on the Goddess already."

He spoke slowly, scanning the room, making eye contact with his audience. "She lived in a house with four or five others. The ones who left The Genus before. They created chaos and violence, as some of you will remember."

People nodded their heads.

"It caused us all a lot of hurt and heartache. Did we not fast and pray and sacrifice ourselves on their behalf?"

Murmurs of agreement filled the hall. He turned his head to look at Mother Abi and nodded for her to proceed.

"Did you realise what you were doing?"

"No, I didn't understand how it would be out there."

"Did you regret leaving?"

"Almost immediately."

"What did you do out there?"

"I found work and duties. I cleaned the house and did the laundry while the others went out to work. Just like you, Mother."

"You did not! You went to college, to work, jogging in the park, drinking alcohol, seeing men!" Sy roared. The whole hall vibrated with an explosion of roars of disapproval, and then suddenly fell silent. He continued with less volume.

"Don't tell us lies. You know I spoke to the victim of your witchery before you permanently maimed him."

"Sir, Father, Abe was very violent. He drank alcohol and took illegal substances. He locked me into his home and ..."

"Yes, of course he did! He realised what a delinquent you were, and that you needed to be controlled. He contacted me to tell me he was willing to marry you, despite your whore ways. He wanted to make you clean again."

And so, it went for some time after. Finally, each member of the panel got to summarise their points.

Mother Abi spoke to them again of Keziah's repentance, her hard work in study and physical exercise. "Father, Keziah was lost without your guidance. She knew to come home. Surely, the Goddess would be satisfied she saw the light."

Charity spoke of Keziah being untrustworthy and Guard Isaac summed up by saying despite how wicked Unclean was, the Goddess would want them to try to clean her. The people spoke among themselves, questioning each other. Through it all, her throat was tense and her whole body thumped hard. She stood with her hands together and only looked up occasionally. If she could get through this, she could move forward and start getting information.

Dismissed for the final decision, Mother brought her back to the house and left again quickly. "Eat and stay here. I will be back as soon as possible."

Keziah ran to the room and pulled her rucksack out from under the bed. Breathing heavily, she pushed the button in the pocket.

"Hello? Hello? Anyone there?"

"Keziah, Frank and Simon here."

"The trial just finished. I'm waiting for them to decide on the punishment. I've no idea what they will do next." She heard her shaky breathless voice.

"Amanda here. Keziah, breathe. Remember your techniques."

"Yeah."

"Frank here. How did Sy seem?"

"Not as aggressive as I imagined but the punishment hasn't started yet."

"And Charity?"

"Turned on me. Said I tried to convince her to escape with me. Mother Abi says she's very close to Sy now."

"Is Sy out and about amongst the people normally?", asked Amanda.

"No, he's up in his quarters a lot. He doesn't seem healthy. Charity visits him in the evenings."

She couldn't hear the next question for the shouting outside. She looked out the window A group of women shouting for her to come down.

"Unclean! Come and face your punishment."

"They are calling. I have to go." She didn't say goodbye. She just stuffed her rucksack under her bed and ran down the stairs, hot and trembling.

Chapter Fifteen

She stood at the door, shaking, as she tried to read the faces of the women before her. Some were ugly with spite; others held their hands out with compassion.

Charity walked up the porch to her, took her hand without looking at her and pulled her down the steps. "Father Sy says we must not talk to her."

As they walked in silence to the hall, Keziah could hear herself hyperventilating but did not know how to stop it.

Upon entering the hall, Charity pinched her hand and leaned into her ear. "It looks like they are not going to hurt you. Most of the women voted against a flogging or putting you in the hole."

Keziah's eyes widened and she breathed out a sigh of relief. "Did you?"

Charity ignored her question and looked straight ahead. "This is not going to be easy, either way."

The women scurried over to their groups. Keziah watched Charity whisper to some of the other women, confused by moments of tenderness mixed with her otherwise spiteful behaviour. She looked up to Mother Abi walking towards her, beckoning her to come forward. Halfway up the hall they met. Mother whispered quickly in Keziah's ear. "Repent and agree with everything." Mother took her position on the platform with Sy and the rest of the chosen judges. All eyes were on her. Beads of sweat formed on her brow.

Sy stood up, holding his chest and coughing. "Your people want to give you another chance," he wheezed. "It's unprecedented. What do you say to that?"

"I am truly grateful, Father."

"Are you?" he spat. "Are you remorseful? Are you ready to repent?"

His small dark eyes penetrated her. His mouth was permanently downturned, and he had far more wrinkles than before. In fact, his whole face looked unlike she remembered, in less than a year. Abe's accident (that's what they called it), had taken its toll. He lost his fight to gain custody of Abe despite using their own DNA testing against the department to prove his was his biological father. The government had legal guardianship of Abe until he was deemed fit to look after himself, which looked unlikely at this point.

"Father, I am truly sorry to the Goddess, to you, and to my people. I am ready to repent."

"I do not trust you," he roared theatrically, "but I am willing to go with what the charitable people of The Genus want. You – *Unclean Keziah* – have one more chance."

Keziah dropped to her knees and acted out the scene she'd not only rehearsed with Mother Abi, but she'd imagined for months. It was just as she imagined.

"Thank you, Father. Praise Gena."

"The council will decide your punishment, but for now, you are under Mother Abi's care."

He looked over at Mother Abi. "You are directly responsible for her, and her behaviour."

Mother Abi nodded obediently. His sermon, full of fire and brimstone (a term she learned from Yvonne), went on for some time, and she could hear the restlessness rise in the hall: sniffing and coughing, children crying or talking aloud. Finally, it ended with a prayer of forgiveness. She looked up at Sy. He was looking at his phone.

As they all filed out of the hall, whispering between themselves, Keziah stayed back and waited for Mother Abi's next instructions. Many of the men looked at her in disgust as they passed, scanning her form head to toe. She tried to ignore them, but it hurt, and Keziah realised it scared her. She knew what they were all capable of, trained by Sy himself.

Mother Abi took her by the arm and turned her around, as if she had seen them. She looked stiff and worried. "You are very blessed. You have the women of your community, and the Goddess, to thank."

"Yes, Mother."

"Be aware, your room will be searched regularly. I believe he suspects contact. He does not know about your rucksack. We need to get rid of it."

Keziah froze. Her only way to stay in touch was gone. "Okay."

"He is likely to make your life very difficult. He has yet to decide your punishment. So, if you have a plan, I suggest you carry it out sooner rather than later."

It was the first time she heard her call Sy 'he'.

She took Keziah by both shoulders and looked closely into her eyes. "Do you understand, Keziah?"

"I understand, and you are correct. There is a plan."

Mother Abi looked around the hall and back at Keziah. "You'll tell me everything later."

Oh, to go back to the innocent girl she once was and stay here under Mother Abi's care forever. If The Genus was liberated, would her mother feel free? What would the older people do? Could they stay and live their lives out the way they wanted, the way they always lived? Mother Abi would be lost on the outside, but she'd look after her. Surely Ish would help anyone in need of help. Maybe they could form a small community: Get a large flat, or even two, close to each other. She couldn't imagine Mother Abi debriefing with Yvonne the way she had. She might refuse, just like Abe did.

They walked briskly towards the house.

"Go straight upstairs and put the rucksack under the bed in my room. I will dispose of it later."

"How?"

Looking straight ahead she replied. "I will burn it."

Keziah ran upstairs, grabbed the rucksack, and ran into Mother Abi's room next door. She sat on the floor behind the door and pushed the button.

"Hello. Who's there?"

"Simon here. Hello."

"We have to burn the rucksack."

"Okay. The trial, Keziah. What happened?"

"Better than expected, but punishment hasn't been decided yet. A lot of the women fought for me."

"Very good news. What are the chances of getting to the next pack?"

"Mother Abi might help me."

"You're sure she's with you?"

"Yes."

"Good. Are you okay?"

"Yes. All good. Mother is taking care of me."
"Everyone will be happy to hear that."
"I have to go."
"Get to the next pack soon."
"Okay. I'll try. Bye."

She sat for a moment against the wall. Maybe it wasn't such a good idea to drag Mother Abi into this further. Keziah wanted to look after her, but the reverse was happening. Maybe she'd just let things settle and try to get the pack herself when she could. The woman needed some peace. She advocated so hard for Keziah, but she could see the stress it was causing her.

Chapter Sixteen

Empty laundry basket in hand, Keziah made her way down to the end of the yard where white sheets flapped high against the blue sky. Looking around for signs of life, she left the basket on the ground and walked through the border of leylandii. The place was deserted. The closest wire and pack was hidden at the top of the slope, amongst the trees, by the lake. Fast walking soon turned into a sprint and before she knew it, she was at the base of an old tree trying to catch her breath. She looked around, recalling that fateful night, running in such fear down the slope and jumping into the lake. The urge to run and do it all over again was bubbling on the surface but she'd come too far.

On her knees, she rummaged through the moss and fungus-ridden mulch with her hands until she heard the rustle of the plastic. She pulled a transparent sealed bag up. It contained two other small packs. Keziah guessed one was a wire. Opening it quickly she took one package out. Inside the smaller package was a little square device with a screen and a keyboard. It wasn't a phone, exactly. showed her this before. It was a pager, with text only. She shoved it back into the larger bag and hid it under her apron.

Brushing herself off as well as she could, Keziah rushed back to the yard. As she arrived, she spotted movement up at the house. She lowered the line and pulled the first sheet down, folded it and then pulled the pack out, letting it fall into the base of the basket. It wouldn't be seen under the sheet. She spotted Charity by the side of her eye but pretended to be engrossed in the folding. Keziah placed the first sheet over the pack and looked up.

"Charity! Charity! I'm here," she called as she waved up to her.

She could see her scowl as she approached.

"You were told to stay inside," she complained, as she eyed Keziah, "What in Gena's name has happened to you?"

Keziah looked confused and followed her gaze down onto her soiled apron.

"Oh! What is that?" She brushed herself down and examined the stains as if she had no idea at all what it could be before looking back up at Charity, who was still staring at her.

"Maybe it's from the barn." Keziah shrugged casually and continued on, folding the next sheet.

"Do they not fold sheets over the wall?" Charity snarked looking at the basket.

They stared at each other for some seconds before bursting out laughing, just like old times. They laughed for a minute solid. What a relief.

"Anyway, they've finished, and you're to come to the hall."

Keziah flushed and dropped the next sheet into the basket.

"I'll just drop these inside."

"Change your apron or take that one off, while you're there," Charity called after her.

Running into the house, she held onto the packet underneath her apron to prevent it from falling out. She jumped three stairs at a time and ran into Mother Abi's room to put her bed. If her room was going to be checked randomly, she'd best not risk having it there. The rucksack was gone already. Her mother moved fast.

The nervous energy running through her body made her feel like she'd had several strong coffees. She ran back down to meet Charity, who'd ambled up the yard and waited for her on the porch. She'd managed to keep a contact device at all times. So far so good. Now to face the punishment, another hour professing her guilt loomed. She could do it, but theses in the dining hall exhausted her physically and drained her emotionally. What would she do if she didn't have Mother Abi?

This time, only Guard Isaac stood on the platform with a sheet of paper in his hand. The crowd were murmuring among themselves, and he was reading the page, as if practicing for a great performance. But where was Sy?

She walked up the aisle slowly. Mother Abi sat in the first row to her left beside Charity. She looked over and her mother mouthed the words to wait where she was, before the senior guard.

"*Unclean* will now be known as Keziah again: The name chosen for her by the Goddess." He read directly from the page.

"Keziah will remain in silence for thirty days."

She inhaled sharply. Please let it be over now.

"During this time, no person male or female should speak to her, or communicate with her in any way. Should any person be found to do so, they will be severely punished themselves."

"Keziah," he looked down at her sternly. "Part of your punishment will be one to one lessons with Father Sy, at a time of his choosing."

Oh no!

"Do you understand?"

"Yes, sir."

"Mother Abi will remain your day to day mentor and will facilitate your punishment."

Keziah held her breath. Was there more?

"Charity will bring a daily report to Father Sy, noting any discrepancies in Keziah's behaviour."

She could hear whispering behind her but could not tell if the women were happy with this.

"Charity will also report any person who is found communicating with Keziah, besides Mother Abi. Is everyone clear?"

A mumbling incoherent *yes* came forward. Keziah looked over at Charity who sat looking forward with a wide grin on her face. She switched so often Keziah found it impossible to read her.

"Dismissed." The guard shouted and exited quickly via a side door.

Both Mother and Charity walked over to Keziah.

"Gena is good." Mother Abi moved forward and squeezed her hand with a smile.

"I think you've been very lucky. You've practically gotten away with murder," sneered Charity.

"I didn't –

"Ah!"

"Sorry. I forgot!"

"Please Keziah." Mother Abi sighed as she implored her to be careful.

Keziah nodded apologetically. This was not going to be easy. Charity knew all the time what the punishment would be. She somehow had authority over her, and it looked like she had authority over Mother Abi too. Something very strange was happening.

The chill arrived just as the sun was setting, but the Autumn evenings were still mild enough for them to sit on the porch for a while. The house was only occupied by younger children right now. Her and Mother Abi were the only adults that slept there, and she felt like this was the way it was always meant to be. If she was chosen to be a Carer she wouldn't have left. She would have continued, naïve and in fear of being berated for every action. It was her who made contact with the ex-members in the first place.

Mother Abi rocked on her chair as she darned. A large basket of children's clothes sat beside her, and she worked through them swiftly but without urgency. All the clothes for the younger children were of white, grey and beige tones, heavy cotton or burlap type fabrics. Mother Abi soaked the fabric before she made the clothes to soften them. Keziah remembered being allowed to swirl them in their buckets of soapy water when she was little. Colour was a privilege in The Genus. Women in favour (about to wed or give birth) were allowed to wear brighter colours, but in general the generic eggshell and taupe shades of clothes were the norm. Mother Abi and the other senior mothers always wore dark greens or blues.

"I have a wire." She just blurted it out. Even if she didn't want to involve her, she should at least be honest with her. Mother looked up at her and nodded for her to go on.

"They want me to get information. About him."

Her mother looked out into the yard as she listened.

"They have reports about crimes he committed in the past. I mean, before The Genus."

Mother Abi said nothing.

"Mother, he is not a good man. He was married before, and he hurt his wife."

"Stop!"

Keziah flushed and tried to compose herself. She must stay calm and listen. She couldn't be emotional.

"Keziah, I do not need to hear such things. I cannot. I just can't." She gasped and dropped her head.

"I'm so sorry Mother. I want to be honest with you." A stinging lump built in her throat.

They sat in silences for a few minutes. "What have I put all these poor children through over the years." She shook her head. "I really believed-I really thought…"

Keziah moved to her mother and bent down to hug her, but she pushed her off instantly, so she backed away and sat back on her chair.

"Mother, it wasn't your fault. You believed what he told you."

The woman became agitated and threw her sewing back in the basket. "Don't you see? They can put me in jail too, and many more of us."

"No-no, you have been coerced, brainwashed".

Mother snorted and Keziah watched her face change to one of anger and frustration.

"Well? What is the plan?"

"I didn't mean to turn your world upside down."

"Too late now. What do you need, Keziah?"

'I need proof. I need to catch him talking about what he does; the punishments, the rituals, what happens to the children and well, record him, if I can. I also need to find out more about his business."

"What business?"

"Apparently, he's involved in various money making schemes that are against the law. He doesn't pay tax."

Mother Abi took a piece of clothing back from the basket and began sewing again. "Let me think it over. Now be careful, there are enquiring eyes all around us."

In her room, she switched the device on, and the little screen lit up. There was a message moving across it on repeat. Her hands began to shake in excitement. Things were moving.

Happy to see you've managed to get to the packet. This is a pager. We can send short messages to each other. There is a wire in the other packet. If the opportunity arises you can use it like Jim trained you. You're doing great. Stay safe. Amanda.

Chapter Seventeen

Every morning the bell in The Fulcrum chimed at five and life began to stir in The Genus. Children and teenagers arrived to collect their breakfast before getting on with their daily activities. The chuckling and scolding filled the house as the younger children waited in line. Mother Abi, with the other Carers, prepared the children for their days; breakfast, lunch, clean clothes including cardigans in case it got chilly. Most of them were off to The Fulcrum for bible study or the little junior school which had been built to try to cater for the growing number of children. Some had extra duties as punishment, or training projects for the older children. They all left with smiles on their faces, touched by the nurturing love of the Carers.

Making her way downstairs to join in with the duties, she resolved to put some actions in place today. It had been days since Mother said she would 'think about it'. They needed a plan before Sy moved. As the women cleaned up after the stampede, they laughed and talked between themselves. She stood at the door quietly until they spotted her.

The room feel silent, but acted fast. "Come Keziah, I've checked with Father, and I am allowed to speak to you with instructions. Now, these potatoes need peeling for the dinner tonight."

The others looked on but said nothing. Some scowled and glared at her; others pretended she didn't exist at all. Keziah walked in and pulled her sleeves up. She looked around the room and smiled in the hopes of seeing a return. Charity was at the sink with her back to her.

"Oh, Keziah has arrived. Protect us all, Gena."

A few women chuckled quietly.

"Enough Charity, or you will have to report yourself."

More chuckling followed and then everyone got back to work, chatting as they went. It wasn't long until the awkward silence was forgotten.

By the end of the of the morning, things relaxed significantly and as they all sat around the thick wooden table with a cup of tea, she was more or less included in the chit chat although no one spoke directly to her. She could listen and that was important. She was beginning to integrate.

It was the season for foraging in the woods. There was always a day or two every year where the whole community of women and children spent their days picking blackberries and wild raspberries as well as cob nuts and mushrooms. Mother she would take Keziah out to assess what was ready for picking. The rest of the group finished up the laundry and were ordered to make their way to the schools and fulcrum for community duties and prayer before lunch.

They carried their baskets on their back as they waded through the foliage and loose rocks. Keziah thanked her mother for the guidance earlier, in the hopes of starting a pointed conversation.

"It's best they get used to you being any risks."

They stopped under a nut tree, and Mother took her stick with a hook out of her basket. Pulling down branches and examining the nuts as she went. She continued to talk.

"They must trust you. They will not share anything with you unless they trust you. It's not going to happen overnight."

They continued on to a small paddock where there was an abundance of blackberries ripe and juicy and ready for picking.

They picked in silence for some time until Keziah cleared her throat. "What is going on with Charity? She seems very odd."

"Yes."

"Is she trustable?"

"No, I expect not. Like I told you before, be careful with her."

"Mother, what happened to her?"

"She never really got over it. Your escape and the punishment took its toll on her."

"

"She is scarred."

"What did they do to her?"

"Well," she said quietly, "They whipped her. They ordered her to eat but once a day, and she spent months alone and in silence. It damaged her."

"Oh no, poor Charity. No wonder she wanted to see me punished harshly. But, why then, does she have such newfound power?"

"She is damaged enough to be manipulated." Mother pulled a huge bramble vigorously. Keziah wondered if she was avoiding answering her questions honestly.

"But what does that mean?"

"I suspect Father has her spying. She has private visits with him now. Only Gena knows what goes on behind those doors."

Keziah squirmed. She dreaded to think what he was doing to her.

As they moved on to the pines, Keziah wondered whether to tell her mother about the second pack, hidden somewhere close by. She didn't need it yet but maybe they should find it and mark the location.

She watched as her mother bent down at the foot of a tree, uncovering moss, and smiling in delight when she found the best types of mushrooms. "Look at ."

"Fantastic, Mother."

"Yes, we definitely have to get everyone up here soon. Look at them!"

She couldn't have anyone else find the pack.

"There's a pack planted here somewhere." There was no other way to say it, but to say it.

"A pack?"

"A device to communicate with them."

She looked blankly at Keziah.

"Probably a bug, like a recording device, and a text device to send messages."

"Oh, for goodness sake Keziah!" The woman sighed slapped her free hand down on her leg. "It never ends."

It took over an hour of searching to find it. They searched each tree individually while collecting any mushrooms they found, since they couldn't arrive home with nothing in their baskets after such a long time.

It was almost six before they began to make their way back. Mother was quiet and didn't engage with Keziah unless the conversation moved to foraging, children or duties. As they passed the lake near the house and the way back up Keziah could stick it no more.

"My memories of escaping that night haunt me."

Mother walked on with a clenched jaw.

"Mother! What will we do? I cannot stay here forever."

"It seems no one can. Bide your time, Keziah," she called back to her as she rushed ahead to a large pine in the hopes of finding more milky caps.

"Where is Zadie's daughter? How can I see her at least?"

Mother stopped in her tracks and turned to Keziah. "Laura?" Why would you involve Laura? She is a sensitive young girl at the best of times."

She got a pang of homesickness, and it stifled her for a moment.

"Zadie would like to know something about her."

The woman sighed again, exhausted by the whole thing. The years of hard work and obedience on her mother's face no longer showed pride, but sorrow. She was using her mother, involving her in this, to get her own job done. But she needed to get to the job at hand done once and for all. the only person who truly had her best interests at heart on this side of the wall, the only one she could trust.

Chapter Eighteen

Keziah lay on her bed with the window open watching the muslin curtain breathe in and out with the gentle breeze. She breathed with it and wondered what the day had in store. Sy still hadn't arranged a meeting. She was determined not to let him stress her. Keeping a low profile was imperative.

As she rose to change from her nightdress into her long-sleeved, high-necked day dress, her device beeped. She sat back on the bed, pulling it from the little gap between the mattress and the wall.

We are here for the day. Any contact with Sy yet? Keep in touch.

She quickly replied. *Nothing yet. Have to get up. Will update you later.*

She heard noise downstairs and opened her door quietly. It was Charity, talking with excitement. Keziah's body tensed as she tried to focus on the muffled words. Mother Abi asked questions as if she was unsure of what she was being told. She thought she made out the word *punishment* but couldn't hear well enough to be sure. Although the kitchen was right under her room, the house was old, solid, and thick. This might be it – time for punishment. She may be facing a beating. Maybe they will make her marry someone? Or try to make her take part in another ceremony. Keziah heard her own rapid breathing and shuddered. Goosebumps formed on her skin, and she suddenly had the sensation of being becoming distant, outside the world and outside herself. The queasiness brought her to her knees for a moment. She took her time to get her breathing in check and slowly sat down on the side of the bed.

Hearing the door slam Keziah jumped up to the window to watch Charity disappear around the side of the porch. Perhaps she was running back to Sy.

No sooner had there been a knock on the door than Mother Abi swung it open and reached her torso in. "You have to go to see him immediately. Hurry up and get dressed."

The door closed and Keziah jumped from the bed to finish dressing. She rushed down the stairs into the kitchen where her mother stood by the stove stirring porridge.

"Mother, is he going to hurt me?"

She didn't turn to comfort Keziah or give her a sympathetic smile. Instead, she kept stirring, looking intently at the pot.

"Sit down and eat. You can't go on an empty stomach."

Keziah obediently sat in silence, her head hazy, waiting for further instructions. As her mother put the bowl in front of her, she automatically began eating despite having no appetite.

Her mother sat opposite and watched her. "He sent Charity. The punishment will not be announced." Mother gazed out the window thoughtfully. "If it was flogging or whipping, I'm sure he would do it in public."

"Can you come with me?"

"I will try, but he might make me wait outside."

Keziah nodded. She sat back on her chair. "I'm ready."

Sy's quarters didn't look like much from the outside: a higgledy-piggledy barn, patched up with various materials, and extending in different directions. The old part of the building looked dry and tired. The small intimate story times of her childhood took place here. The children were brought in the dark evenings in a line. A stove always burned in the corner, and he'd give out hot toast with jam before he started. They lived for these moments; to be in his presence, and to be treated by him as someone important, one of his people. He was softer then. Less cynical and bitter, and certainly less crazy. She stepped into the tiny square hall at the foot of the narrow steps. It was dark, but she could just about make out someone standing at the top of the stairs.

"Hello? Father Sy?"

"It's me, Charity. Come on up."

She looked back at her mother who was ushering her inside.

"What are you doing here, Charity?" called Mother, up into the darkness.

"I am Father's personal assistant now."

Mother Abi pushed her from behind and they both started their ascent to the unknown.

"Sorry Mother, only Keziah."

Dismissively, Mother Abi kept climbing. "I'll talk to Father directly. Don't let it concern you."

"No, he says I am the only one to be in the room."

"Don't be silly, Child." Mother passed Keziah and made her way to the top of the stairs, puffing her chest in front of Charity, who stood back clearly unsure how to proceed. Wide-eyed, Charity knocked the door as if to announce Mother's presence. Mother Abi did not hesitate. She walked right in and closed the door behind her. Charity stomped her foot like a child and sat on the little wooden stool, folding her arms. She smiled wryly at Keziah as she arrived at the top.

"Do you know what he will do to me?"

"Do to you? What an odd way to word an opportunity for retribution. I'd say you are very lucky."

Keziah sighed. "I didn't mean it to sound disrespectful. Do you know what it is?"

"Not exactly."

The door swung open, and Mother Abi walked out.

"Charity, leave me here with Keziah for a moment, please."

her eyebrows. "-

"Do as you are told, or I will be reporting you for repetitive insolence, personal assistant or not!"

She stomped down the stairs. Mother Abi waited and watched. When Charity snuck back and took a peep up the stairs she was ready.

"Charity! Go away from here, right now."

"Go in and kneel in front of him. I think it will be more of a verbal rebuke, but he is in a very bad mood. Submit, implore, and beg for forgiveness. Do not try to explain anything."

"What if he insists?" Keziah voice trembled.

"Answer in submission and respect. Choose your words carefully."

"Will you be out here, Mother?"

"I will try to be." She knocked the door, opened it just enough for Keziah to enter and then closed it again quickly.

The only light came from two small windows at one end of the room. As her eyes adjusted, she spotted him in a large leather armchair on a low wooden platform. He sat in it, but she couldn't see his face. As she walked slowly towards the platform, his mirthless smile became visible, and she immediately knew he would show no mercy. She dropped to her knees.

"Father, thank you for seeing me."

He coughed but said nothing. After a moment, she raised her head slightly to see what he was doing, and jumped when he began to talk.

"One option I considered was the black box."

Silence again. Should she reply? This was going to be long and drawn out. Her neck was starting to ache from keeping it down.

"...a small dark cell, for days," he finally continued in a low gravelly voice. "We haven't done that yet, but then, no one inside The Genus has ever behaved as you have behaved."

She took a deep breath in; her neck still bowed.

"No one has ran from my bed, no one has refused my hand in marriage. Me, your leader, the only person who received messages for you from the Goddess. Why would you refuse it?"

The leather of his chair squeaked as he shuffled around.

"I've thought long and hard about why you would purposefully remove yourself from this wonderful, protected life," he continued. "And the conclusion I've some to..."

He paused. Keziah tried not to breathe heavily because it was sure to lead to tears and she couldn't afford to wail now.

"Ego. Your curse is ego."

outside. Think of Lila and Joe. The library. Baby Rachel.

"I'm just not sure you have the capacity to rehabilitate, quite frankly."

Where was he going with this?

"It's apparent from your actions. Once out there, everything you did was grounded in evil."

She heard movement again, but daren't look up.

"Ish. Now he's a piece of work isn't he? He took more than you from the Goddess. He took another of my brides, Zadie. Zadie happily left her baby in here, happily left her child of Gena. Imagine? And now I believe the two have joined in sin and created a bastard, yes?"

"Yes, Father."

"He took Dorcus, a timid vulnerable girl, Eli, a hard worker, and he took Abe."

She heard him get up from his seat and slowly make his way down to where she knelt. As he approached her, so did the smell of his stale body odour. His wheezing told her he was just a few steps away.

"Abe. Tell me about Abe. When did you meet him?"

"Sir," she began.

"I am not your Sir. I am your father, your leader, your God!" His voice shook. "Answer me."

"Father, I wanted to see him to find out why he left the group."

"Had Ish not told you he had been banished?"

"No Father. No one would tell me what happened."

"So, dark-willed as you are, you went against your precious Ish, and you found him. Always working against the rules, are you not? Against those who are trying to protect you."

Keziah sobbed inwardly. He was right. She always went against those who tried to help her. Yvonne, so full of love and concern, had risked her own job. She'd refused to heed her warnings.

"And then, once you'd found him, once you snared him. He told you he wanted to come home. But still, when he tried to look after you and protect you, you used violence against him."

His breath reached ear and she winced.

"Father," she whimpered.

"What?" he roared. "You raised his passions, teasing him about his future with you until he could no longer cope."

She finally broke down, sobbing over his erratic breathing.

"But you couldn't run away this time, could you?"

"No Father," she wept.

"Why not?"

"He locked me inside his flat, Father."

"So, what did you do instead? Nasty little Keziah, tell me out loud."

She began to talk when he roared again. "Look at me"

She raised her head and looked him in the eye. He stood directly above her staring down with black eyes. Her shoulders bowed and the dizziness came in waves.

"I want you to tell me what you did to your brother. I want you to say it out loud. What did you do to your husband to be? The man who wanted to have babies with you. What did you do to the man who was trying to protect you?"

She tried to calm herself enough to talk but her knotted throat wouldn't allow any words through.

"Tell me," he whispered into her ear.

"I stabbed him." She managed to get it out.

"Louder."

"I stabbed Abe but..."

Don't say but.

He circled her like a hawk ready to pounce on its prey. She wondered if he would hit her from behind and braced herself for a blow.

"Every man who tried to protect you, you have and betrayed them. You even stabbed one.

Tell me, how should you be punished?"

"I do not know, Father."

"How convenient." His tone changed. Hopefully he had calmed a little.

She waited in silence, but he was letting her sweat, and she knew it.

Eventually, after a chesty cough and spit up, he cleared his throat. "Retribution will help deterrence."

Back at his armchair, Sy proceeded to pour a cup of tea from a silver teapot into china cup with saucer. She watched him suck the tea, his face pallid and moist. She'd barely had a chance to see him properly since she came back, either her head was always down, or she was disoriented or distracted. Even in the low light, she could see his eyes darting from side to side. He took another sip, his little finger in the air. The man oozed lunacy, and his unpredictability terrified her. He set the cup back onto the table and placed his hands on his knees with a sickly smile.

"Yes, retribution is a funny one. Your community, the one who decided to save you, well, they need to know that our system works, don't they?"

"Yes, Father."

"The punishment must let the others understand what will happen if they behave as you have."

She inhaled sharply.

"The women say they don't want you stripped and flogged. Only Gena knows why. I personally think it would do for starters." He chuckled manically. "Interestingly, they don't want to see you humiliated, even after the disrespect you have shown them. Good clean women, they are."

She heard some movement outside the door and then a knock.

"Charity, come in please and take note."

Keziah heard her open the door creak open.

"Yes Father. Mother Abi is still here."

"Oh, tell that damn stubborn woman to come in too."

Once they both shuffled into the dark room and took their places, he continued.

"One last thing you little reprobate before we talk punishments."

She looked up at him again. His mouth was twitching, and he was still sweating.

"Let's talk about the night you ran away."

Her breathing deepened.

"The night you refused to marry your father."

"Father it - I..."

"Yes? You what?"

"It wasn't just..."

Stop talking. Stop talking.

"I am truly repentant."

"Stand up."

Keziah stood up and watched him heave his body out of his chair again and walk towards her. She held his glare. As he got closer he raised his arm and before she knew it she was back on the floor holding her stinging throbbing jaw. She could hear him panting.

"Get up," he screamed.

Stars whirred around her as she got up on one knee, then another, and stood staggering in front of him.

"Take your hand from your face, coward!"

"Father please, she is about to fall unconscious." Mother Abi came forward.

But he came again harder, and this time she knew . Her chest took a hard bang, and she curled up tight as she waited for the next blow. Did she just faint and come to? He spoke again from the chair, and she wondered how he got over there. The taste of blood was strong on her lips. She heard herself panting.

He cleared his throat and now spoke in a whisper. "You have gotten off lightly. But I wanted to give you just a teeny tiny taste of your future if I catch you taking one step out of line."

"Yes Father. Thank you, Father," she slurred as she looked over to see the stunned faces of Mother Abi and Charity.

"Now get her out of my sight, and do not let me see her again unless I say so."

She managed to stand up, focusing on each painful slow movement. Still swaying, she found the door. The door was her target. The door. Mother Abi ran and stood in front, catching her as she fell.

Chapter Nineteen

Keziah woke in the dark to mumbling whispers. She focused her eyes and looked down to see Mother Abi, sitting on the end of her bed rocking and praying. Her head spiked with a sudden dart of pain, and she groaned.

"Keziah." Mother moved up and put her hand on her forehead. "Are you alright, my dear?"

Keziah opened her mouth to talk but struggled with what felt like a small golf ball attached to her lip. Her mother stood up to help her, propping pillows behind her. After a few sips of water, she sat back and looked at her squarely.

"You are badly injured. I think some ribs are broken. Your face..." She looked down and a tear slid down her face.

"Mother, it's okay. It was to be expected." Keziah dribbled from the swollen side of her mouth. Mother quickly mopped it up with a handkerchief.

She sighed and shook her head. "Why would you do this to yourself? Why would you do any of this, Keziah?"

"Would you have preferred me to let him assault me?"

She got up to fix the bed. "Stay where you are for today. He wants them all to see you like this, but I've insisted you need a doctor."

Keziah's heart raced. This could be an excellent opportunity for a doctor to report back. Even a receipt or source of payment to the doctor might help them.

"Yes, please. I want to see a doctor. Are there any who come inside The Genus?'

"There's one but he's very disapproving of our life here."

"Please Mother, do you know his name? Who is he?"

Mother took a small notepad and pencil from her apron and began to write. When she was done, she ripped the page and handed it to Keziah. "Give this back to me to destroy when you are finished with it."

Keziah nodded. "Convince him to let the doctor in. I need painkillers."

"Try to sleep." Mother Abi disappeared out the door.

Keziah tried to move but the burning shooting pain stopped her in her tracks. Shuffling down the bed a bit, she managed to reach her arm underneath for the plastic package. She cried out as she pulled it up in front of her and with both hands opened the package and took out the device.

Hello. Anyone there? she texted.

Are you Okay? It's Yvonne.

How come you are connected?

I have one of the backup devices. Are you okay? What's going on?

Keziah hesitated. Where on earth could she start?

I have a doctor's name. They might call him to come to examine me. What have they done to you? Shall we send the police in?

No, no, just a punishment. Nothing too serious. It's over now. Could have been worse.

What did he do?

He hit me, in private. I'm okay. It's over now.

Stay strong honey.

I don't have much time. Here's the doctor's name.

Keziah typed the doctors details into the pager quickly, gasping in pain with her arm. Now her *punishment* was over, she wanted to get on with the tasks at hand. She pushed the device under her pillow. If anyone else came into the room, she could record them and send it to the detective. Just as she was resettling her sore body, the door swung open and in walked Charity.

Her jaw dropped. "Sweet Gena have mercy on you." She came in and shut the door. "He sent me to see how bad you are."

"I don't understand what is going on with you."

"I didn't know *this* was going to happen."

Keziah smiled benevolently. "It's okay. I understand. You have to look out for yourself."

Sy had taken Charity under his wing and was trying to mould her. The trauma she endured after Keziah left clearly made her unstable, and no wonder. No doubt he was manipulating her, and probably abusing her.

Keziah's lips cracked as she spoke. "Does it look very bad?"

"It looks terrible. Does it hurt?"

"Very much."

"I'll tell Father you need the doctor."

"Please do."

Later, as Mother Abi fed her some soup, Keziah told her about the wire, and how the detectives would get in touch with the doctor. She didn't seem to like it.

"Mother, please understand. This needs to stop."

"What does? Our way of living?" Her forehead wrinkled and she looked like a forlorn child.

"Not necessarily, but Sy is an evil abuser, and he needs to go to prison. No one should be here against their will."

"Come now, eat up."

"Mother, if the community was open and everyone had a choice to be here or not, wouldn't it be a ?" she persisted. "What a beautiful community we could have."

"Things are not so simple, child. I don't even know who owns this land. Where would we go?"

"You will get help. The authorities on the outside will help. I promise, it's not like he always told us."

Mother took another spoon of soup from the bowl and slowly moved it towards Keziah's swollen mouth. "For now, concentrate on getting stronger. Hopefully we'll get a doctor in to you later this evening."

Later, when things were dark and still, Keziah messaged the detectives to let them know the doctor had not arrived. They replied to say they were having difficulty contacting him. She hadn't heard from anyone in the house since one of the younger women brought up some bread and cheese for supper a couple of hours before. After a long sleep, still no one had come to collect the tray. She suspected Mother Abi was somehow incapacitated because she usually made a point of wishing her a goodnight.

Just as Keziah nodded off again, she heard the main door downstairs open, and people talk as if it was in the middle of the day. She tried to sit upright but a sharp pain in her shoulder stunned her, and she called out in agony. As people moved upstairs she recognised

Mother Abi's voice. The door opened quietly and in came Mother Abi, Charity, and a man she supposed was the doctor.

"Now, Keziah. Doctor Armenia will examine you to make sure you are alright."

She turned on the light. Charity stood at the door watching as the man sat down at the end of the bed, putting his leather bag on the floor. He was a dark balding man with a well-groomed moustache.

He looked directly into her eyes. "Hello, Keziah, I have spoken with Father Sy, and there must be no talk of how these injuries happened if I am to examine you. Do you understand?"

"Yes."

He spent some time checking her all over; every bruise was examined and every joint mobilised. He shone light in her eyes and down her throat. His touch was firm but comforting. She hobbled by the bedside, trying to bend, and raise her arms. When he touched her ribs she involuntarily squealed. When he was finished she got back into bed, and he took out a pad and pen and began to write.

"Her cuts should be redressed every day, especially the busted lip and brow. I'm writing down instructions".

"Yes, Doctor. And her ribs?"

He looked up at Mother Abi with disdain. "I suspect three of her ribs are cracked, and I would not be surprised if the clavicle is sprained too."

Mother Abi sighed and covered her mouth with her shaking hand. Keziah looked up at her and then over at Charity who stood in silence, taking everything in to report back.

Charity cleared her throat. "Doctor, how long will it take Keziah to heal? To be able to get out of bed and do her duties?"

He didn't even turn to look at Charity. He looked at Keziah again and proceeded to talk "You must rest. Your ribs will not heal if you don't rest. It can take up to six weeks."

"Doctor, can't I leave this room?" Thoughts immediately moved to getting on with finding useful information. Six weeks inside this little bedroom would be torture.

"Day by day you will be able to do a little more. It's clearly very painful for you to move at all. Your cuts, although manageable with regular clean dressings must not get infected. You must not lift or carry anything, and if the shoulder issue persists, you should really get an Xray at a hospital or clinic."

He looked up to make sure Mother Abi had gotten all the information. She nodded.

"Now, I have some medicine but not enough to last long enough, so Father Sy promised me he would arrange a collection of anything you need from a local pharmacy."

He pulled his leather bag up onto the bed and pulled out different types of dressings, and antiseptic cream. She recognised the anti-inflammatory gel she sometimes used if she hurt herself running.

Finally, he handed some jars to Mother Abi. "These are painkillers. They are strong. She needs them three times per day, at least every four to six hours, for as long as needed. And then these are the anti-inflammatory pills. You can give her these in between the painkillers if she needs them. I expect she will."

He looked at her again and touched her hand. "Keziah, it is very important you rest if you want to fully recover. Do you understand me?"

"Yes, sir."

"You are going to be okay. There's nothing here that cannot be healed with rest and time." He squeezed her hand and she almost cried for the compassionate he was trying to give her.

As they walked down the stairs she heard him say "this girl should be in the hospital. She will not be fit for full duties for at least eight weeks if she heals well."

It was all so frustrating and shocking. Keziah thought of pulling out the pager to send an update but didn't want Charity barging in on her. The door opened. Sure enough, it was Charity.

"Mother Abi is walking the doctor to his car. She told me to come and check on you."

"Oh. Okay. So, it's worse than I thought."

"Yes. You have taken a hard beating."

Keziah turned her head sideways and looked at Charity. What in Gena's name was going on in her head.

"So, we can call it a beating now?"

Charity didn't answer.

"Anyway, I'm fine. I need to sleep."

"Well, I think you'll need to take some of these medicines first. Mother said she will be back."

"Okay."

"The doctor was a bit grumpy, wasn't he?"

"What do you mean?"

"I mean, he clearly doesn't approve of our life, the way we live in here." She pursed her lips.

"Well in fairness, getting a beating like this usually does cause alarm over the wall. I'd be in a hospital being closely monitored. Anyway, I found him very good."

"Why am I not surprised?"

"Charity, do you think you could just leave me alone, given my current state? Could you do that, please?" She felt like telling her to fuck off, but that wouldn't do.

The door opened again, and Mother Abi entered. "I told you to go to bed, Charity."

"Father said I had to oversee everything."

"Don't be ridiculous. You cannot be here every moment. Now I need to re-dress the cuts and give Keziah the medication. Be gone with you until the morning."

She left, slamming the door. They looked at each other knowingly. Mother got up from the bed and opened the door.

She looked out and left the door open and went back to the bed.

"Charity, seeing as you're still hovering, please go downstairs and get a glass of water for Keziah to take her pills."

Mother Abi's hand shook as she unbandage Keziah's wrist. "Let's get this sorted so we can all get some sleep."

"Sounds good."

"The doctor says they are considering taking you out of here. Or they may get him to report the injury to the police, so they don't have to reveal your undercover position."

"I'm fine. I've got these meds now and I'm being well cared for." She whimpered desperately. Surely they weren't going to take her out at the first hurdle.

Charity entered the room and put the glass of water down on the bedside table. She watched Mother Abi intently as she gently removed the dressings and rinsed the wounds. She began to work on some of the smaller scratches. Both women worked silently and tenderly, and Keziah suddenly found herself trying to swallow her sobs.

"Hush now, Keziah. Gena is looking down on you and protecting you. Everything will be fine." Mother pushed her hair behind her ears and got back to work

They continued until every graze, nick and bruise had be tended to. Once tucked in, the medication kicked in quickly. She did not see the women leave her bedroom.

Chapter Twenty

Over the next two weeks, her days were filled with nourishing meals, visits from some of the women and children, who read prayers from their scripts aloud in their best and most cute voices. Most of them were friendly and Keziah prayed with them just to keep the peace. They usually stayed for a chat and asked her if she needed anything. Some of the older women, the more orthodox types, watched her with tight lips and furrowed brows. She remained quiet and polite at all times.

"Mother, can't Zadie's mother speak to me? Dorothy, isn't it? Can't I see Laura?"

"Now is the time for healing, not to start your other escapades."

Keziah laughed. "How do you know about escapades?"

"Seniors occasionally watch films in the hall." She smiled at Keziah's reaction.

"Really? We had no entertainment when I was here! How is it allowed?"

"Who knows. No one complains. Perhaps he just wants to watch them himself," she chuckled.

"What other films did you watch? Surely no romance or violence or ?"

"No. Of course not. Mostly cartoons and the odd action film."

Keziah shook her head in disbelief. Nothing made sense in here anymore.

"Mother, can't you send Mother Dorothy with one of the meals? I won't say anything to her. I just want to see how she is, and how she reacts to me."

"We'll see."

Every few hours Keziah got help to move to the side of the bed, just to change positions for a while. The pager was still under her pillow, and she also had the time to pull out the wire and set it up. It was nice to hear their voices from time to time, but they agreed it was risky speaking aloud in case someone walked in on her. She left it on so they could get an idea of what kind of care she was getting, but she only used it when she was sure there was no one in the house. Anyway, there wasn't much to say while she was stuck in her bed.

Try to get a sense of people's feelings towards Sy, and Charity too, but don't push anyone if they seem detached or angry with you. Detective Frank had advised.

. I'm bored here. The days are so long so don't hesitate to make a list of questions and I will try to find out the answers.

You are relentless, Keziah!" It was Yvonne. A lump formed in her throat. She missed Yvonne so much. *Do you get the concept of resting?*

I do, and it's boring.

I'll come in there and get you myself, young woman, she teased.

Keziah, Amanda here. What we're looking for is more people who are doubting him, but as Frank says, be very careful how you approach.

The other thing of course is his finances. What is he paying for and from where? Money in and money out. Do you get me?

I get it. Charity seems to be in his quarters a lot and calls herself his assistant now. I'm trying to gain her trust, but she blows hot and cold.

Okay. Good. Slowly does it!

And they are allowed to watch movies here now sometimes. Can you believe it?

Someone was walking up the stairs, she called out as she pushed the pager under her pillow, but no one answered. Whoever it was reached the top of the stairs. The board on the landing creaked. Surely it wasn't Sy? A man in black peeped his head in. A guard.

"Hi Keziah, don't panic." He held his gloved hands up for her to stay calm. "I'm in touch with the police too. I think they told you about me?"

"They did. What's your name?"

"Richard. Look, I haven't got long. I just wanted to check how you are. Getting better?"

"Yes thanks. They are looking after me."

"Good. I'll keep an eye on you so if anything happens and you cannot get in touch with your contacts, I will be able to."

"Okay."

"I've got to go now. I just had a few minutes alone."

"Thanks, Richard."

He waved and walked quietly back down the stairs and out the door. Between the doctor and Richard, the detectives were seriously keeping eyes on her. Mother Abi was caring for her so well too. She appreciated it all. They all risked their own punishments if they were caught doing anything they shouldn't be.

Chapter Twenty One

By week three, she spent an hour or two every day sitting in the kitchen with the women. The silence was lifted, although neither Charity nor Mother were willing to explain anything about how the lifting came about. She could shell peas and wash vegetables, but her shoulder ached when she tried to peel potatoes. Mother Abi usually sent her back to bed when she noticed her getting tired. She enjoyed the atmosphere; the front door wide open with children running in and out, the women doing a host of tasks both in the house and in the yard. It hadn't been so long since she left, so Keziah remembered most of them, and got on well with the same characters she liked before. It was strange to observe the social world of the women now she knew the truth about The Genus, about the original concept and how women were very much free to do as they pleased under Mother Sarah's guidance.

These women, some of them in their fifties, were still very girlish and naïve. The Bearers, who really didn't have the same pressure as the Carers, were especially silly. Even though the Carers never had relationships with men, they understood life better, perhaps through their strict regimes and their laborious lives. The mothers, or Bearers as they were called, often popped in for nappies or other baby supplies. They'd stay around to chat or make a huge pot of tea for everyone. The Carers moved in a more focused and organised manner, to look after the mass of youngsters, ensuring to meet their needs at certain times of the day.

It occurred to Keziah for the first time these older Carers were virgins. She wondered if secret relationships went on between Carers and the guards or labourers. To spend your life without feeling another's lips on yours, or touch your loved ones skin, well, it seemed unnatural. Not that her only experience of it had been healthy. She'd like to talk to Mother about it, but it might be too embarrassing for her. Mother was one of the oldest apart from two very elderly retired Mothers who spent their days praying and sitting on benches chatting. She guessed she was in her late fifties, but they didn't celebrate birthdays.

"Hello! Keziah! Are you on another planet?"

She came round to many of the women looking at her and smiling. She looked up to see Mother Abi hand her a sandwich and put a cup of tea down in front of her. "After this, you must go and rest."

"Keziah, was the beating worth all this lovely attention you're getting?" It was Charity, standing at the kitchen entrance observing the scene.

"Charity!" said Mother Abi in disgust. "You should be ashamed of yourself."

"It's okay Mother. It's true. I am being looked after very well, despite my punishment being deserved."

As far as she could tell, the women did not approve of Charity's sarcastic behaviour, and no doubt they were very weary of her close relationship with Father Sy. They did not react, instead they turned their back on her and continued with their tasks.

Charity sat down opposite Keziah at the large oak table. "It was a joke."

"I know. Don't worry."

As the noise in the big kitchen rose again, she heard one of the women speak to another.

"Dorothy, can you pass me the sieve please?"

She looked up immediately. A tall slender woman passed the utensil to another woman prepping ingredients for baking. Mother Dorothy looked at Keziah and looked away quickly. Zadie's mother.

"Keziah, eat up now. We need the table to roll out pastry for pies."

She suspected Mother was trying to avoid this meeting altogether.

"Yes Mother."

Keziah looked over at Charity who grinned.

"Whatever are you grinning at?"

"Oh, nothing," she replied as she sauntered out the door.

"That girl," said Mother Abi with a sigh, "What will become of her?"

The other mothers mumbled in agreement.

"Is Charity a Carer, Mother? She never really answered me when I asked."

"There's been a bit of a pause on her long term role for the moment. Now she is in this new role to assist Father Sy on a day to day basis, I am not sure what her next role will be."

"I see."

Charity was vulnerable. She tried to escape with Keziah already. She sent a note to Ish not long after Keziah managed to escape. She remembered Charity's note said her life was terrible and she had been shunned. What changed? And what was Sy's for her?

Later as Mother Abi dressed Keziah's wounds she asked about Dorothy.

"So, Dorothy seems like a nice woman."

"Dorothy is a hardworking strong woman."

"Have you talked to her about me?"

Mother continued to dab her cuts with cotton dipped in antiseptic. "It was very hard for her – when Zadie left."

"I can only imagine."

"But little Laura gave her strength to carry on."

Keziah could see where this was going.

"I think Zadie would just like to know Laura is doing well, her parents are okay."

"You can see for yourself they are doing just fine."

"But –

"Keziah, stay still please!"

"Sorry."

"You know you don't seem to realise tearing this whole community apart will have detrimental consequences. You take for granted that everyone will be happy about it."

Keziah was silenced and she knew her mother was right. It didn't occur to her outside. All she could think about was getting Sy into prison so the abuse would stop. It was all very well and good to feel like you were saving people, but what if they didn't want to be saved?

"I do understand, but I know you agree he cannot be allowed to continue abuse and imprison people any longer."

"I agree with the sentiment, yes."

"Mother, maybe Dorothy would like to send a message to Zadie. I can do that for her."

"I have already spoken to her. When there is something to tell you, I will tell you." Her tone changed and Keziah immediately regretted pushing it.

That night she sent a message to the detectives to say she had seen Dorothy and she looked well. She asked them to let Zadie know. She didn't want to tease her to say there might be a message just yet.

Chapter Twenty Two

Every day Keziah gained strength. The furthest she went was to the barn or the bottom of the yard with some of the women to feed the hens. She helped with the laundry by folding the children's clothes too but was permanently consumed with trying to come up with a plan to get into Sy's office. The detectives told her to bide her time and focus on recovery. Of course, the advice made sense, but it was frustrating, thinking about the next marriage set up, or the next poor young person who was desperate to leave. It was all happening under her nose, and there was no way to help anyone in need. Then there was Charity who clearly wasn't in a good place. Things were moving far too slowly.

"Up to bed with you," Mother Abi would say every afternoon after lunch, and she would rest until someone brought the evening meal. Then she would do a little walk around the house just before sunset, to get out again. Her ribs hurt less and less, and some of the cuts completely healed. Her shoulder still gave her trouble, but it was low grade pain and nothing she couldn't handle.

"Dorothy will bring your dinner up this evening."

"That's wonderful, Mother."

"Go easy. She might get upset or frustrated. Let her lead the conversation. Do you understand?"

The tall slender woman entered the room carrying a tray with a bowl of casserole and some bread. "Hello, Keziah."

She didn't even look at her as she placed the tray down on the side table. She walked back over to the door and closed it quietly before turning to look at her. She kept her hand on the doorknob.

"Mother Abi said you wanted to talk to me."

"Mother Dorothy, I thought you might like some news of Zadie."

The woman's eyes were tired. She sighed and looked down.

"I don't want to upset you," continued Keziah, "It's just I've been living with her, and she was eager to know Laura and you were well."

"She didn't think about Laura when she ran off in the dead of night. She left her own daughter to the fate of the same community she turned her back on."

"I'm sure she trusted Laura would be taken care of by you."

"Have you forgotten what is asked of us by the Goddess? Laura is owned by the Goddess and guided by Father Sy."

"Of course. Sorry. I-I just wanted you to know you have a new grandbaby." Keziah smiled at Dorothy, hoping to lighten the conversation.

"Well, it is no grandbaby of mine. Zadie chose to leave her family, and The Genus."

"She was scared and unhappy, Mother Dorothy. She made a very good life for herself out there. She works hard and helps other people, and now is a mother again."

Dorothy looked at Keziah and smiled gently. "It is good to know. What is the child's name?"

"Rachel. She's beautiful."

"." She got ready to leave when Keziah spoke quickly before the door opened.

"If you were to send a message, what would you say?"

"You are on the wrong side of the Goddess young woman." Mother Dorothy flushed and marched out of the room.

Keziah let her face fall into the palm of her hand. Bad move. She could have left it until the next time they spoke.

Later Mother Abi appeared to collect the tray and help Keziah up for the last evening walk. "I told you not to push her, Keziah."

"I'm sorry. She asked Zadie's baby's name so I thought she might want to go further."

"Give people time or your whatever it's called will fail." She waved her hand in the air. "People are scared! They know what he is capable of, and now they have the proof, you!"

"I'm sorry. I get too excited sometimes. She wanted to know more."

"Maybe she does, but you need to let her digest things."

"I hope she won't report me."

"She won't. Dorothy is a good woman."

After some morning chores, Keziah sat on a bench in the sun, watching the children play. Just considering going back indoors, Dorothy approached hand in hand with a little girl.

"Good morning, Keziah."

"Good morning, Mother Dorothy."

"This is Laura. Say hello, Laura".

"Good morning, Mother Keziah."

"Oh, I'm not a Mother, Laura. Not yet anyway." She looked at Dorothy and smiled. "It's lovely to meet her."

"Laura is five years old now."

"Five. You are a very pretty girl. Do you like learning?"

The child nodded and smiled.

"She is a very good girl. Praise Gena."

"You certainly seem to be, Laura. Well done!"

Laura smiled again and ran off to join her friends.

"Thank you for letting me meet her."

Dorothy nodded slowly. "You can tell her the child is well. She is healthy and clever, and I always have eyes on her. She lives in the same house as me."

"I will tell her. Thank you."

"Let that be that Keziah, please."

"Yes, Mother."

Dorothy turned to see Mother Abi come down the yard. She smiled and waved and walked towards her. They met and walked off together around the side of the house, with Laura in tow. Zadie would be so happy to get this message. She'd send it on the pager later to be sent directly to her.

MESSAGE FOR ZADIE

Zadie, I spoke with your Mother. She was hesitant to talk at first, although happy to hear you had a good life. When I told her you had a baby she asked the name. Today she brought Laura to meet me. She is a beautiful little girl, full of smiles. Your mother said to tell you she is healthy and clever, and they both live in the same house so she can always watch over her. She asked me to leave things at that. But if you want to send a message back I'm sure she will receive it over time. She's now another person who knows I have contact outside, but Mother Abi says she will not report it.

Chapter Twenty Three

Arriving at the police station, Yvonne glanced at her phone once more before pocketing it—no messages, a rare occurrence. The past few days had been nothing short of chaotic. After locking her car, she headed towards the reception area.

"I'm here to see Detective Frank Power. He's expecting me."

The receptionist checked her off the visitors list, gave her an access card on a lanyard and asked her to sign in on a page stuck to a clipboard. She obliged stiffly and waited until she was told to go ahead. By now she knew the way.

"Yvonne! Nice to see you. Please take a seat. We've just been discussing the project with the powers that be."

She sighed and took a seat. "Glad to hear it. This project looks like it's falling on its face, Frank. Keziah is in over her head."

"We've had the doctor check her over. She's perfectly fine and stable, despite her injuries."

"Oh, come on Frank! How could she be? And you have no way of knowing this isn't going to happen again."

He sat back and folded his arms. "Well, we can take an educated guess, can't we? Look, Sy's back is against the wall. He went too far, and he knows it. He sent Charity to check *how bad it was*, and he let the doctor in. These are signs he is weakening."

"So, what now? She sits tight until she's better, and then tries to steal some files from his office, or grabs a few photos of – of what?"

Frank looked at her blankly, but she refused to lie down.

"It's all so vague! None of it seems worth this. I'm really surprised you're letting her go through this, to be honest."

"Yvonne, there are things you don't know, things we can't share with you right now. Once Keziah is better, the guard, our mole, will be working closely with her. He'll brief her on exactly what we're looking for."

"So, there's something else going on?"

Again, he just looked at her but said nothing.

"What are we talking about here, Frank? Drugs, and what else? Weapons?"

"Yvonne..."

"All of the above?"

"Pretty much. Look, Keziah is well trained. She's very capable. Once she's up and about, things will start happening and we'll be able to go in and swoop Sy within a couple of hours if we need to, along with anyone needing urgent assistance."

"She could be dead by then, and you know it. He's completely unstable. He didn't just slap her across the face. He broke her ribs! Don't forget it's not the first savage beating she's had. She's already trying to deal with so much trauma..."

Amanda knocked on the door and entered. "Hi Yvonne."

"Hello. Any updates?" She was determined to remain steadfast.

"Actually, Zadie's mother has been responsive. She allowed Keziah to meet the child and send a message to Zadie."

Yvonne smacked her lips. "Zadie is not in good shape right now. She's suffering with postpartum depression and has enough on her plate."

Amanda let her head hang sideways. "But you knew the plan all along. There's no point in e three weeks later complaining. Anyway, this is something positive for one of your people."

"It's not going to help Keziah."

Amanda shook her head. "Keziah had a proper psychological evaluation. She was given all the training and preparation she needed, and then some. She's doing fine."

Yvonne looked at Detective Frank and raised an eyebrow. "Really?"

"I agree. There are no surprises here."

"Okay." She took a deep breath in and put her hands flat on the desk. "If it looks like Sy is going to hurt her again, will you 'swoop' as you put it, in and get her?"

"It's very possible. Or we'd get our mole in there to take her out."

Amanda cleared her throat. "I don't mean to be rude Yvonne, but you have no say in this. We didn't even need to give you access to her pager or wire messages. Let us do our job."

Yvonne stood up and leaned over the desk, pointing her finger at Detective Frank. "If something happens to her, I'll go in there myself. Do you understand?"

"Yvonne..."

She grabbed her bag and slammed the door on the way out.

Amanda looked at Frank. "That woman is a liability, Frank. I told you we gave her too much leeway from the beginning."

Frank, always stoic, shrugged his shoulders. "You didn't help things. I've known Yvonne for a long time. She works hard for her young people."

"We don't need her dictating to us. This project could go big."

"Believe me, you're better having Yvonne on your side."

Chapter Twenty Four

Charity crawled up the stairs, dreading having to disturbing him. You just never knew how Father would react. Even though he sent her on a mission, he might still be angry with her intruding on him. She knocked gently.

"Enter."

She opened the door and put her head in first. "It is Charity, Father. I checked on Keziah."

"Come in."

She closed the door behind her and approached him as he sat in his throne drinking what smelled of some kind of alcohol. He did it a lot these days. "Well?"

"Father, she looks very bad. Her mouth and eyes are both very swollen. There's still some blood on her face and arms and she does not seem to be able to move without pain."

"Is that so, dear Charity?"

"Yes, Father."

"And do you think it's just reward for her behaviour?"

"Oh yes, Father. I really do. I was just reporting-"

"And do you think we should allow a doctor to come in and see her?"

"Yes, Father. She will be of no use if here is long term damage."

"Yes. Good girl, Charity. Come and give your father a kiss goodnight."

This was another new habit. Especially on the nights he drank his foul-smelling whisky. She kneeled beside his chair, leaned into his face and waited with her eyes closed. She breathed in through her nose as he forced his sloppy mouth hard onto hers, pressing into her lips.

"Off you go."

She hesitate at the door. "Father?"

"What?"

"Have you had any more thought on my request to be a Carer?"

"No, I have not. What is this obsession with you women to be Carers. It is for the ugly women; the carers will make ugly babies. It is for the strong women who can work hard and do some heavy lifting. Surely, that is not for you Charity?"

"I just – I think I can be a very useful Carer. I love to guide the children and I'm a hard worker. Even though I don't have a set of duties at the moment, I tend to the hens, and I help with the-"

"Go to bed."

"Yes, Father."

With a heavy heart Charity snuck into the dormitory so as not to wake anyone. She didn't fit anywhere. The other women were starting to resent her. Why had her attempts at escape never worked? Even those on the outside didn't trust her. She detested being Father Sy's spy, his goodnight kisser. She hated it.

Chapter Twenty Five

Still stiff and sore from the punishment, Keziah lay on her bed doing some leg stretches. She'd gone from being extremely fit to moderately active in her chores, to bedridden all in three months. Joe wouldn't be impressed. Smiling at the thought of him, she wondered how he was getting on. Their date, just the week before she left, went well but they agreed to get on with their own things and see what happened. There was something about him that made her think she could be herself, and together they could encourage each other in their individual endeavours. Experiencing someone's genuine attraction towards her as a woman was a novel sensation. Abe suffocated her. Love-bombing Yvonne called it. It certainly was nothing like this. Even if her and Joe never got it together, it will have been worth the good night kiss, and touching his sweet soft lips with hers. It will have been worth seeing his smile as he moved closer to her. The way he held her, tenderly but firmly.

Keziah sat on a stool in the laundry room to the side, folding pillowcases and towels. The other Carers were off tending to their chores or caring for the children, or in The Fulcrum praying. The aromas of the bread baking in the oven, and the stew bubbling away in a huge pot on the stove made her hungry wafted through the kitchen. She appreciated the homecooked food much more now since she tasted the processed microwaved rubbish out there. Most people just didn't have time to cook from scratch, or they were too tired when they got home from work.

She heard footsteps and some low talking as people entered the kitchen. to see Mother Abi and Mother Dorothy, standing close to one another.

"Honestly Dorothy, I don't know where it will all end, but I can't see it happening any other way at this point."

"Praise Gena, it is for our own good."

"I hope so. I worry about the children. I've heard awful things about these children's homes and social workers. They could never get a life as good as this one, but..."

"Indeed. I worry for little Laura. Wouldn't it be wonderful for her to be reunited with her mother though? Keziah says Zadie is doing very well."

"Yes that's what she says, but I worry Keziah's version of what is well, is different. She is strong, but she is young and some of the things she told me about out there would stand your hair on end."

Dorothy sighed. "But we cannot go on like this. He is taking too many young women as brides without taking family lines into consideration. Before long we will have a serious issue with illnesses."

Keziah held her hand up to her mouth. So, they were talking between themselves and acknowledged the problems – certainly progress, although she was a little hurt to hear Mother didn't trust her one hundred percent.

She quietly stepped out of the laundry room. "I'm sorry, Mothers. I didn't mean to pry. I couldn't help but overhear your conversation. I thought it best to make myself known."

Dorothy looked at Mother Abi with panic. Mother Abi, calm as usual, blinked slowly at her friend.

"Thank you for making yourself known, Keziah. Mother Dorothy and I do sometimes share some private conversation. Is the laundry folded?"

"Most of it."

"Well on you get and finish it, please."

Keziah obeyed. She couldn't help but wonder how many more people felt this way. The thoughts of moving to the dormitory filled her with dread, but maybe she'd have better opportunities to get information, and perhaps the office would be more accessible. However, privacy was a privilege in here, and it would be much more difficult to send messages on the pager or the wire. It would be hard to leave Mother's protection, sleeping in the room next to her, always under her wing.

Charity floated around during the day, until Sy called her with a task. Perhaps spending more time together might help her to open up. Keziah couldn't help but feel bad for her, even though she couldn't trust her. The girl had two failed attempts at escape: first with her originally, and second when she sent a note to Ish asking for help. The only one ready to give her a chance was Ish, the rest, including herself, were up in arms about it. The general consensus was no one wanted to open their home to another Abe, another troubled person. She thought momentarily of Abe but then pushed him out of her mind. She couldn't afford those emotions right now.

No matter what, Keziah and Charity had been together since they were babies. They shared the same nursery. They played together in the same yard and prayed together on the same bench. Charity was an insecure little girl who struggled with sharing friends. She told tales and was cruel to the other children at times. Keziah resolved to try to help her, even if it meant trying to get her out. But she'd play a slow game. She didn't want her to get angry and flippantly report something to Sy. The power game she played came from hurt and fear. Of that, Keziah had no doubt.

Chapter Twenty Six

After lunch, Mother Abi did not tell her to go to bed to rest, so Keziah happily got involved in some cleaning after the baking.

"Keziah, you're to go to The Fulcrum to pray," said Mother Abi stiffly.

"What?"

"Don't *what* me, Keziah. It's time you started to get back into your prayer routine. Do you need guidance?"

"I'm not sure. It's just it has been so long since I have been out of this area. I do pray but…"

"I can walk with her, Mother." It was Charity. She stood watching quietly at the door, as usual, observing without any attention.

"She does not need a babysitter, Charity."

"No, it's okay. Thanks Charity. Having you accompany me would be good."

Mother Abi gave Keziah a disapproving look. She chose to ignore it until she could speak with her later.

As they walked, Charity prattled on about a very handsome guard she liked.

"Don't let anyone catch you flirting, Charity."

"Oh, don't be silly. He smiled at me once or twice and I smiled back. That's all."

"Which guard?" Keziah observed her chitchatting and giggling. She could change her tone and mood so quickly.

"His name is Richard. He has only been with us for five years."

"Really? How unusual."

"It is. But I think Father needed more men to help with guarding."

"Oh, I see. Are new people allowed to join us now?"

"Well, I wouldn't say so, but there are a few males who joined over the years. One brought a wife and a child."

They sounded more like soldiers than guards for The Genus.

"Are all the new male guards here now?"

"I think so. Some of them have regular meetings with him. They leave quite often too. For supplies and things."

She was already getting new information, affirming she really needed to move to the dormitory. At The Fulcrum entrance they stopped for a moment.

"Would you like me to come in with you?"

"I think I need a private moment with the Goddess. It has been a while..."

"They might have prayer school going on in there. It might not be very peaceful."

Keziah smiled. "I'm fine."

Charity lingered for a few minutes more, and it was hard to know if she wanted information for Sy, or she was looking for some company. Perhaps she remembered the last time Keziah was in The Fulcrum, the night she ran from the marriage ceremony. When Charity finally walked away, Keziah entered the hall. The silence brought with it a sense of serenity. She looked up at the giant image of the Goddess, swathed in beautiful white robes, a garland of flowers around her head, almost like a halo. Gena's kind face, pink lips and rosy cheeks, had always served as the ideal woman for Keziah. Since she was a child, she was told she looked like the Goddess. When she got out she would change her hair colour for a while. Lila was always dying her hair colour and it looked like fun.

Now she knew the full history of The Genus, she appreciated it more than ever. The Goddess represented the sacredness of women. The importance of women's roles in society, in free will to all. The huge mural covered the whole gable wall, behind the pedestal, on the platform. The Fulcrum likened a traditional church, with it's rows and rows of seats and places to kneel to pray. There were candles and flowers too. Gena's hand reached out in front of her, as if beckoning her people to come to her, to trust her and to be themselves. Her soft smile pulled Keziah in so strongly. Overwhelmed by the sadness, the grief of losing her faith she thought instead about remembering Mother Sarah, and *her* ideals. Women *were* important. The women of The Genus needed to be protected. They needed to be saved from him.

She never made it onto the altar the evening she was supposed to marry him. She told Mother Abi she was sick, and then she bolted. It was the beginning of everything: getting trapped in the cold lake, climbing the wall, the car speeding off. Goosebumps rose all over her body as she recalled her efforts at tracking down Abe, and all the uncomfortable feelings that ensued. She didn't have the mechanisms to cope with everything then. For Christ sake, she was still healing from all the trauma of the escape, let alone what happened with Abe.

If only she knew to stay away from him. If only she had heeded the warnings of the people who tried to protect her.

"Hello"

She jumped and turned around to see Richard, standing there.

"Oh, hello."

"Take a seat and wait for me."

She walked to the front of the temple where a few pews from some old church had been used for as long as she could remember. Behind the pews were a row of foldable chairs and behind some almost threadbare mats for people to sit on.

She heard him behind her. "Are you okay?"

"Yes. I think so. Eager to get on with things."

"Physically, are you doing better?"

"Much. I was considering moving to the main dormitories soon, if I can."

"Sounds like a good plan. The detectives want to know you are strong enough to continue."

"I'm fine."

"Good. If you start spending time in the more public sections we can begin to work."

"Charity told me there are new men here. Why? How did you get in?"

"It's a very long story, but Sy is involved with some pretty hardcore stuff."

"I know about the tax fraud, and the criminal incest laws he's breaking. The detectives mentioned drugs but...."

"Things have become more serious. More complicated."

"How so?"

"I can't tell you very much yet. I am waiting for more intel myself."

"Right."

"Don't worry too much. When I know more, you will too."

They sat there in silence for a moment.

"Charity likes you," she stated, waiting for an explanation.

"It might be on the cards. A way to keep an eye on her if you get me."

"I should tell you she's already very messed up. I'm worried about what Sy is doing to her."

"More of a reason to get close. We can protect her too."

"We as in...? Is there a plan?"

"Listen, move to the dormitory. Leave your devices in Mother Abi's house. I've spoken with her and she knows."

The change in his tone made her feel uneasy. He was giving her orders instead now, of the detectives.

"Okay. When will you tell me the plan?"

"Soon."

His footsteps trailed back down the tiled aisle, and she heard the exit door close. Confused, Keziah looked behind her to make sure there was no one else listening. What did he mean? Everything was so cryptic. She suspected there was a plan she was not privy too. She was merely a cog in a wheel of a bigger operation. Richard joined The Genus five years ago, and yet she had no memory of ever seeing him before. Something else was happening. Also, If Richard got involved with Charity, would he really protect her?

She heard the door open and turned around. It was Mother Abi. She walked up and sat beside her.

"How was your prayer time?"

"You knew, didn't you?"

"Yes." She kept her eyes on the Goddess.

"What has he told you?"

"Father is in trouble in a very serious way it seems, outside of The Genus."

"Yes. I believe so, but I'm unclear of my role now."

"I am sure all will be revealed in time. There is no going back now, Keziah, for you or I." Mother Abi took Keziah's hand and squeezed it. "So long as we can keep the children safe. You'll help us to protect them, won't you?"

"I promise, Mother."

She snuck to bedroom before supper and took the wire out.

"Hello? It's me. Anyone there?"

"Keziah, it's Simon."

"Hello. Just wanted to report a few things."

"I'm just getting Frank in here. One second."

While she waited she watched the sun set through the window. She'd missed the views from this house. It was north facing so didn't get the sunrise, but the sunsets over the expanse at the end of the yard, were always stunning.

"Keziah. Frank here. How are you holding up?"

"Hi Frank. I spoke with Richard."

"Great."

She expected more from him.

"So, it seems there's a larger plan in the making, right?"

"Richard has been working with another police department for some years now. He's building a large case."

"Why didn't you tell me?"

"I told you he was in there. You knew he was going to keep an eye."

"Yes but it seems I'm now taking orders from him."

"I wouldn't say so, but *Richard has a lot of experience. He has been involved in undercover work with some of Sy's associates for a while now."*

"Okay."

"How are you? How's life on a day to day basis?"

She could tell he was trying to change the subject.

"It's fine. I'll be moving to the dormitory soon. Tomorrow maybe. It'll be better to try to get information."

"Good. Any more contact with Sy?"

"No, thankfully. But I will be taking in part in all ceremonies from now on and eating in the dining hall with the others."

"How are things with Charity?"

"I think I'm getting closer. She changes all the time though. I suspect he's really playing with her mind. Listen, I think Richard is going to start some kind of affair with her and I'm not sure –

"Keziah don't worry. Charity is in safe hands, and when this thing all comes falling down, she'll be looked after very well."

"I get it. But I think she's already in trouble. If Sy finds out he'll really hurt her."

"We won't let that happen."

She clenched her jaw. He thought she couldn't see through his indifference. Seriously some people were so transparent without realising.

"I won't let it happen either."

"Rest assured, there'll be no need to get involved."

"What's the plan now?"

"Take your time, get better, get on with your daily life and get closer to Charity. If you see or hear anything you think might be interesting to us, let us know. Otherwise, Richard will make you aware of anything else. Sound okay for now?"

"I suppose. One more thing. Did you know Sy has recruited other men from outside as guards? Charity says they leave the grounds often."

"Right."

She blushed. Of course, they knew.

"So, will Richard tell me the 'big' plan?"

"Yep, it's all still in the making but he will be in touch with you, and of course we will be in constant contact."

"And if I get into the office, you're looking for files or anything to do with finances, right?"

"Yes, but hold it for now. You need to recover. We don't want you walking yourself into more injuries. You could keep your eyes peeled in any of the outdoor storage units or barns for anything strange or unidentifiable."

"Like what?"

"You know, vehicles, heavy machinery, those kind of thing."

"Okay. One more thing Frank?"

"Sure"

"Did Zadie get the message?"

The pause unsettled Keziah.

"Is something wrong?"

"Not at all. I just don't know if she got the message yet. Amanda will have the answer to that. I'll ask her to message you about it."

"Yes please. It would be nice to know she got it, and it made her happy. Also, I have more opportunities to talk with her mother so...."

"Well, let's focus on the task at hand, yeah?"

The change in tone made her feel uneasy. So now, Richard was the big chief? He was planned on faking a relationship with Charity, and she didn't even know if the message got to Zadie.

"Is Yvonne still seeing my messages?"

"Again, that's something for Amanda to check in with you about. Perhaps we can start arranging times so she can be here."

"Okay. I have to be honest; something feels off."

"Everything is fine. There are just delays in the strategy building now that another department are involved. That's why I'm saying to take your time. You've got time."

"Alright then. I'll get on with settling down here. I'm eager to get something useful for you. The sooner the better this is all over."

"You're doing a great job, Keziah. Speak soon."

She switched the pager off and lay on the bed playing the conversation over and over in her head. First, Richard was suddenly more involved in a plan she couldn't know about, and second she would have expected a response from Zadie almost instantly. She really wanted to hear something of Laura. Yvonne would have been the one to bring the message to her, but she hadn't spoken with Yvonne in over a week. What the hell was going on out there?

Chapter Twenty Seven

Keziah walked across the yard with a few pieces of clothing and a nice feather pillow Mother gave her when she was recovering. She was to report to the mother in charge of the dormitories, Mother Michelle. The women who did not frequent Mother's house, only knew her as the one who was punished, the one who ran away and stabbed someone. They tattled among themselves, bitchier and more distrusting than she ever remembered. Hopefully Charity would help her acclimatise.

For women, dormitories were divided into two: the Bearers section was marked B and Carers section was marked C, with large white square signs near each entrance of the barn-like buildings. The ground floors usually held a cloakroom, a few showers, and toilet area to the front. At the back, the more senior mothers had their sleeping space, divided by a thin wall. They managed the coming and goings and oversaw anything needing supervision.

The dormitories for Bearers were for women who were still breast-feeding their new-borns and did not live with their husbands for one reason or another. Some Bearers had guards for husbands, and the guards always slept in the guard's quarters. If a husband was not a guard, but decided he did not want to live with the wife he was assigned to, he could often choose another wife. This meant a woman could be a Bearer just once, and then never have another baby, or never be assigned to another husband. What a sad, lonely life it must be. Sometimes they were transferred to a Carers role but that was rare. Sometimes they were left in limbo and just helped out wherever they could. That being said, Keziah heard some passing comments about women now being assigned to Father Sy after already birthing another man's baby. It would have been unthinkable before.

The Carer's dormitories had a very different feel to them. There were no babies crying, and the women slept peacefully every night until it was time to start their day of prayer and duties again. They tended not to be so stressed because they had quite a strict routine and worked closely with other women. All things considered; they were the engine of The Genus and part of a strong sub-community. Being a Carer was all Keziah aspired to as a young girl, and all Mother had hoped for her. And here she was. It was all quite surreal.

Mother Michelle walked towards her as she entered. "Keziah, follow me please."

She followed obediently, past the cloakroom and into the senior mother's sleeping area. It looked like a living room despite the four single beds at one end. It had a desk, a nice armchair, with a little corner table with a fancy table lamp.

"Now, take a seat by the desk please. I want to talk to you."

Keziah sat down and waited. The woman gathered some papers from the desk and put them aside.

She sat down and looked into Keziah's eyes. "This is a new beginning for you, a chance to become a member of the team of wonderful Carers. I hope you appreciate this."

"Mother Michelle, it's all I ever wanted since I was a child. Thank you for accepting me here."

She inhaled and changed her position as she watched Keziah. She'd always had a downturned mouth. "My point is you should be very grateful. When Mother Abi suggested it was time for you to integrate again I was hesitant to agree. But Mother Abi knows best and tells me you have been working hard and you are trustworthy."

Keziah nodded eagerly.

"It remains to be seen."

"I promise I won't let you down."

"You will report to Mother Abi every morning at eight am after your prayers, and she will assign you your tasks for the day. I have spoken to the other young women you will share quarters with. I've told them there must be no hostility. You have repented and you have taken your punishment, so you deserve a chance in the name of Gena."

"Thank you, Mother".

"I want to stress, you only have once chance though, and I will not tolerate any misbehaving. Understood?"

"Yes, Mother."

"I see you have some clothes with you. Beside every bed, you'll see three hooks. You will also have a small bedside locker with two drawers for underwear and the likes. You'll probably remember tunics, aprons, and scarves are part of communal laundry. You can speak to a mother at the cloakroom when you need fresh items, but don't overdo it. We go through tons of laundry every week. One fruit stain on your apron does not entitle you to a fresh one."

"Yes, Mother."

"Your bed number is four and you are beside Charity. I'm not sure about this arrangement so I'll be monitoring you. Charity is a little flighty at times. Remember, this space is for rest and prayer only, and you should not disturb the other women."

How many more times could she say yes mother, thanks you mother. If she nodded anymore she'd strain her neck.

"Off with you then."

Keziah sat on her bed and took a deep breath in. Some women lay resting in silence, but otherwise the large room was empty. The brick and metal walls were painted white, but over time the paint had faded and chipped. The whole room looked tired and in need of a revamp. At the very end were bunk beds. Thankfully she was assigned her own decent sized bed, not too far from the exit. Once her things were hung and her new pillow down, there was still time to go back to Mother Abi's house to check on the pager. Maybe there was news about Zadie and Yvonne, from Amanda. Yvonne must be very busy not to have been in touch. She might have visited Abe. Maybe he was showing some new signs of recovery. It had only been about eight weeks, but it felt like a year since she came back in.

She was just about to get up and leave when Charity arrived, walking like a little girl that just got a big bag of sweets.

"I was the one who asked if you could be beside me," she beamed.

Keziah smiled. "Thank you. I was wondering if they'd let us be together."

"They had to. I got permission from Father Sy, but I said it was because I could keep a close eye on you," she giggled.

"Oh, don't tell me you're going to follow me around everywhere!" Keziah joked with her, but her heart thumped faster. She didn't need the burden of Charity following her around everywhere. She wanted to explore a bit without constantly looking over her shoulder. Maybe her getting involved with Richard would be a good thing after all. She was as bad as him then.

"Hello! Keziah!"

"Sorry. What?"

"Why are you always daydreaming mid-conversation?"

"I don't know. So many new things are happening. I'm good. What did you say?"

"I was just saying Elizabeth over there is a misery to deal with. She'd report you if you sneezed too loudly."

Keziah glanced over and saw Elizabeth, one of the ladies who was lying down, look up and shake her head.

"Hey! Don't get me in trouble Charity. I need to stay quiet and get on with my life, please."

Charity smacked her lips and laughed as she walked away.

"Where are you going?"

She walked back and leaned into her ear. "I'm meeting Richard around the back of the old garage." She looked at Keziah with an impish grin, waiting for a reaction.

"Be careful! If Richard is so serious why can't he ask Father Sy for your hand?"

"It might happen." She tottered off, delighted with herself.

In recent years, they bought new vans for the guards, and a minibus for the market. They parked in the new parking bay near the storeroom. The old garage, referred to as such because it was the one they parked their vehicles years ago. She guessed it was there they stored some older vehicles and parts now. She'd try to have a stroll around the area later.

Chapter Twenty Eight

After her first day of work in the mainstream of things, she discreetly made it upstairs to Mother Abi's bedroom. A quick check in with the pager was on the cards before heading to the dining hall to eat for the first time since her trial. Mother told her the pager and wire were now hiding under her own bed. Keziah reached under to find a small wooden chest. Inside the chest was the pager and the wire, in their original sealed plastic bag. Alongside it, she found some pictures, crocheted lace items, and a little carved wooden bird Abe made when he was young, as she recalled. She held it in her hand for a moment and perceived the love and sadness Mother Abi had for Abe, once her little boy.

Feeling quite unsettled about this creeping around to get messages out, she decided to use the pager rather than the wire for fear of being overheard. She sat on the side of the bed and typed quickly.

Hello. Keziah here. All okay. I'm in the dormitory and back to communal dining today. Mother is storing the devices in her bedroom. I won't have as much freedom to message but will make an effort to check in at least once per day. I am going to have a stroll around an area Charity mentioned later. I think it may be of interest. I would like to hear from Yvonne. Did Zadie get her message?

She waited a few minutes but there was no response. Usually, it was instant or within a minute. Keziah tapped her foot as she sat on the edge of the bed, thinking about what could possibly go wrong from here. Why are they no longer so enthusiastic about her project? Why had the atmosphere completely changed? They cut her loose.

Hello? I can't wait, or I will get in trouble. I am feeling nervous about the lack of contact and the lack of instructions. Please let me know what's going on. Am I still of use?"

She heard the quiet buzz instantly.

Keziah, It's Simon. Having a few technical issues today. Please don't worry. Wait for more information from Richard. Don't forget timing is everything. Just give it a day or two to settle back into group life."

Okay.

She inhaled sharply, switched off the pager and placed it back in the box. As she walked down the stairs, Mother Abi waited for her.

"Come on. They've already said their food prayers. This will never do, Keziah!"

They walked quickly towards the dining hall.

"Mother, has Richard told you anything?"

"Not now, Keziah."

"You know something I don't?"

"We will talk later."

Nothing seemed real anymore. Suddenly Mother Abi, and this new guard was involved in a scheme she had no knowledge about.

Rushing into the dining hall, she looked around to realise it was a bigger event than she imagined. Everyone was quiet and Mother Abi directed her to one of the long tables with other Mothers of her age group.

"Thank you, Mother."

Charity watched with a smile of encouragement as she made her way over to the table. Everyone moved up so there was no space beside them for her to sit. Finally, there was a small space at the edge of a bench. She looked at the women sitting at the table. Some of them smiled and others looked at her in spite. She smiled and said thank you to the young woman beside her. A tray was put in front of her with a plate of vegetables, a small bowl of rice and a yoghurt. She had no appetite, but in order to avoid more attention she put all her focus on mixing some of the rice into her vegetables. The whispers turned into quiet chatting and soon the normal buzz resumed.

The woman beside her passed her some salt with a smile. "We get salt every time we get rice now. Praise Gena."

Keziah responded eagerly. "Oh, that's wonderful. Thank you."

She took some salt and tried to pass it to the girl in front of her, but the girl purposely looked away as if she didn't see her. The next woman at the table smiled and took it. Keziah could see a lot of kindness around the table, but there were some diehards who still didn't accept her back into the fold. She ate slowly and in silence, waiting for the minute she could leave the hall and go to her bed.

The chairs scraped along the tiled floor and people slowly rose. Keziah followed suit and looked up to see Sy and Guard Isaac walk in. They made their way to the platform where their food would be served. Richard and two more guards followed. They looked like nothing more than bouncers. Richard scanned the room. At first, she thought he was locking eyes with her, but she looked over her shoulder to see Charity smiling. She looked back at Richard who winked and smiled ever so slightly before returning to his stoic expression.

Sy remained upright but swayed subtly. One of the guards touched his hand and he shrugged it away.

"Have you all eaten yet?" He looked around the room.

Silence.

"Are you deaf?" he shouted.

"We are eating, Father. Praise Gena, called out a mother. Probably an elder who was trying to pacify him.

"So, you are not deaf?"

"No, Father." The response came in unison.

He cackled darkly as if someone had told him a joke. One of the mothers, who cooked especially for him and the higher guards, came out to serve the food. She went to serve Sy first as usual, but he swung his arm upwards sending a hot pot of what looked like soup all over her. She squealed in alarm. He stood up and slapped her face before she could step away. The senior guards stood up and Richard brought the woman through the side door back into the kitchen. Sy, seeing the reaction of the guards and the shock of all in the dining hall dropped his head and started to shout.

"Praise Gena for the food"

"Praise Gena," came the response in unison.

Keziah could not believe what was happening before her eyes. She looked over at Mother Abi. Her head was down as she listened intently to another Mother speaking into her ear. She rose, and left discreetly, out the same side door. A few minutes later returned and walked down the aisles along the tables, telling everyone to eat up quickly and to watch for her signal. What on earth was going on? Was Sy drunk? Did Mother speak to Richard back there?

Everyone ate quickly and sat waiting apprehensively. The guards were now eating purposefully, ignoring all around them. Sy ranted and laughed at them, despite their serious faces.

Guard Isaac rose. "Mother Abi, can you please lead the prayer and have everyone leave in an orderly fashion."

Mother Abi nodded and began the gratitude prayer. Everyone joined in. Once finished, the mothers quickly got up and helped people to queue table by table. Keziah was grateful of how close her table was to the door. Just as she stood to leave, she looked up to the platform where Sy collapsed onto his plate. It was hard to know whether he was asleep or drugged or unconscious, but the guards remained stoic and simply watched everyone leave.

As she got out into the fresh air, a hand pulled at her shoulder.

"Did you see? It's shocking."

It was Charity. The elated expression on her face unsettled Keziah.

"What is wrong with Father? Do you know? Is he ill?"

"Richard says he drinks too much alcohol."

"It is shocking! What does Richard think of all of this?"

"Richard says maybe there will be a new leader in the future."

"What? Who?"

"Well, I don't know. Father is getting older anyway. At some stage the Goddess will speak to someone else, won't she?"

Keziah looked into Charity's eyes. She really believed in what she said.

"Yes. Praise Gena. Did you meet Richard yesterday?"

"Yes," she giggled, and ran off to catch up on some other younger women who came together to gossip as they walked back to their places of duty or prayer for the rest of the day.

Keziah looked back at the entrance to see Mother Abi standing at the door watching and guiding all the women out of the main entrance. She looked at Keziah and waved her off with her hand. There was nothing to do but go to the house and wait.

Chapter Twenty Nine

Sy was drunk in the dining hall, she typed. *Guards were very serious. Tried to get the situation under control. We ate and left early. His head was on his plate of food. Don't need answer as I cannot wait.*

Keziah didn't even know if any of this was useful. She suspected Richard was in constant contact with the detectives. When she heard movement downstairs, she made her way to the kitchen where Mother was putting on a pot of tea.

"Mother! What in the world is going on?"

"Things are changing before our very eyes, Keziah."

"Do you have new information?" Keziah folded her arms and stood against a press waiting, but Mother Abi continued with the tea and then started to slice bread in silence.

"Mother! What should I do? Are we in danger?"

She finally stopped what she was doing. "This guard - Richard."

"What about him? Who is he? I'm beginning to think his motives are not necessarily good. He is secretly meeting with Charity and-

"He is a member of a large criminal organisation. But he is also spying on the group for the police." She spoke very quietly and did not look at Keziah.

"Is he dangerous?"

"He seems to want to help. Only Gena knows."

"But why was Sy in that state?"

"I believe some of the guards are infiltrating The Genus."

"Did Richard tell you this?"

"He implied it. Once he found out from the police I knew your reason to come back, he decided it was better I know 'the bigger' picture as he put it."

Keziah shook her head as she tried to process it all.

"But what does it mean for us? For you?"

"Keziah," she threw her hands up in frustration, "I don't know any more than you! What I do know is we must protect the children, and we must make a plan should anything bad happen." She sat down at the table with a huge plate of sandwiches. "Now, some of the mothers are coming here this evening for a little discussion."

"But you cannot tell them anything."

"You don't have to worry about it now. I will imply certain things without causing a panic. We will, as Mothers, prepare just in case."

"Can I be here?"

"Of course not! It would rouse suspicion."

"True." She paused for a moment. "I think we should record your conversation and send it to the police."

"Why?"

"Because if they know your plan, and you need to use your plan they might be able to help."

"Go and set it up then, Child."

As Keziah ran up the stairs she heard her mother sigh. She must be so stressed. What was about to descend upon The Genus? She took the pager out, quickly sent another message to make the detectives aware the conversation would be recorded and then she put it in her underwear. She must carry it at all times now. Keziah brought the wire downstairs to the kitchen, deciding the dresser was a reasonable distance from the table. It generally needed to be no more than two metres from the conversation. She sat at the table and watched her mother, opposite her, sorting cutlery. She got up and took some cups from the big old oak dresser.

As she laid them on the table she leaned over to Keziah and touched her cheek softly. "Be brave and wait. Your moment will come!"

In the dormitory later, there was some general chitchat, but no one openly discussed what happened in the dining hall earlier. Keziah was relieved she received less hostility at bedtime compared to dinner. The atmosphere was generally tense, but they settled down early. It was, generally speaking, a peaceful space, but not as peaceful as sleeping in her own little box room beside Mother Abi's room.

If only she could sleep. Instead, all she could think of was about the gang taking over The Genus. She wondered if they drugged Sy or tricked him into getting drunk so his people would begin to doubt him. These new guards had been around for years though, and Mother Abi had already questioned the changes in his behaviour before Keziah arrived back. It certainly appeared to be building up to something big. Were these criminals just using the space, or did they have other plans The Genus? She needed to see Richard. Charity was fluttering around still trying to chat to people as they were preparing to sleep.

She beckoned her over. "Are you seeing Richard tomorrow?"

"Probably. Why?"

"Just wondering. Do you always meet at the old garage?"

"Yeah, mostly. He has a friend there who keeps an eye."

"Friend?"

"Yeah there are two mechanics, and another man who washes cars."

Charity was starting to drip-feed her new information.

"Are they from The Genus?"

"No, they mustn't be, because I never see them at The Fulcrum or dining hall."

"Don't you find it weird?"

"Keziah, I have been assisting Father with lots of weird things lately. Everything is weird now. Everything."

"What do you mean?"

"I can't talk here," she whispered. "Tomorrow."

Keziah thought about running more than once that day. She imagined taking Laura and running to Mother Sarah's secret bunker. Would she find it again though? Ish made a map for her escape. It was deep in the frontier, the furthest woods. Maybe Charity could accompany her. They could easily fit three or four people: Maybe Dorothy could bring Laura. Zadie would be so happy. Mother Abi might insist on staying and caring for the children, no matter what happened next. These thoughts spun around and around until she finally fell asleep from sheer exhaustion.

Chapter Thirty

She sat up in her bed to see a few mothers walking around talking to the carers with instructions. What now? By the time everyone was awake, Mother Michelle rang the bell at the top of the room and waited for everyone's attention.

"Everybody, please listen closely. Quickly get up, dressed, and washed. Then make your way to the dining area. There is a talk before breakfast."

Charity looked over at Keziah with a big grin, her eyes wide with excitement.

As they rushed across the grounds in groups, guards were installing poles throughout the grounds, from The Fulcrum to the dining hall, to the dormitories. Keziah thought they looked like the poles for holding streetlamps in the City, but she couldn't be sure. All the guards were in black, which was new. While the tended towards darker clothes they didn't all wear black like a uniform.

The men were already seated in the dining hall, talking among themselves. The platform, free of tables, looked ready for something other than eating. Women rushed in and found their place quickly, while some settled younger children into their seats. The hall changed from clamour and agitation to complete silence within just a few minutes. Keziah looked up to see a group of guards walk up onto the platform. They stood waiting as the Guard Isaac walked up and stood in front of them. He turned and mumbled something to them, and they all nodded.

"In the name of Gena, we have some news. It may be upsetting but be assured everything will be just fine." He took a deep breath in before he continued. "Father Sy, our dear leader, is unwell." He put his hands up automatically as he spoke as if to calm the masses. "Father is getting the medical attention he needs, and we're sure he'll be back up and running very soon."

Is this just a ruse to take over? Guard Isaac had been in The Genus since he was young. Surely he was not part of this new organisation.

"You must all be strong and carry out your prayer and duties as normal. We, the guards with the help of the senior mothers, will oversee things in Father's absence. Hopefully it won't be for too long. Enjoy your breakfast. Praise Gena." He walked off the stage so quickly even the guards behind him were surprised.

There was no time to question anything about his vague message. She looked over to see Mother Abi was not in her usual seat. Some of the other Senior Mothers were absent too.

The women around did not react to the announcement as she expected. Their Father and leader was ill, so naturally the senior guards who worked closely with him would help out until he was better. She even overheard someone asking what the drama was about. No one seemed suspicious, or sensed something was awry. Perhaps they did, but didn't dare to speak up? When she looked over again, Mother Abi was there eating casually and chatting with the other mothers.

After breakfast, everyone had a half an hour to spend as they wished. Some people prayed, more went back to the dormitory and others went straight to the houses they worked in during the day. It was the perfect time to go for a walk. Keziah wanted to slip away without Charity noticing, but she was like a hawk, always watching and ready to pounce. She walked quickly out of the dining hall and down the path as if heading to the dormitory, but instead took a sharp left. She slipped through a hedge to a grassy area at the side of The Fulcrum where no one ever went. Her feet were sodden from the morning dew. Behind The Fulcrum she joined another path running around the perimeter of the main communal area. Keziah walked on it as if heading back around to the front the temple, but instead once she arrived to a less used path towards the old garage she turned again.

Rusty old car engines bordered a path leading her under a galvanised roof with two large garages on each side, into what they used to call the parade area. Weeds pushed up through the gravel and dehydrated bits of metal were strewn in all directions. She watched weathered cans of cola and cigarette packets flitter around the ground. After the garages, came a row of makeshift wooden shelters with tin roofs. Those buildings weren't there before, were they? A couple of faded plant pots held some dying geraniums and in front of a door with blue peeling paint stood a little pink trike. Who on earth lived here? She heard people talking in a different language and turned around to see one of the garage's large doors were wide open. She squinted in the morning sun to see a man bent over an engine of a car. Another was working at a bench, and a third was under a car on a roller. Keziah froze for a second but quickly realised they hadn't spotted her. She walked quickly through the open area but didn't dare run in case she raised attention. Once behind an old oak tree to the left, she turned to observe from safe distance. These people did not seem to be a part of The Genus, like Charity said. They spoke in a different language, which was not unusual over the wall, but in here everyone was from the same ilk. In fact, Father Sy prided The Genus on this point, and mentioned it often. The lack of registration was supposedly one of the reasons she was back in here, after all. Sy had been on the detectives radar for not registering births for a starter. The DNA test she had once over the wall confirmed Ish was her brother. Shivers ran through her as she remembered sneaking hair from Abe's brush to get his DNA tested. Keziah had no regrets on that front. His test revealed he was Sy's blood son. It just didn't make sense, new people being allowed in, let alone live here. What was their purpose? They worked on the cars, but they'd always had their own mechanics.

The blue door opened and out came Charity with a little girl. She sat on the rickety old bench and watched the child hop up onto the trike. The little girl rode around in circles, laughing and shouting for Charity to watch her. Keziah leaned back against the tree as she let everything sink in. Charity knew exactly what was going on in here. Who included her? Sy or Richard? A woman appeared, spoke to Charity for a moment, then waved goodbye to them. She walked over to the other garage, the one closed up, and disappeared through a heavy metal side door. While Keziah longed to walk over to Charity and declare her presence, she knew better. Charity was obviously in this deeper than she could ever imagine; minding this child while this woman went in there. Was she getting into a vehicle to leave?

Realising her thirty minutes must be up, Keziah walked the long way around the whole area, showing up again at the front of The Fulcrum. She went straight to Mother Abi's house to pick up the wire and check in with the detectives.

Chapter Thirty One

"What on earth is going on with your feet, Keziah. They're wet?"

Keziah looked down at her soaked canvas pumps and looked back up sheepishly. Her mother handed her a fresh pair of socks.

As Keziah sat down at the table to change them, she stood over her and spoke quietly. "He is still in his quarters. As far as I know, no doctor has been called in."

She took the wet items, placed the shoes beside open fire and dropped the socks into a basket in the laundry room.

"How did the meeting go?," asked Keziah.

"Overall, it went well. It panicked some of the women of course, but I presented it as Father Sy's new idea to have a plan for fires and such things. Some knew better and understood perfectly well."

"Dorothy, of course."

"Yes, of course."

"Mother, do you know of Mother Sarah's earth room?"

"The bunker? I heard of it when I was younger, but we never knew if it was true or not. Why?"

"It's true. That's how we all got out. By staying in there before climbing the wall."

Her mother looked at her, waiting for more information.

"It's past the rocks at the old pine woods, near the wall on the south side."

"How big is it?"

She was thinking about using it already. This woman never ceased to amaze Keziah.

"It's very small. Maybe in an emergency, you might fit six adults. It would be tight."

"I understand." She went back to the stove and stirred a huge pot. "So, it really exists." She shook her head as she stirred. "What is it like?"

"Well, it's dark but there are candles and lamps. There is water and a few food supplies there already."

"Space for eating and sleeping?"

"There's a little table and bench and small platform for sleeping one or two."

"Might it be worth getting some more supplies out there?" She stood at the pot with her back to Keziah.

"I think it might be an option in an emergency."

"Could you find it again?"

"I can find my way to the rocky cave and then to the huge red cedar. After that I'd struggle."

Mother turned to her. "Perhaps you can contact someone who knows the way?"

Keziah nodded. "Ish. He planned all our escapes."

"Ish," she muttered to herself as she stoked the fire. Keziah watched her. The tight scarf across her forehead gave a fierce impression of Mother Abi, but Keziah had seen her soft curls underneath. By the end of the day, falling whisps of blonde turning grey were pushed behind her ears. She was strong, unmoved and pragmatic in a time of crisis. Her pleasure was hard work, nurturing children and sticking to rules. She never went to a cinema or stuffed herself with chocolate. She never kissed a man, as far as she knew.

Charity walked straight in and stood at the fire heating her hands. Keziah most definitely didn't want Charity to know she knew about the garage people yet. She'd prefer Charity to confide in her, to show her.

"It's getting cold out there. It's almost time for the heavier dresses and overcoats!"

"Why are you outside so much Charity? Does Father not have work for you to do, because if not, I can find plenty here." Mother's tone was always so sardonic with Charity. It amused Keziah.

"No Mother," she replied sarcastically, "I am on a different schedule than you, and I'm currently on a break."

Mother Abi ignored her and carried on with her work, but Keziah took the opportunity.

"Charity, do you know anything of Father Sy? Is he getting better."

"I don't know much. The guards are close to him, looking after him. They've asked me to do a couple of things, like check stock and supplies."

Mother Abi's ear cocked. She looked up and clenched her jaw. "What supplies are you talking of Child? Food?"

"Flour and cereals mostly, but also some hygiene products, car oil, those kind of things. So, of course I'm cold. That big old garage might as well be outdoors."

"And how is the stock?" Mother Abi persisted.

"We are low on some things. A guard usually assists Father Sy on these matters is also sick. Maybe they have some kind of bug."

"And will they be replacing the low stock?" asked Keziah.

Charity shrugged her shoulders. "I suppose so. I just counted and handed back the totals."

Keziah guessed the big old garage she referred to, was the one the woman walked into earlier. What was she doing in there? It might be true Charity counted the stock, but other people were moving in and out of the garage too, for some reason.

"Is that over near the old garage?"

"Yep. Mother, can I have a cup of tea and maybe some bread."

"You can of course, but you must look after yourself. It's also time for me to sit down with a cup of tea for five minutes."

They sat chatting for a while before getting into some serious work. Charity left claiming some very important tasks needed to be finished. Other mothers arrived to make snacks for the junior children, and Keziah returned to the laundry room to fold clothes. She would try to catch Mother alone before she made her evening contact. She wanted to discuss the walk she took earlier, and if they needed to start pilfering supplies for Mother Sarah's hermitage.

Keziah here. Anyone there?

Amanda here Keziah. How are you holding up?

So much seems to be happening in here. I'm sure Richard has updated you.

Please, give us your version.

Sy is still sick, they say. One of the senior guards says he is getting medical attention, but I heard no doctor has come in yet. Around the old garages there are new people. I've seen mechanics and a woman with a child. Charity minds the child. She doesn't know I know her yet. I am working at getting closer to her.

Okay. Anything else? Keziah sensed an odd coldness from Amanda.

Mother Abi is determined to make a backup plan. You've got her conversation with the mothers I take it? There's also talk of dwindling supplies, so she's worried about it.

Please tell Mother Abi not to make plans. We are watching and will protect everyone.

Well, surely you can understand she just wants to protect the youngsters.

Please encourage her to stop all plans. It may clash with undercover work.

Keziah paused in thought for a moment. She determined there and then not tell these people anything else about Mother's plans.

Okay. I have to go.

Sitting back on the bed for a moment, trying to digest it all, she bit her nails. How could Mother's plans clash with theirs? Her suspicion grew by the day. She needed to look after Mother and Laura. They were her priorities now, along with, Charity and Dorothy if she could. She'd keep reporting and working on Charity but that was it. No more information about Mother Abi would be shared. Who knew if this was their plan all along or whether it changed? Something felt really off.

Thanks Keziah. Please keep working on Charity and let us know of any new people you see. We need to know what area they are in and what they are doing. Okay?"

Yes, bye.

Chapter Thirty Two

She jumped with fright when the bell rang loudly. She would never get used to sharing a dormitory at this pace.

"Good morning, Miss Keziah," Charity chimed.

"Morning. What are you up to today?"

She scrunched her face up. "What do you mean?"

"I mean, what tasks have you got today? Maybe I can help. I'm so bored with the laundry."

"Oh, I'm not sure it would work actually."

"Okay." Keziah got on with dressing as if to say it didn't matter anyway.

"I'll ask though. Or if anyone else is needed I'll suggest you. Okay?" She looked at Keziah hopefully.

"Sounds great!" Keziah gave her a big smiled.

Once washed and dressed, they said their morning prayer, and walked out together towards the dining hall.

"It's weird in here now, without Father Sy, isn't it?" Keziah probed.

Again, Charity looked at her oddly, as if she suspected she knew something. Maybe she was pushing her too far.

"Do you think? we still have to say our prayers and do our chores so not much has changed."

"How ill is he? Will he die, Charity?" Keziah feigned concern as best as she could.

"Keziah, I don't know what you think I do all day but I'm not in his inner circle. While Father is ill, I assist the guards with any miscellaneous tasks. There's no more to it."

"Yeah, but you see him more than most other Carers."

"I suppose."

They walked in silence for a moment. The guards were still working on the new poles. Some were on ladders hanging some kind of speaker system on the poles they'd laid just days before. People passing by looked up at them in disbelief. They never needed such things before.

"You know, the guards have stopped his cooks bringing him his food directly."

Keziah stopped and looked at her "Why?"

Charity shrugged her shoulders. I don't know. Maybe he is so unwell they want to preserve his dignity.

"Dignity? When was the last time you saw him?"

She sighed and rolled her eyes. "About three days after the dining hall event."

"Was he worse?"

"Do you think I am some kind of spy or something?" She stomped off, exasperated.

"Charity, come back. Sorry."

Charity turned on her heel with a smile and walked back to her, took her hand, and walked up the path to the entrance with her. This constant change in mood unnerved Keziah.

"I know you're looking for answers, but I don't have them." Charity stated boldly as they walked.

"Okay. I believe you. You've been a good friend to me since I came back. I appreciate and trust you."

Charity smirked sarcastically, but when Keziah squeezed her hand, she squeezed it back.

Just before they separated and went to their assigned tables, Charity leaned over. "They think he is losing his mind. Going crazy."

She marched off and left Keziah to sit on the edge of her table as usual. Portraying him as crazy would work very well if they were drugging him. He did seem drunk that day. But who is doing it? The guards?

The usual senior guards walked in led by Guard Isaac whose face was ashen and tired. Since the first day he spoke about Sy's illness, Keziah picked up on his stress. Perhaps he was under duress.

"Quiet now, people! Quiet please!"

Everyone settled down except some younger kids the mothers tended to instantly.

"The sooner I speak, the sooner you can eat."

Four other guards including Richard stood behind him on the platform like before.

"You may have noticed; we have installed some speakers across the main paths." He waited for a moment before continuing. "Father Sy suggested this great new system of communication. While he is still recovering, he can speak to the people of The Genus."

"Praise Gena," led the mothers, looking around encouragingly.

"These telecom systems will soon be installed inside too: The Fulcrum, here in the dining area, as well as the houses and dormitories. Father will be able to give sermons and messages as we go along our daily lives." His head dropped as if he had just told the crowd Sy was dead.

He raised his head and looked around the room. "I ask you good people of The Genus, to cooperate during this difficult time and pray for Father Sy to recover quickly. We will have a special ceremony in The Fulcrum at the end of the week." He looked around at the guard who nodded at him. "That is all for now. Mother Abi will lead with prayer. Enjoy your meal. Praise Gena."

He walked off the platform quickly, with the others following suit. She should try to be at the side entrance the next time they spoke like this.

Chapter Thirty Three

Keziah walked towards The Fulcrum as she contemplated whether to run over to the old garage again to see if anything was going on. She'd like to try to enter the mysterious closed garage, but maybe from the other side. She walked into the temple and up the aisle to the top. She chose the same seat as last time. Within seconds she heard Richard speak just behind her.

"Hello."

She turned around with surprise. "What are you doing here?"

"Thought it might be a good chance to have a quick word."

"Yes?" she was determined to play her cards close to her chest this time.

"So, you know about the old garage?"

"Know what?"

"Come, Keziah, we are on the same side."

"Are we?. In fact, I barely know what side *I* am on anymore."

"I understand. Things have changed dramatically."

"It seems so."

"Sy is behaving erratically. I'm pretty sure he's being manipulated."

"By your crime gang?"

He sniggered. "It's not my crime gang. Do you know anything about it?"

"Well, you seem to have quite an important role. Enough to know everything I report back to the detectives. Enough to stand behind the Senior guard on the platform when he speaks."

"I have been a part of the Arma Bloods since I was in my late teens. My father was too."

"What a legacy. You should be proud."

"I'm not proud. Why do you think I work with the police?"

She turned around angrily. "I am sick to the teeth of all of these obscure conversations. What is going on? Who do I need to protect? Do you think I came back in here for a joke?"

"Certainly not. I'm well aware of how you've spent the last year or two. I admire your courage."

"Well then use me, or I am leaving."

He inhaled sharply. "Look, we were both supposed to try to find some evidence of fraudulent tax claims, forced or underage marriage nonregistration of births, things like –"

"Are you really going to sit there and talk this rubbish to me? I already know that, and I already know something has changed."

He sniffed and continued. "I have been passing bits and pieces to the police for about three years now."

"Yes. That was my understanding." She got up to leave, so exasperated by the way he spoke around things.

"Keziah, please sit down. I'll answer any questions."

She sat back down and stared at him. She didn't trust him, but she needed information.

"Who are the people living at the old garage?"

"They are immigrants – mostly Eastern Europeans – nice people."

"Why are they here?"

"Cheap labour. Crime organisations like to keep workers close to hand. They feed and house them in a basic way and work them hard."

"What are they working at?"

"All sorts. Packing, cleaning, there are mechanics as you know."

"Packing what? Why do we need other mechanics?"

"These people have nothing to do with The Genus. They pack for us, and they, em, they get stolen cars in and take off the serial number, spray them, change engines around, that kind of thing."

Her heart was thumping in her ears, but she pushed on. "What do they pack?"

"They pack contraband things. Illegal things. They get them ready to sell and deliver."

"They dispatch from the other garage?"

"Yes. They also have taken some stock of The Genus."

"Charity mentioned something vaguely. Food and toiletries."

"Yes. We're in discussions now."

"What? Discussions with who?"

"Well, Sy wants us, I mean them, to replace what they've taken for their own people, or to sell."

"I thought Sy was incapacitated?"

"Well, he seems high to me, but still talking."

"Are there any other people, slaves, working inside The Genus?" She couldn't believe what she was hearing. "And do the police know all of this?"

"Yes and yes."

Keziah sighed and shook her head. She wished she'd never come back.

"Look, things are tense," continued Richard, "I am unsure what's going to happen. Sy is taking all sorts of stuff, and they are taking advantage of his weaknesses."

"Where is he getting the stuff, and what is he taking it for?"

"He's a mess. Some of it is prescribed medicine. He has high blood pressure, gout, pain in his joints. He's on all sorts including some heavy pain meds."

"You said some of it."

"He's partial to whisky now I hear and no doubt if he wanted anything else it wouldn't be a problem to get it from my associates."

"Oh yes, and-

The door banged. Keziah stood up immediately and went to leave. It was Charity walking towards her up the aisle, red faced. She looked from Richard to her angrily.

"What is going on here?"

"What do you mean?"

"Do you think I am stupid?"

Richard stood up and walked towards Charity with a smile. He put his arm around her and kissed her forehead. She pouted like an infant.

"You have a very loyal friend in that one, Charity."

"I'm not sure."

"She just interrogated me about my intentions with you. She was making sure I am not taking advantage of her friend."

Oh, he's good.

"Charity, I'm sorry but I just needed to know you won't get hurt." Keziah walked over to her and gave her a hug. "I should be going. Mother Abi will be looking for me."

She rushed over to the house, panting as she went. She needed to let Mother Abi know about her conversation even though she was left feeling very unsatisfied. It's a shame Charity interrupted. She wanted

INTO THE OLD

to walk away with more information. She needed to talk with Richard again very soon. She reached the kitchen door breathing heavily. The Mothers looked over at her.

"What's wrong, Keziah?" asked Dorothy.

"Oh, nothing I just realised how late I was. I came from The Fulcrum."

"Come and help me dry these dishes. Mother Abi is over in the storeroom with the guards."

Keziah smiled to herself. Her mother worked fast. She was straight into the storeroom to assess things for herself.

Keziah slipped to the bathroom to use the pager.

I know everything. If I am no longer useful I want to come out.

Hi Keziah, it's Frank here.

He hadn't shown his presence in a while. She continued with purpose.

I spoke with Richard just now. If you do not share the plan with me I will run.

Please do not do that. It is not safe.

What kind of charade is this? Do you think being in here with a drugged leaders and car thieves is safe?

I understand you are upset, Keziah. We have been working out a new plan. There has been nothing to update you on yet.

Rubbish!

We are now working with the Government Crime Investigation department. It's bigger than us. They asked us to hold out for now.

Why and until when?

They are just waiting for a little more evidence, and we are all working very hard on the strategy. The timing needs to be right.

How come Richard is being updated and I am not?

He is a GCI informant. They do things differently.

I want to join them instead then.

Keziah, please sit tight.

No.

She shut the device down altogether, slipped it back in her undergarments and walked back into the crowd of women. Mother Abi was back, directing some of the younger mothers on some cooking.

She looked over at Keziah. "Keziah, I want you to stay back and help me prepare for a foraging expedition with the young ones tomorrow. Seeing as you were late to your duties today, it's only fair the others get off on time this evening."

Keziah looked at Mother Abi knowingly. "Of course, Mother."

Chapter Thirty Four

By the time everyone left the kitchen, Keziah was about done with the laundry, finally. It was so monotonous. She needed to ask for other chores.

"Mother, what's happening tomorrow?"

"We will carry some dried foods as far as we can, maybe to the cave you spoke of, and have a look for the hermitage. We'll come home with some nuts and berries if there are any left."

"And we bring little ones?"

"Just a couple of youngsters who could do with a day off school. Mother Dorothy may come if she can get away without suspicion."

"Mother, do you know there are other people here who have been have been enslaved by a gang?"

"Around the old garage, yes. Richard told me when we last spoke."

"I saw him today. I asked if there are more and he said yes. We might see some on our walk tomorrow."

She looked at Keziah for a moment. "Do not tell Charity or anyone else about our plans."

"I think we're going to need Charity more than we first realised. I worry about her Mother. She doesn't seems very balanced at the moment. Maybe Richard's taking her under his wing is a good thing." She looked down "I believe so".

"Do you think it is a real relationship?"

"Who knows Keziah. Maybe, but my only focus is getting some supplies hidden in case we need them. From there, we will assess what happens next. I have arranged a meeting with Richard tomorrow evening."

Keziah, dumbfounded, just nodded. Mother Abi was now in cahoots with Richard and now knew more than her.

"Mother, do you know he is a spy? He can turn on the police at any time. He was practically born into that group."

"Like you were born into The Genus, Keziah? And here you are trying to disband it."

A lump formed in her throat. "It's not the same."

"Well, Richard seems to think the police want to minimise any further stress to you until completely necessary, and it makes perfect sense to me."

"I just want Sy to stop hurting people."

"I know, she replied with a sigh. "Get to bed and I'll see you at 7.30 am sharp."

She walked in the dusk back to the dormitory, her mind in a race with her body. She lost control of everything. When she finished undercover training she was so determined to come in here and help, but she was scared and alone, and needing help herself. Unlike Charity and Mother Abi who had a place in this world, she was lost in limbo, somewhere in between this world and the other. Now, abandoned by the police, and Yvonne. She hadn't heard from Yvonne in a longtime which made her sad to the bottom of her stomach. Sad and lonely.

A squealing echoed around the sky and Keziah let herself fall, covering her head just like Joe taught her in self-defence classes. A loud but mumbling voice sounded in the sky. She looked up to one of the speakers.

"Watch out people of the Goddess. Watch out for the baaaad men. They are here – wait – stop that! No!"

She could just about make out a struggle between the whistling and thumps over the mic. She looked around to see some men running to The Fulcrum. It was closer than the dormitories, and there was a speaker in there too. She looked behind to see a group of mothers running. They caught up with her at the entrance. Mother Abi was among them. She hung back and let another open the door. Keziah could not believe her eyes. Two guards were on each side of Sy, carrying him by his elbows down the aisle as he roared in anguish.

"They are killing me! Help me! They are trespassing! They are invading the people of the Goddess. Gena, please save us."

She stood with Mother out of the way as they sped past. Sy's face was red and bloated and saliva dribbled down his chin as he struggled unsuccessfully out of his captor's arms.

Finally free just at the door he ran back up the aisle and collapsed in sobs at the step of the altar. "Goddess Gena, forgive me. I repent."

Keziah watched the guards closely as they talked discreetly among themselves, as they walked slowly back up the aisle. One younger guard sat down on the steps and touched Sy's shoulder as he leaned into him, speaking gently. Sy rose slowly. Sitting up on the steps, he looked down The Fulcrum to see a small crowd at the end of the aisle watching him. He hung his head and after a moment tried to get up. The guards moved towards him, and he gestured he didn't need help. He walked out the door to the side of the altar, the guards behind him.

"I'm going to follow them," she announced.

"Be careful, for Gena's sake!"

Keziah ran out the main door quickly, and around the back to see the guards walk with Sy towards his quarters. They walked him around the back of his place, and up the stairs. The rickety old front door was left open, and she wondered whether or not she should follow up. She stood in the hall looking up to Charity who stood at the top of the stairs in alarm.

Spotting Keziah she ran down the stairs and tool her by the shoulder. "What happened?"

"He went mad. He just completely broke down and he shouted over the speakers about bad men invading us." Charity's red face crumpled up and tears fall down her cheeks.

"What? Charity, what is it?"

"Everything." She collapsed into Keziah's arms, and she held her tightly. When she came up for air Keziah rubbed her shoulders. "How about a cup of something warm in Mother's house?"

Charity nodded. "Yeah."

The three of them sat at the kitchen table. Keziah broke the silence.

"Charity, you know you can confide in us, don't you? You know Mother and I understand things may have gotten very complicated for you. You can tell us anything without getting in trouble."

"What is said here and now between us three will remain so," said Mother Abi as she took Charity's hand. "We need to look after each other now, dear."

Charity took a deep breath in and a gulp of her sweet tea. "You know, don't you?"

"We know something is changing and it doesn't seem very good. We know there are some new people over at the garage." Keziah spoke quietly.

Charity's eyes widened. "You do?"

"It's going to be just fine, dear. Tell us everything."

"So, you know I know." She pursed her lips.

Keziah took her other hand. "It's okay. We just want to be able to protect ourselves. They are with these other people – the new guards, aren't they?"

She sighed. "Well, yes but they don't want to be. They were promised a good life, but now they are imprisoned by them, working all hours and – and - they are really nice. It's not fair." Tears started to stream down her face again.

"But you've been helping them."

"Richard wanted me to be away from Father. He said they needed help with the children, and it was safer."

"Safer why?" asked Keziah.

"I don't know. Father has been drinking a lot of alcohol and acting strange. I think it's the mix of medication and whisky. I don't know."

"Where does he get it?" asked Mother Abi.

"There's a man. I think he is the leader of those new guards. I think he's Richard's old manager, or something. He visited lots of times. At first it was all very good. Father had special meals prepared. I sometimes waited on them. He always gifted him these bottles of alcohol."

"When did the people arrive? Have you seen anymore?"

She nodded. "Once I was driven into the woods to mind some children. There are little cabins there and those people are not well. They – " She began to sob but spoke through it "they burn some liquids. I don't know. There's a big barn there with chimneys. Even the little children are continuously coughing, and they are hungry."

Keziah interrupted. "Do people come and go? Do they bring people out?"

"Yes, mostly women."

"What about the stock you mentioned the other day? , asked Mother. " Is it going to these people?"

"Some of it, but father is not allowed to buy more. I overheard one of the guards say so. He said we have to use up what's already here."

"Not allowed?" Keziah raised her voice. "But we are running low on flour and important things," she persisted.

Mother Abi remained quiet, and focused on what Charity was saying, and Keziah realised she should not allow her emotions to run ahead of her.

"Father told him we need flour, and he said when we use all the other grains we can get more."

Mother Abi sat back in the chair, but she did not take her hand away from Charity's. "What do you think is happening, Charity?" she asked softly.

"At first I thought it was great. Something to ease the boredom but then I realised these new people were suffering. Father was changing. The guards - the newer guards – they give the orders now. Father sleeps a lot and takes lots of pills."

"Why? Why do you think they are taking over?"

"Mother, I think they want the land. I don't know for sure, but I think they want to build factories and use us to work for them. I overheard some of them talking about building a factory, I don't know where - and they mentioned some of us would work in it. Father got angry and said it couldn't happen and they shouted at him."

What a weird twist of faith that Sy ended up like this, being bullied and abused by people with more power than him.

"What are the speakers for?" Mother Abi leaned into the table again, ready for more answers.

"I don't know but Richard thinks they might just stop ceremonies or group gathering and just do alarms for work and breaks."

"What about prayer? Leisure time?" asked Keziah.

Charity shrugged her shoulders. "It's all I know."

"You have done very well, Charity," said Mother, "you will be rewarded for your courage."

"Keziah, I think we shall go ahead to try to find the hermitage tomorrow, and also try to find this set up in the woods."

"Mother, we might get our hands on another pack with devices."

Mother Abi sighed. "Not that they are doing much to help us anyway. Can you also please insist on talking to your Yvonne? I think she might very well be the only one we can trust now. The detectives have now prioritised getting to the Arma Bloods, not Father Sy. Their mission has clearly changed, which leaves all of us here in danger."

Charity glared at her. "You are a spy?"

Keziah blushed. She meant for Charity to find out differently. To tell her gently. "Not exactly. Well, kind of. Look, so is Richard."

"I know but...." She shook her head in disbelief.

"I have been meaning to tell you, Charity. I promise."

Charity pursed her lips and nodded. "Life will never be the same again."

"It will certainly not be boring, Charity." Mother Abi smiled sweetly at the broken girl in front of her. "Now, it's time to sleep. Charity, see if Richard can help you to disappear with us tomorrow but be vague. Richard is fine but we have our own little plan to build now."

Chapter Thirty Five

They made their way from the dormitories quickly, and without a word. The big drops of rains splattered on their thick plastic raincoats and dripped down to meet their dresses. At the end of the garden, past the clothesline, Mother Abi waited in a poncho with a waterproof bag on her own shoulder and a foraging basket on her back.

She handed them a shoulder bag each full of tins of food and a small hand basket. "It will brighten up later. We'll return with some mushrooms at least!"

They walked down through the first patch of pines, past the lake and the last boardwalk. Every time she passed the lake, Keziah could not help thinking about the repercussions of the night she ran away, and the effect of her escape on the two women beside her. She never asked either of them directly what happened afterwards, or about their specific punishments. Mother had told her of Charity's punishment, but she wondered what happened to her when she trusted Keziah to go to the toilet?

When they were a safe distance away from anyone Mother Abi began to talk. "We must be always prepared to appear like we are foraging, understood? There will be people in areas we don't usually have people."

"When I came before there were no guards around, but I think they check on the workers a few times per day," said Charity.

"If we are caught in the act, we must all say we came to forage and do not know about anything else going on." Mother Abi marched along determined to get to the cave early.

Everyone agreed. The morning was already clearing up by the time they reached the next part of the forest. Mother Abi found a spot under a huge chestnut tree. They took their raincoats off and let them hang on branches to dry. The air was still damp, but the sun was making a huge effort. She took a waterproof blanket out and laid it down. She kneeled and doled out some bread and cheese to Keziah and Charity. They ate it gratefully.

"In your bags you have tins. I suggest we leave them in the cave until we are sure of the hermitage location. I have not taken anything low in stock. We don't was to raise any alarms. In my bag, I have some cooked food and bread in case these people need it. However, we wait and decide if we communicate with them once we get a bit closer."

They nodded as they ate. Mother Abi continued.

"At no time, shall any of us separate from each other. At no time shall any of us act in the spur of the moment. Everything shall be agreed between us.'

"What if a guard sees us?" asked Charity.

"Are you listening to me, Charity? If we are seen, we will explain we are out here foraging for mushrooms, late berries, wild herbs and rosehip for teas and medicines. That covers all the areas."

"But what if they are angry and don't believe us?"

"The same applies. You must keep to the story."

"Some of them know I know about the workers."

"We will say you didn't tell us. I insisted you came and when we stumbled across these people we shared our food with them."

"We must keep our eyes out for all of these things and add them to our baskets as we go," added Keziah.

The shoulder bags were heavy and by the time they were up and walking again Keziah was already switching sides.

The sun shone strongly through the canopy and the birds chirped cheerfully. Keziah and Charity each managed to find some berries for their baskets. Mother was such an expert forager. She found mushrooms under every new pine tree. She hummed to herself as she worked with her special little knife she'd had for years. Keziah tried to recall how much further it was to the rocky terrain, or the cave. As far as she remembered, they were coming from the other side so should see the cave before the people.

At midday they stopped again in a little grassy opening. They had a quick bite and some water and got on back on their feet quickly. Charity found a glut of wild raspberries. They were almost dried out, but she took the good ones while Mother stripped the leaves for tea.

"Good Girls. We're doing well."

Keziah wondered how she could be so cheerful and upbeat given what they were about to face. It wasn't long before the rock face appeared, silver glinting streaks between the trees made themselves known in the sun. Keziah tried to run ahead but Mother reminded her they must stay together. When they made it up through the smaller lose rocks they got on their knees to get into the cave. Mother crawled in first. She took her bags off her back and sighed in relief. Keziah passed her shoulder bag to her and then Charity's. They pushed the bags down to the back of the cave as far as they would go, into a little nook. Charity passed some loose stones in to make a little fake wall. The bags would be safe. They had a little sip of water before it was time to go again.

"Uh oh." It was Charity who'd just crawled out of the cave.

"What's wrong?" called Keziah from behind.

They all crawled out to see a group of five little children staring at them. Dressed in rags and dirt dried into their faces, they all smiled. A little girl walked forward and waved at Charity.

"She remembers me. What do I do?"

"Do they speak English?" asked Mother Abi.

A little boy giggled and replied "a leetle bit."

Keziah smiled. "We'd better be careful of what we say then."

"Look at the state of the poor little things. They can't be more than five or six years old," said Keziah.

The same little boy announced how old each one of the children were and then stood proud waiting.

"Are you hungry?" asked Mother as she put her hand to her mouth to explain.

They all nodded their heads and as she opened her bag they got swarmed her with their hands out. She smiled and passed them each a piece of bread. They gobbled the bread as if they hadn't eaten in a long time.

Looking over at the boy she asked, "How do you say thank you?"

The boy spoke with some authority to the rest of the children in his own tongue, and they all sang in unison "thank you meesuz".

It was clear they were learning fast.

"Where are your mothers and fathers?" asked Mother.

Given Mother Abi's experience of people outside The Genus amounted only to the days she went to market, Keziah was impressed both with her communication skills and her openness to these unfortunate children.

"Working," he answered as he pointed his shoulder.

"We go?" she continued, and he smiled and took her hand to walk her to his home.

Charity walked just behind holding the little girls hand, and Keziah followed with the remaining three, who looked up at her with smiles. They needed help. Yvonne would not let this go on if she knew about it. Something had to change, and fast.

Chapter Thirty Six

White smoke billowed into the clouds up ahead and sounds of more children playing rang in the air. They walked right into the centre of an encampment to a cooking-fire made from cement blocks with some kind of small animal cooking on rotary. Beside it were a heap of five litre water bottles. Keziah counted as she turned three-sixty. They were surrounded by fifteen small wooden huts. A few men sat on a bench talking. One stood up in alarm as they approached.

Mother Abi looked back. "Charity, go ahead and talk to them."

Inquisitive people stood at their doors watching.

"I can't believe it, Mother. This can't have been here long," said Keziah under her breath.

"It is a sight for sore eyes. Keep smiling."

They caught up to Charity. She stood using her hands to explain they were friends and had food. A woman joined them. She knew Charity, and she spoke a little bit of English.

"They are afraid they will get in trouble."

"Why?" asked Keziah.

"Guards say not to talk with us. It's rules," explained the woman.

"Mother is a senior member of the community and just wants to help." Charity waved to where mother stood with a smile.

"Guards, no," said Mother as she stepped forward. She put a finger to her mouth to show it was a secret.

The little boy who led Mother to the encampment stood in front of the woman.

"My mama. Mudder."

The woman smiled and put her hand to her heart.

"Your mother?" asked Keziah with a smile.

Within minutes the people began to smile and talk to each other, although they remained wary, they were clearly in need of help. The woman brought them to her house and showed how she was living on the floor with her husband and three children. A couple of old cushions and blankets were folded up in the corner. They didn't even have a mattress. There was no running water and only battery lamps for light. The woman explained they often ran out of batteries. A tiny plastic table sat in the corner with a bottle of water and a half packet of crackers. Mother Abi took out a large slice of pie, a couple of slices of bread and a little square of cheese. The woman almost cried and continuously thanked them. Keziah observed Mother Abi taking a deep breath. She hugged the woman; told her she would be back and walked outside back into the centre.

"We don't have enough for everyone. I'll divide what I have for the remaining huts. Fourteen more, let me see."

Keziah staved off the hungry children, and tried to explain they would give them more food. Mother sat flat on the ground; her skirt fixed right to her ankles as she counted out small bundles of food. Keziah and Charity brought each bundle inside each doors of the shacks.

Mother walked back over to the men. Keziah and Charity followed her lead.

"You work?"

The man who initially stood up answered. "Work in factory." He pointed over the huts to where they'd seen the smoking chimneys.

"It was dark when I came, but I suppose it's the factory with the chimney."

"Are there guards in the factory?" asked Mother.

The man looked at his wrist as if he had a watch.

"Later?" came Mother again.

"Yes layta."

"Now, factory, no guards?"

"No guards."

"Show us, please."

"Mother are you sure?," asked Keziah, wary of what they may find.

Her mother talked to her quietly. "This might be our only chance to see for ourselves."

The man said something under his breath to the other men and lead them through the other side of the encampment. The smell of human waste stifled Keziah. She held her hand over her mouth and nose as they were led through a corridor with walls of plastic flapping in the wind.

The man, noticing their reaction to the smell, nodded. "Toilet. too close."

"Yes, toilet should be far away, in the woods," agreed Mother pragmatically.

"Yes." He nodded and led onwards.

The corridor opened out and just before the next woodland a barn appeared in a massive pasture opening. A tall thin metallic chimney puffed white smoke out into the clouds. Outside the entrance were huge barrels and crates.

"What is inside?"

The man smiled and shook his head ashamedly, but Mother Abi persisted.

"What is in there?"

"Bad things." He looked down and walked on. When he got to the door he stopped and turned to them. "Just a little."

"Yes, dear, just one moment. Let us see."

First Mother peeped her head in and then stood inside the door. Keziah watched her mouth drop open and her hand cover it almost in slow motion. She stepped inside beside her.

Another world lay before them. About twenty men and women, wearing goggles and cloth tied around their faces, bent over intently on makeshift benches that ran along the walls in a U shape. The benches held containers of all types: conical flasks, glass tubes and pipes. Some people wore gloves as they mixed in bowls, others weighed something out. A stainless steel stairs led to a mezzanine with huge steel cylinders and vats. Keziah's eyes began to sting so she stepped out and pulled Mother with her.

"It's not safe in there, Mother Abi, please come out."

"What is it? What is it?" insisted Charity.

"Smells like ammonia to me. It's toxic."

The man observed them and beckoned for them to come out nodding in agreement. "Toxic. Yes. Toxic."

They took a moment. Mother took out her bottle of water, poured some out and rinsed her face. She passed it around to the others, and then walked around the whole building, looking at the sacks and barrels and waste.

When they arrived back at the front of the building she shook the man's hand. "What is your name?"

"Jan."

"Well, thank you Jan. Remember. It's secret." She put her finger to her mouth again and touched the man on his shoulder with a smile.

"Secret yes. More food?"

"Yes more food soon." She nodded and he led them all back to the main circle where the little boy guarded their baskets carefully.

Mother handed him some berries for his good work, and he stuffed them in his mouth and swallowed them within a second.

"What is your name, young man?"

"Me, Davit," he smiled.

"Good boy, Davit. You are very helpful."

The child beamed in pride. They waved goodbye to everyone still outside as marched out of the circle of huts. The children followed them until the edge of the woods. They had to run them back a couple of times until eventually, they stayed behind.

They walked home in silence, stunned by what they'd just witnessed. The magnitude of it all was overwhelming. When they arrived at the hedge at the bottom of Mother's yard she stopped and hugged them both strongly.

"I am very proud of you both. Please, do not even whisper about what we've seen today. It could get us in serious trouble."

"Killed even," announced Charity.

Mother inhaled sharply. "Indeed."

"I won't even tell Richard. I swear to Gena."

As soon as they arrived to Mother's kitchen and greeted a few Carers working away, they put all their findings on the table and bid everyone a good evening. Keziah remembered she still needed to try to contact Yvonne, but it might be too late. She'd try anyway. She didn't want to let Charity know about the device firmly placed between her hip and the elastic of her underwear. Once she arrived to the dormitories, she ran ahead into a toilet cubicle. She turned the pager on and received three messages instantly.

"Keziah, please do not turn your pager off again. It could be dangerous."

She could not see who it was from. The next one was from Amanda.

"Keziah, please let us know you are okay. Turning the pager off is not a good idea. We appreciate your concerns and have some updates." Amanda.

And lastly came a message from Detective Frank.

"When you turn your pager on, send us a message. It is a tracking device so we can ensure we always know where you are. It's for your own safety." Frank

She typed a response quickly.

"I'm back on and won't turn it off again. Amanda mentioned an update. I'm off to bed now. I hope to see it when I wake in the morning."

An update on what exactly? More rubbish to appease her? Those people were being poisoned and starved out there. The police or the GCI, or whatever they are, should swoop in and get them to safety. No doubt they know damn well what is going on. She'd look for Richard first thing in the morning to see what if he has any updates.

Chapter Thirty Seven

Yvonne sat at her desk shoving a sandwich down her neck before her next appointment. Checking her phone for messages, she sighed. Another visit to Frank was on the cards, and this time to make a formal complaint. An email had already been sent to his director about her concerns, with no reply. She was trying to stay composed but was genuinely starting to worry about Keziah. Since the last visit to the police station, and her angry exit, they'd completely cut her out of the loop. Her little pager thing was off all the time. Why would they do that? Cut Keziah's support contact off completely? She supposed the whole operation was now out of Frank's hands. He was a small fish in a big pond and Keziah's well-being was no longer in his remit. It had to be the reason. Frank made promises to Yvonne he could no longer keep. What if Keziah is in trouble? What if she wants to leave but can't? It really wasn't good enough. None of the people in there were safe.

She picked up the phone and dialled. "Ish, can we meet?"

"No. I've heard nothing. Absolutely nothing."

"Agreed. Maybe it's time to start thinking about what we discussed before."

"We can't. They've stopped doing the markets again."

"Okay, speak soon."

She put the phone down on the desk and stared out the window. She couldn't believe she was considering doing this.

That evening, as she pulled up outside the station, she hoped Frank was ready to be honest with her and what was happening. Keziah was her number one priority. Yvonne did not care about mafias and cult leaders. One ex-ember was already deemed incapable. She'd do her damnedest to make sure it didn't happen to another.

"Yvonne, it's good to see you," he said, with a big grin as he walked towards her, at reception.

He held his hand out for a shake, and she obliged. *Better start this conversation off civilly as it might go downhill fast.*

"Frank. How are you?"

"Oh fine. Glad you came down. Let's head to my office for a chat."

"No Amanda today?"

"She's over in GCI working on Project G."

"I see. Project G."

Once in his office, he sat down in one of the chairs for guests. She thought it was a nice move. Smiling she sat down opposite him, no desk in between.

"Look Frank. I was upset the last day."

He put his hands up as he closed his eyes. "It's behind us. You have a right to advocate for one of your clients."

"She's more than a client to me. You know this. I'm so upset, and quite frankly, suspicious that you would cut me off like that. Keziah needs me."

"She does. And we're going to put you back on the communication line."

"What happened?"

"Things got bigger. Much bigger. We have her sitting tight, to protect her, and she is getting very frustrated."

"You have her sitting tight because she is of no use yet. Don't play me, Frank."

"Look, Yvonne, GCI are over the case now. We have some major criminal activity going on beyond those walls."

"Is she safe?"

"She is safe but she's getting angsty. She shut down her pager for over twenty four hours. I think she's very overwhelmed. She has asked for you and we're happy to have you back in touch.

"Aaaah. Now I understand. You need me to get her to play on your side, so I'm back in the loop."

He laughed. "In a nutshell, yes. But you have to realise, when GCI took over, we had to reassess everything. Every single part of our approach and plan had to be redesigned. It's a different project now."

"Tell me what's going on in there. I already signed away my rights to share any of this with anyone."

"Where to start. Trafficking is probably the biggest one after the drug production."

"Jesus, Frank!" She raised her voice and slapped her leg.

"Who the fuck is he trafficking and to where?"

"It's not him. It's this criminal organisation. The Arma Bloods. And they're not moving anyone from The Genus, so far. They've moved people in. Refugees, immigrants, missing people from the streets. Whoever they can manipulate into their factories."

She couldn't believe what he was saying. "Does Keziah know?"

"Richard reckons she, along with Mother Abi and Charity, are finding out more every day, but we don't know for sure. Keziah has begun to play her cards very close to her chest."

"Can you blame her? Let me speak to her. Now!"

"Wait." Frank stood up and grabbed some papers from his desk. "We've been instructed to discuss the following."

She took the pages from him, and her eyes widened as she read. "You're giving me a script?"

"GCI are giving you a script. This is not my project anymore. I am merely facilitating their plan now."

"Which is?"

"To build enough evidence for the drug Squad to swoop in."

"Why do you not have enough yet?"

"We will. Very soon. They have a drone ready to go in just before they dismantle the whole thing, but remember, this is complicated."

"Oh, do go on," she said dryly.

"We have to provide safety and shelter to The Genus, and the other people in there."

"And?"

"We need resources organised out here, and ready to go."

"Are you saying it would have happened before now if someone's boss's boss had signed off on funding for these poor unfortunates?"

"Logistics take time. This is not just financial. We also have criminal lawyers working on other things, like the land. It turns out about half of it was left by Mother Sarah to The Genus as a group. The other half is Sy's. The legalities here are intricate, but potentially these people could continue to live in there, provided they change their practices to align with the law. Yvonne, if this is done correctly, we might not have to disrupt the whole community in an acute way."

She sat looking at him directly, processing it as he talked. "What intricacies?"

"Well, we need to make sure we have enough to bring him down properly. He has been completely infiltrated now, and there are whispers he is being manipulated, possibly even drugged. He's certainly not in his right mind."

"I want her out of there, Frank."

"The last thing we want to happen is Sy hiring an excellent defence lawyer and gaining back his assets. We want him in prison, so all of this is not in vain."

"Sounds like he could be dead by then."

"There are no answers yet, but there's a hell of a lot of work going on in the background."

"Just let me talk to her. When will she be available?."

"I sent a message earlier to tell her what time you'd be here."

They walked together to the other side of the building to Simon and Jim. They greeted them with a nod.

"She's here. She just messaged to say she can't get on the wire but has the pager."

"Does she know I'm here?" asked Yvonne as she walked over and stood beside Simon to see what he was doing.

"I told her."

"Can I just type?"

"No," answered Frank quickly. "Simon will type for you. You need to use the page in front of you with the list of questions."

Yvonne smacked her lips and looked at the page.

"Hi honey, It's Yvonne here. How are you doing? Sounds like it has all kicked off in there."

Simon looked at Frank for his go ahead. Yvonne shook her head in disgust.

"Here, check out her answers on the screen," said Simon as he pulled up a chair beside him.

Yvonne sat down and leaned into the screen.

"Hi Yvonne. Yes it's very strange in here. Sy is ill or drugged or something. They are keeping him away from us."

"Look at your page," reminded Frank.

She gave him the filthiest look she could muster up and continued. "I just heard. Are you safe?"

"I suppose so. We just don't know what will happen at any time."

"Yvonne, ask her about the guards. Come on!," said Frank is frustration.

"Hey, can we not have a bit of small talk first for God's sake, Frank. Where is your humanity? Gimme a chance!"

"Okay, Simon: *"Are the guards in charge now? Are they taking care of you all?"*

"Yes, the routine is the same except there are whispers of getting us to do other work soon."

"What kind of work?"

There was silence for nearly a minute.

"She knows damn well." Frank looked down shaking his head.

"Shut up! If you want me to continue, shut up, Frank!"

"Okay, Simon: *"Keziah? Talk to me."*

"I don't know what kind of work. Everything is confusing in here. There's no use in me being here anymore."

"I know honey. Just sit tight. I promise things are going on in the background to get this all over and done with."

"Yeah so I see, but at who's expense?"

"What do you mean, Honey?"

"*Food supplies are low. Mother is worried for the children. You know she had a meeting with some of the senior Carers. They are scared they will have to run.*"

Frank walked forward. "Tell her to tell everyone in the know to sit tight. God damn it, if they start running around hysterically now, it'll all fall flat on its face." Frank's face was red.

She looked back at him in disgust. "You're beginning to show your true colours, Detective Power."

"She's a little girl with a superhero complex because she stabbed her crazy boyfriend. Jesus Christ." He turned around and sighed.

"*Keziah, Detective Frank has assured me they know everything that's going on. They are just tying up some loose ends and then the GCI will close in on Sy, and everyone else involved in this nightmare.*"

"Ask her has she been to the cave." Frank didn't even look at Yvonne this time.

"*Yvonne, I don't trust any of them now. I don't even trust Richard. He could easily be a double agent.*"

"Listen, this has turned into a whole new thing. It's not your fault, and we want to make sure you remain safe by standing down and waiting. If you start planning an escape now, there are chances you will blow your cover and be in serious danger. Do you understand?"

"*I'll give it a little while longer.*"

"Good. Have you been anywhere near the cave or hermitage?"

There was no response for some moments.

Frank sighed. "She's gone to the factory. Her and that busy body Abi woman. This is not good."

Yvonne Persisted. "*It's important to know what's going on out there.*"

"*We went foraging.*"

"*Did you find much?*"

"*Yes.*"

"You need to stay away from anything dangerous. If they see you breaking the rules or, you know Keziah, trying to help anyone."

"I understand Yvonne. Do you understand these people are dangerous and don't care about anyone in here?"

"Yes, I do. It must be terrifying."

"Wrap it up. Tell her you'll be back tomorrow, and we'll let her know the time first thing in the morning. She has not to go wandering around again. Tell her it's an order."

"Keziah, This is an order from the detectives: do not go anywhere but your usual communal buildings from now until you hear more from them."

She looked at Simon. "Can I at least type my own goodbye message?" He nodded.

"Keziah, stay strong. Everything is going to be ok. I will message you every day until you are out of there. Keep your pager on you. And Keziah, the cave. Bye x"

"The cave?" asked Simon.

"Yeah, the order about staying away from the cave." She moved on quickly. "I'll move some meetings around and try to be here at the same time tomorrow."

He looked at her in anger and she walked past him and out of the room, leaving the door open.

Chapter Thirty Eight

Charity banged on the cubicle door. "Oh, come on, Keziah, will you?"

"Can't I have any privacy, Charity?" She quickly stuck the pager between her hip and waistband before and making her way out to wash her hands.

"I'm doing you a favour by waiting for you."

"Hmmmm," she answered looking sideways at Charity who stood with her hands crossed.

"Let's get on to Mother's house then. Do you have any other tasks scheduled today?"

"I have to go over to Father's quarters every day at 9.30 am to see if I am needed to run any errands or carry out any tasks. Have you realized most of the Carers eat breakfast in their Senior Mother's house lately?"

"Yeah, everyone is avoiding the dining hall, or seeing him."

"And the guards don't seem to mind."

"We haven't heard anything else on the speakers yet either. Are the controls in Father's room?"

"Yes but he is in bed all the time now."

Later, as Keziah folded clothes in the laundry room, she played back her conversation with Yvonne. The cave. She emphasized the cave. Why? She also made it clear the order was from the detectives, not her. Maybe she was reading into it too much, but what if Yvonne was trying to send her a message. What if Yvonne was encouraging her to go back to the cave and wait, or there'd be something waiting for her there. She wished she could speak to her alone, unsupervised. She'd suggest Mother Sarah's hermitage instead. It would be safer, further away from the factory and the new people.

"You should use the word hermitage in your message tomorrow, in the very same way Yvonne used the word cave to you," said Mother after listening to the whole story.

"Good idea. But I don't know how to tell her I need to know where it is first."

"It will be another while before we can get back there and explore further."

"Mother, I'm still so shocked at what we found there. The fear on the people's faces. The hunger of the children."

"We must dwell on how we can help them, not how shocked we are."

"True. Why do you think they don't want us to communicate with them?"

"Well, the more communication we have with them, the stronger we are."

"A united front?"

"It is possible. When people are starving, they will fight for their children, and rightly so."

"But surely the detectives want what's best for us all?"

"They want to catch the criminals. If they can keep us out of their way, even better, but we are not the priority."

"Do we have enough supplies to bring more food to them?"

"Yes, I am baking corn biscuits in small batches at night and storing them in airtight containers. We have lots of hazelnuts from years of foraging, so I've managed to pilfer a couple of large jars. I'll see what else I can come up with. We have some jams and ferments out in the back too."

"Pilfering, Mother? That's not very wholesome of you."

Mother looked down at the stocking she was darning. "Needs must, Keziah. The Goddess would want us to do right by those poor families."

Charity arrived and changed the mood of the room as usual.

"Whatever are you doing out so late, Charity?," asked Mother.

Keziah immediately saw something was wrong. Charity looked different, her face tired and her lips pursed tightly. She quickly looked away to the fire.

"Charity? What is it? " She jumped up and sat her down at the table.

"I think they will take some of us away."

"What are you talking about?"

"They asked me to clean out Father's quarters just as I was about to leave for dinner. So, I started to clean. Father was sleeping so I couldn't use the hoover and I - and, but, that man came again. The senior man who used to be Richard's boss."

Keziah looked over at Mother and then back to Charity. "Tell us everything."

"He came and spoke to Father while he was still in bed. I wasn't told to leave so I swept out and dusted his living quarters. It was filthy.

Then a guard asked me to go and make some beef sandwiches and bring some glasses."

"More alcohol?" asked Keziah.

Charity nodded and continued. "He was sitting in an armchair at the end of Sy's bed. I put everything down on the table beside him. I looked over at Father and asked him if he needed anything and the man told me to leave."

"How did Father seem?," asked Mother.

"He recognised me. I'm sure. But he seemed sad. His face was ashen, Mother. I continued wiping down the counters and banging the cushions in the salon when I heard Father shout something like "It was not part of the deal," to which the man shouted back "There is no deal anymore." Charity dropped her head and began to cry.

Mother moved over to her and put her arm around her shoulder. Charity let her head drop into her chest.

"Go on, dear."

"He said he needed at least ten women," she cried.

"For what?"

"I don't know but it was for something outside The Genus, so not for the factory because he said they had to be ready by next week and they'd be brought out in the minibus on market day so as not to raise suspicion."

"Mother, it has started," cried Keziah. She stood up not knowing where to go and sat down again. "If this is the way things are going I will take the wire right now and threaten to take everyone to the factory with tools as weapons and then we can all fight –

"Keziah, sit down and be quiet, please." Mother's voice was stern, and Keziah flushed and sat down.

"They have guns," sobbed Charity.

"What else did you hear, Charity?" Mother probed gently.

"A lot of it was muffled. Father said something about taking his land but not his people. The man said he owed him."

Keziah sat back in her chair. What now? If they have no power how can they protect each other?

"Where is Richard?"

"In the guards quarters, I expect."

"Do you have any way to reach him?"

"Not at this hour, Keziah. What do you think I am?"

"No, I just meant we need to talk to him. If you knew a way…"

"Some of the other guards know I see him, so I suppose I could ask them to fetch him, but for what? What can Richard do?"

"I've been talking with Richard, Charity," interrupted Mother Abi. "He has been telling me things."

Charity flushed.

"Like you have, about things going on behind the scenes."

"Oh. I just don't know how to tell you. ."

"He used to be a part of a huge crime gang, the one infiltrating The Genus, the one holding these people captive, and the one wanting to take some of our women," continued Mother.

"."

"I'm not accusing you of anything. I know he wants to look after you and that's fine. He seems to want to help us. Do you agree?"

"Yes Mother. I agree. He is a good man. I've seen him get some of the workers out of trouble and he snuck them food a couple of times. And he got permission for me to care for the children when the adults have to work sometimes."

Mother Abi nodded in approval as Charity spoke.

Mother continued to explain to Charity. "Unlike Keziah, he is an informant for the GCI. They have more power than Keziah's contacts have. In fact, the GCI are now over the whole operation, now it has become a much bigger thing."

Charity looked satisfied. "So can we get help to get rid of them?"

"The problem is all the groups involved want to do it on their terms, to hit the most criminal activity in one go, instead of what's best for the innocent people, " said Keziah.

"However," continued Mother Abi, "we could certainly ask Richard some questions. Maybe he knows what the plan is for these ten women. Maybe he knows, or can find out, the exact timings."

Keziah looked up at the clock. It's already 9.30. Maybe we should leave it until tomorrow."

Mother Abi agreed and they arranged to meet in The Fulcrum after breakfast, and after the children were settled. If Charity could get in touch with him first thing in the morning, she could ask him to come there and meet them.

Chapter Thirty Nine

Zadie came back out to the sofa where Yvonne was waiting. "She's down finally. I wish she'd get her teeth all in one go!"

"Wouldn't it be so much better than them having to suffer for so long?"

Zadie sat down next to her on the sofa and turned into her. "You have news from Keziah, don't you?"

"Sort of. I've been out of the loop, but they brought me back in this morning. She's – em – not cooperating with them."

"She's gone rogue?" Zadie laughed.

"She has, kind of! She's playing her cards close to her chest because things have taken a new direction in there."

"Is she safe? Are *they* safe?"

"Yes, yes, but the investigation has been taken over by the GCI, so things are moving a bit differently."

"Wow, the GCI? What changed?"

"They just found lots of other stuff going on there, so it's a bigger operation."

"Is it about Laura?" She looked at Yvonne plainly, ready to face what was coming.

"Okay, so first, I wanted to let you know I could have told you this weeks ago but as you've been battling with depression, and it wasn't going to make much of a different in the immediate future anyway, I decided to hold off."

"Will you just tell me please?"

"You're doing better. I can see it in your face."

"Yvonne!"

Keziah spoke of you to your mother, Dorothy, and she met Laura."

Zadie took a deep breath in.

"At first your mother was very hesitant to discuss things, but Keziah persisted. She's happy you are doing well and when she found out you had Rachel, she wanted to know her name. It's a good sign, isn't it?"

"I suppose so, yes."

"A few days later, Dorothy brought Laura to meet Keziah."

Zadie's hand shot up to her face and tears spilled down her cheek immediately. "Is she alright?"

"She is doing very well. Your mother said she as her so can always keep an eye on her, and she says Laura is a very clever little girl."

Zadie dropped into Yvonne's embrace.

"It's a lot, honey, but it's positive news."

"It is. It is. It's just, I've waited so long to know something, anything." Zadie sat back up and looked at Yvonne. "Anything else?"

"Not really. Keziah was adamant you get the message. It would be nice to give her some feedback tomorrow."

Zadie sat back and shook her head as she processed this news.

"Your mother, Dorothy, knows what's going on in there. It seems Mother Abi and Keziah and some of the other Carers are trying to make a little plan, should things get messy."

"Messy?"

"I don't know much but Sy is drinking or taking drugs. He is volatile, but the police are aware, and all will come tumbling down soon."

"How soon?"

"I have no idea. Any message back to Keziah?"

"Oh yes!" She thought for a moment. " Well, I suppose just to say thank you and I am very happy to know Laura has my mother to look after her. I'm very grateful to my mother. You could tell her I miss them all so much and if I ever have the chance to see them and spend time with them I would jump at it." The tears fell again, and Zadie took a deep breath in. "Does it sound alright?"

"It sounds wonderful, honey."

Chapter Forty

When Keziah woke the next morning, Charity was nowhere in sight. She presumed she was off looking for Richard and got up to wash and dress. As she made her way over to The Fulcrum she wondered if they'd already be there waiting for her. She opened the heavy door and spotted Mother at the top in the area she usually chose to sit. She quietly made her way up and sat beside her.

"Any sign of Charity?"

"No Mother. She left before I woke."

"That girl," she sighed.

"I know. I constantly worry for her. Do you think Richards intentions are good?

"They seem to be but only Gena knows. Look how quick Sy was to bring her into the fold. How quickly Richard singled her out, as someone who could be charmed. She has been dragged right into the heart of the problems from the beginning."

The door opened and Charity walked up to where they were and sat beside them. "Richard will be here soon. He says they've been called to some important meeting."

"What on earth could it be about?"

"I do not know, but I overheard one of the guards talk about one of the senior guards having a heart attack."

Mother's face flushed. "Which one?"

"I don't know. I heard no more."

"Did they die? Was a doctor called?"

"I'm sorry, Mother. I don't know."

"I want to leave to find out, but I will give Richard a few minutes."

When he did arrive, he clomped noisily up the aisle and sat behind them. "Sorry, I can't stay long. How can I help?"

Mother Abi started. "We have got wind Sy has been ordered to release ten females to your gang."

"I told you, it's not my gang."

"Do you know anything of it?" Mother persisted.

He sighed. "Yes, they say he owes them for some favours he got from them."

"What will they do to them? Where will they go?"

"I'm trying to find out more, but they have several nightclubs, you know, gentleman's clubs, one of them in the City. They are short staffed."

Only Keziah could understand what kind of club it was. "Prostitution? They want us for prostitution?"

"I don't know. It might only be for dancing or bar work. I honestly don't know."

"What does it mean?" cried Charity in alarm.

Mother let her head drop. "How will they choose the women from here?"

"Well, with anything like that."

"I understand, but in your opinion, what type of women will they choose?"

"Young, pretty, sassy." He shook his head. "Look, I can't confirm anything. I'll try to find out more."

"How can we stop it?" asked Keziah.

He sat quietly for a moment. "You could have someone on the outside, ready to interrupt their plan."

Keziah turned to Mother Abi. "We can do it. need..."

She stopped abruptly and looked at Richard. What was she doing? She couldn't let him know their plan.

"Oh, I don't know. When is this hell going to end?"

"Soon, hopefully. Look, I have to go, one of the guards is very ill and I might have to drive him to hospital."

"Who is it?" asked Mother.

"I don't know yet. I try not to be in the centre of every drama happening in this Goddam place."

He got up to leave and Keziah gestured for the others to remain.

"Look, he called from the door. I'll try to find out more."

"Thank you, Richard," called Mother Abi without turning around.

When Keziah was confident he was gone, she began talking excitedly. "I know Yvonne and Ish will help us to get those girls away from them. They will try to intercept them. They will kidnap them if they need to. I know they will."

Mother Abi stood up. "It is something to be considered but be careful in the words you use to her in your conversation this morning."

Keziah walked out of The Fulcrum alone, and she did not see her mother until very later on the same night.

Keziah stopped her laundry and ran upstairs to her mother's bedroom. She closed the door and took out her pager. It needed charging, so she plugged it in and began typing.

Yvonne, are you there?

I'm here, honey. How are you today?

Alright. I think one of the guards is dying or had a heart attack.

Is he one of them or part of The Genus?

I don't know yet.

I spoke with Zadie this morning.

How is she? Did you ever give her the message?

I waited until this morning because she as a little depressed, but better now.

How did she take it?

It made her happy to know Laura was doing well and cared for by her mother. She said to say she misses them so much and to see them.

She might get a chance soon!

What do you mean, Keziah?

Well, are they not working away trying to resolve this mess?

Of course, they are. I just thought you had some exciting news.

I wish.

How will you spend your day?

Probably folding laundry as usual. It's very boring.

Anything else on the grapevine?"

I heard Sy might allow some women to go to the market.

Why did he change his mind? I thought you were low in stock.

Not this kind of stock.

Oh?

Yeah, there'll be lots of heavy stuff I expect, so they need more people. Big jars of pickles and jams.

Honey, Frank wants to know dates and times.

I don't have dates and times.

Why so many women, Keziah? Usually there are more guards than women at the market, right?

True. Maybe I heard wrong. There are so many stories and whispers in here lately.

It's to be expected given the circumstances. So many things seem to be changing. It makes .

I miss the days of going downtown to eat with you. Remember the Lebanese Restaurant. You know the one across from the gentleman's club? The food was something else. I'm so tired of vegetables and rice.

What? Ah yes, I remember. Amazing hummus there.

It won't be long until we're back there together.

They said their goodbyes and Keziah sat on the bed reliving the conversation. Had she done enough to let Yvonne know she was trying to send a message? Or had she said too much so Frank had caught on to it? Only time would tell.

Chapter Forty One

When the conversation was over, Yvonne went to leave the room like the day before.

"Before you go," said Frank as he leaned back on the door again, "what restaurant was she referring to?"

"Oh, what was the name of it again? I'd need to look it up."

"Across from the Gentleman's club?" He let his head fall to the side and looked into her eyes. "Is there something else I need to know here?"

"Like what? Seriously this case has you festering from the inside. She's a young woman who lived most of her life imprisoned and controlled, so on this side of the wall she is naturally inquisitive, always asking questions."

"Okay, but wasn't it odd that she brought it up now?"

She stared at him blankly.

"Come on. It was out of place."

"She was remembering good times at a restaurant. What are you talking about?" She looked at him in disdain.

Frank held her glare for a few seconds. "See you tomorrow." He opened the door, and she walked out without saying goodbye.

As she walked out of the station she worked through the conversation: ten women in the minibus at market day. As she sat into the car it dawned on her. She took her phone out of her bag and dialled.

"Ish? We need to meet, asap."

Chapter Forty Two

She sat at the fire, poking the sticks, and moving the red coals around. It was pitch black outside and the glow of the fire was the only light in the kitchen. Looking up at the clock, she sighed. It was after 9pm and she had not seen Mother since earlier in The Fulcrum. She was clearly upset when she found out one of the guards were ill, but it was so unlike her to disappear for so long.

Mother Dorothy managed the kitchen in her absence and just said she'd be back when she could, obviously knowing what was going on. Despite Keziah's protest she was told the same over and over again. She'd come back when she could.

"What on earth are you doing still here, Keziah?"

"Mother! What happened. Where have you been?"

Her Mother walked in and took off her coat, hanging it as she spoke. "You should not have waited for me."

"Why not?"

"After I spoke with you this morning, I went back out to those people."

"Alone? Mother it's not safe. At least one of us should go with you!"

"It was fine, Child." I made up the little bundles so just had to leave them inside each door."

"But it was too much to carry alone! What if a guard arrived?"

"I have better chances of getting away with it without you and Charity hovering on my periphery. Neither of you have a good reputation exactly now do you?"

"I suppose not. Here let me get you some tea and bread while you tell me more."

Her mother sat down with a sigh of relief.

"Did you talk to the same people?"

"Yes. They need first aid kits so I will focus on those next."

"For what?"

"Apart from normal day to day accidents with the children, they are getting burns and cuts from working. It's so easy for a small wound to turn into an infection in those conditions."

"Do we have many supplies to share?"

"Well, some antiseptic and bandages won't be missed." She stared into the fire. "I just hope they don't get caught with extra food now. I've warned them but we shall see."

"Surely they understand."

"It only takes one person - one silly person to think they will be let go free, or that their family will be fed if they tell."

Keziah put a big mug of sweet tea on the table in front of her mother, and then brought some bread with butter and cheese to the table. She sat down and watched her mother eat.

"What about the guard from earlier, Mother? Did you find out anything else?"

Mother Abi reddened. "He died. Guard Isaac, one of the senior guards. He had a heart attack in front of all the other guards. Noone called an ambulance."

"Wasn't Richard to bring him to hospital or something?"

She watched her mother's lips tighten and tremble. "He had another attack while they waited on permission."

"Did you know him well, Mother?"

"I did. I grew up with him."

Keziah moved across to her mother and hugged her. "I'm so sorry. Was he your friend?"

"He was a good friend at one point. Before I – Keziah, head off to bed now before Mother Michelle is up in arms. Tell her you stayed to keep the fire stoked."

She leaned down and kissed her mother's cheek before putting her coat on.

"Oh, what of your conversation with Yvonne?"

"I think it was good enough for her to realise what I meant. I just hope the police don't get it too."

"That's good. Goodnight Keziah."

Chapter Forty Three

"How can we be sure?" Ish sat at the kitchen table in the flat.

"We can't. Not really, but the comment about the stock, and then, why would she mentioned the club."

"Yvonne, why can't we just trust the police and the GCI to handle this? What if they know something we don't?"

"They are not prioritising the people in there. That Amanda lady is more interested in getting promotion than getting people to safety. They are interested in the headlines and the shoulder slaps."

"Surely if we tell them this is happening they'll try to save them?"

"Ish, anything could happen at any time. They know it already. Don't you understand? Detective Frank has already made it clear they are letting things slip for the moment while they build a case from the back outwards."

"It doesn't bode well for Keziah, or Laura for that matter."

"It's not safe for anyone in there except Arma Blood members. Look, help me work this out. What else could she mean? She knows I would talk to you about it. She knows you know the timetable for the market. You've been there so often and know the routine, so you'll know the time."

"Yeah, but we'd need to be ready at the gate and follow them. What happens then? Do we let them arrive at the club? I'm just afraid we're not equipped to deal with this. These guys carry guns, Yvonne."

She put her hand to her head. "I was thinking…"

"And," he continued, "what if we're overthinking this and it's not what she meant?"

"We could into her, to the cave, so we can make sure we're all on the same page."

"Bloody hell, Yvonne!"

"It's the only way." She looked into his eyes.

"Okay, great. So, we have five days to get a phone to Keziah, outsmart a cartel and kidnap ten women from a minibus." He shook his head.

"Are you in?" she asked him squarely.

"Do I have a choice?"

"Not really. You'll regret it forever if you don't take this opportunity. Look, you know what you're doing. You've done this before."

He sat back. Give me a day to think it through. There's a whole new village to get past to reach the cave now. I'll need help. Eli would be happy to, I'm, sure. Maybe a couple of guys from work. I don't know."

Yvonne stood up and grabbed her bag. "Let's talk tomorrow at the same time and place."

She kissed him on the head. The headlines of the folded paper grabbed her attention.

She pulled the paper from the table. "I knew it!"

Ish took the paper and read the caption. "Oh my God."

LAP DANCERS AT TEEDY'S GENTLEMAN'S CLUB DIE IN MASS OVERDOSE – SUICIDE NOT SUSPECTED.

Yvonne looked down at him wild-eyed. "Stock. The stock are being replaced."

Chapter Forty Four

The next morning after breakfast, Keziah sat with the carers in the kitchen shelling and blanching some nuts. She guessed Mother planned to use them for the workers in the forest. Mother Dorothy was there, and they were discussing the lack of vegetable oil and how the flour supply was decreasing quickly.

"Well, when there are no loaves or pies or biscuits, maybe they'll stock up."

"Who has the ultimate say on the stock?" asked Keziah.

"It has always been discussed with the cooks, Senior Mothers, and Sy. We'd let him know what was needed. A guard would put the order together and go and get it. Simple"

"Has no one discussed this problem with the senior guards?" asked Keziah.

"They have. But apparently they want us to use up older stock."

"Like what?"

"Well, like nuts and some other grains we have; millet, oats and the likes."

"I see."

At lunch time Keziah went looking for Charity. She hadn't seen her all day. She usually flitted around and showed her face in the morning if she was up and out before her. She walked around the back of The Fulcrum and made her way to the old garage, approaching from the back this time. Three men were in the garage working on the cars, like before. There were more cars now. Four large fancy cars in good condition.

The small metal door to the other side of the garage was ajar, and she was too tempted not to go and have a peek. She walked quietly and quickly up the side of the area, past the door with the blue peeling paint. The low lit ceiling lights were not enough for her to see much from the door. . She heard people talking but couldn't see them. All she could see were high shelves full of food. Tins and jars and packets of all shapes and sizes in piles, stacked on huge metal shelves. This was the first time Keziah had ever seen this food store. The one at the front of the complex held the fresh goods and bread. It looked like a lot to her, but of course there were many people to feed, so she guessed it didn't last long.

She didn't want to be seen but couldn't resist the temptation to step inside and see who was talking at the bottom of the building. She slowly moved behind the shelves to hide herself. at the end of the row, she peered through to four tall tables with women sitting around talking laughing as they wrapped and packed something into transparent bags, and then stacked them like bricks on a crate beside each station. They did it so quickly, automatically, as they chatted. They all wore gloves and some of the women wore cloth around their mouths like the people in the factory. Keziah put her hand over her mouth. They must be packing drugs.

"Keziah. What the hell are you doing here?"

She jumped and turned around to see Richard standing watching her. He shook his head and walked down to where the women were now watching with concern.

"Everything is okay. Back to work please."

They all got back to it, whispering between themselves, and occasionally looking over at Richard who led Keziah through the building and back to the door.

"I didn't know there were people in there," she lied, "I just came to see the food stock everyone is so concerned about."

He sighed and led her out of the main pathway to the back of The Fulcrum in silence. How dare he give her the silent treatment.

"I'm sorry. I didn't realise there was anything going on in there."

"You appeared pretty interested to me."

"Well, of course, once I'd spotted them. What are they packing?"

"Guess."

He beckoned her to walk with him around to the front of The Fulcrum.

He spoke as he walked. "You need to be careful. You really don't understand what you're dealing with here."

"Are you threatening me?" She glared at him. He had not managed to gain her trust yet, and even though Mother Abi and the detectives approved of him, Keziah believed he was capable of turning on them.

He brushed his hand through his hair irritably. "Of course, it's not a threat. I don't want to see any harm come to you."

Determined not to let him see she was worried; she changed the subject. "Any update on these ten girls your people want to traffic?"

"Afraid so. Looks like I'll be taking them downtown in the minibus in a few days. Friday probably."

"And you're just going to do it?"

"I don't think you quite works. I have enough on my mind without trying to look after you."

"Look after me? Are you for real? Look after me?" she laughed wryly.

"Come on, Keziah. Nothing in here is straight forward. You know this by now. I'm not trying to disagree with you for the sake of it. We're on the same team!"

"If so, hear me out. If I could get someone to minibus..."

"Are you fucking mad? Who?"

"I can't say. But I know people willing to stop the minibus and take the women off."

"I can't do it. They would suspect me."

"Are there any other guards in here that know what's going on?"

"One, kind of, but I don't drag him into things. He's a friend. He prefers not to know."

"Oh, you have friends."

"Jesus, give me a break will you?"

"You could bring him, and he could attest to the fact you had no choice. Please Richard. We could stop these women from being forced into...look, just think about it."

She walked off, red faced and anxious. If he decided not to, he now knows about it, and could prevent the women from being saved. She wondered if Detective Frank and company knew about this. She forgot to ask Richard if he told them. Why would he hold it back?

Chapter Forty Five

Yvonne stood with Simon messaging Keziah. She wanted to be careful but also wanted to push a little to see if Keziah was getting the message.

"How is Ish doing? Is he still in the business?"

"You know Ish. He'll never change."

"I bet he's adorable with Rachel. I'm missing so much of her growing up."

"You'll be out soon, Keziah. Be patient. I know it's hard."

"I'd love to be chosen to do the market on Friday, but I doubt I would be given permission. I have to stay with Mother all the time."

"I see. The detective is asking if you have been speaking to Richard over the last two days."

"Yes."

"The detective wants to know if there is anything new."

"Not that I know of. Richard knows everything, more than me."

On her way out this time, Yvonne stopped at the door and looked at the detective.

"Is there any update? Any progress?"

"Yes. going on."

"I know. I know. In the background. The girl is depressed and anxious. She needs out."

"These people need to be handled very carefully, Yvonne. I told you. They are armed, and they don't care ."

"Well, I care about Keziah, and I want her out."

"Did you see the group of girls from the strip club died?"

"Yeah. What about them?"

"They own the strip club, and the girls, and probably the bad batch. This is what we're dealing with here."

"Frank, I understand Keziah was determined to go in, and the project has changed but she's not serving any purpose in there."

"Listen, things are coming to a head. I don't think the GCI will let things go much further." He nodded reassuringly, but it was too late. Yvonne lost all trust in him when he cut her off a few weeks before.

Keziah's talk of Ish still being in the business surely referred to him helping people escape. At least, she hoped so.

Chapter Forty Six

As Keziah approached the dining hall the next morning, a guard stood at the door talking to a group of confused looking women.

"If you are a Carer, or assigned tasks in Carers houses, you can eat your meals there from now on."

Groups of people stood around listening to him answering questions.

"Yes, that's right. If you're in a senior Mother's house during the day, you can have your meals there too."

"If you are a Bearer or a bride of a guard you can eat here in the hall."

"If you're a Bearer but spend time in a mother's house you can eat there."

"Why?" a few people asked," What's wrong?"

"There's nothing wrong. The guards just want to make sure the food supplies in the houses are used to full potential.

"For Bearers, farm hands, labourers and guards, there will be food as usual, here in the hall."

"All the meals throughout the day will be served here in the dining hall for those who do not work at, or frequent, a Mother's house."

It was a huge change to most people's daily routines.

"What if the Mother's homes do not have enough food?" asked Keziah.

"Mother's will have eggs and they bake in their own kitchens, don't they?"

"Yes, but Mother Abi dines here for lunch and dinner. She has enough for breakfast, for some children's snacks and lunches, but she and all of us at her house will need meals here."

He replied quickly. "If any Mothers have issues with supply of food they should talk to a senior guard."

The stragglers eventually walked away confused and unsure.

Keziah went straight to Mother's house and spotted her from the small hen houses.

"Hello dear! I'm trying to collect these early before anyone claims them."

"Do you think things will get so bad?"

"If one house has more eggs than another they may be asked to share, but I would like to use a few for baking for the factory people."

"I see. Aren't you worried about them sending people away from the dining hall?"

"They will do anything now but give us money to eat. We foraged and cured and fermented food all our lives. We still have plenty of food yet, but eggs might very well become valuable."

"They could become a currency."

"Who knows! Now, do you speak with Yvonne today?"

They walked up the yard together, dodging young children playing just outside the house on the lawn, with younger Carers running around after them.

"I am mulling over how to tell her Richard will drive. It's Tuesday. We have until Friday to make a plan."

"Use the market. She might realise by market you mean they are moving people out. Mention the minibus and tell her Richard is driving. Then later on, mention him again."

"The detectives can easily cop this though."

"Knowing about it and stopping it are two different things. Did your Detective Frank seem like a bad man?"

"No. Not at all. But he's not in charge anymore."

Mother sighed. Her tired face reminded Keziah of all she had been through. Her features were softer now, the lines hung lower on her face. She appreciated this time with Mother, to rekindle their bond under new circumstances was important. Who knew what the future held.

"They keep saying for me to sit tight but things are getting worse by the day."

"Now is the time for taking risks, Keziah. Things have become unpredictable".

"Richard is annoyed with me. I spoke with him, and he said he will get in a lot of trouble if the bus is pulled over. I suggested he take a guard he trusts so there are witnesses to show it was not his fault."

Keziah held her mother's hand and they walked into the kitchen together. Mother went straight to the storeroom off the kitchen and Keziah watched her take four eggs from her basket and put them under a shelf at her feet.

"When will you get back to the factory people again?"

"Before Friday I hope. The man said on Fridays they collect the stock."

"So, on Fridays there will be lots of coming and going, including this plan to bring these women to the market."

"It seems so. They had bread and apples the last time. The guards brought them. Still not enough, but better. They need more sustenance, both the hardworking adults and the little growing children. And first aid. I'm putting together two kits. One for the factory and one to share in the women's hut.

"Will I accompany you, Mother?"

"Let's see what happens in the coming days."

Keziah headed upstairs to start her chat with Yvonne.

Hello, Yvonne.

Hello Darlin'. How are you doing?

Oh fine, they've stopped lots of people eating in the dining hall. They're trying to spare food they say.

Really? So where will you eat?

Well, the Carer's in the houses run by senior Mothers, usually bake and have chickens and other dried food stuffs."

Okay. It sounds like a big change.

It is, but the guard explaining it was very polite and said it was just a way to make the food last.

And who's decision is this?

Who knows.

Detective Frank wants to know why they are planning a market this week if they are low on food.

Tell him, there's a separate market store with conserves and dried mushrooms and all sorts of things.

So, supplies aren't that low?

We're low on things like flour and oil, things we really need to for baking and general cooking. Now we are using other cereals for breads and pies. The Senior Mothers will need to arrange more baking.

Okay. I suppose they're not quite in crisis but heading there.

Yes. Maybe the idea behind the market is to get more money for food.

Maybe

That guy Richard drives the vans and minibuses a lot of the time.

Okay.

Maybe one of you could go to the market on the day?

The detective says they won't approach yet. A few more details need to be worked out.

Keziah sighed and began to bite her nails. How can she know for sure they understand what she is saying? If she tries to insist it will begin to look suspicious. She waited pensively for Yvonne to say something.

"*Do they head out early on Fridays to the market. I'd love if you could go. I'd nearly do a sneaky visit* "

Keziah laughed. She's getting it. She was sure.

I wish. I'm doomed to the laundry these days. Yeah I think they leave early enough. I'll check if the detective wants? :)

No harm to pass it on if you can.

Keziah cringed. She knew Richard was giving them information and she had no idea if he was telling tales on her. The Detective might know exactly what was going on."

After the chat she ran down the stairs giddily and looked a Mother Abi with a smile.

"So, your headache is gone?" Mother glared at her, and Keziah froze in confusion, before noticing a guard in the pantry inspecting the shelves.

"What is this? Our nuts are being counted now. Do we have to share our raspberry leaves?"

"Don't be insolent, Keziah."

She shut her mouth quickly. The guards did not like back talking. This one was young. She didn't recognise him. He wore a modern ribbed black polo with nice jeans. The Genus did not have access to this kind of style. He backed out of the pantry and nodded at Mother Abi before walking out the front door quickly.

"How did your conversation go with Yvonne?"

"I think she got it. She asked about the times. I need Richard to confirm it." She sat down at the table, her shoulders slumped. "He won't tell me. I'm sure of it."

"Leave Richard to me," she said as she took off her apron and put on her overcoat. "Can you please move those eggs upstairs to my box?"

"Of course."

Mother walked out determinedly not far behind the guard.

Chapter Forty Seven

Keziah walked out of the dormitory to see people buzzing around, looking confused and stressed. She just missed the end of a message over the speakers. She took the arm of a passing young woman, a Bearer she thought.

"What's wrong? What did they say?"

The girl looked at her, full of fear. "They say there's a list of names in The Fulcrum reception."

"For what?"

"New jobs."

"In what?"

"I don't know," she said pulling her arm away and running towards The Fulcrum.

Keziah followed the people to the front entrance. She pushed and shoved to get to the papers posted on a notice board, just beside the door. There were three A4 pages of handwritten names in lists. Three columns on each page – so many names. Roughly forty five per page. What the hell? Keziah scanned the list quickly. Relieved there was no sign of her name, she turned around to look for a guard to ask some questions. She spotted Richard with another guard standing outside the main door, so walked over.

"Excuse me, I missed the announcement. What is going on with the people on the list?"

The guard with Richard reacted quickly. " Are you on the list?"

"No, but I-"

"Then you have nothing to worry about."

"But what if my friends or sisters are on the lists. What does it mean?"

The guard scowled at her and was about to go off when Richard interrupted.

"New jobs. Now off with you and get your duties done."

"What kind of jobs? Where?"

This was horrific. Were they moving people out? Or over to the factory in the woods?

"Listen, Ma'am, the people involved will find out about soon enough, and then everyone will know. Off with you now and stop loitering."

She glared at him for a moment and then marched off to Mother's house. When she arrived, Keziah found a large group piling right outside of the kitchen onto the porch. They were distraught and all talking over each other in high pitch. She heard mother's voice shouting and trying to control them, but it wasn't working.

She yelled as loud as she could "Women, please stop. One at a time. Mother can't speak with you all at once."

Their heads turned and the noise abated, Mother came out onto the porch to see who was shouting.

She walked over to where Keziah stood in the yard and spoke quickly under her breath, "Some of their names are on the list."

"Alright ladies! Please slow down and breathe. Then, come over here and form a circle," called Mother.

The women obeyed. Some were very young and had just started their Carer roles. The faces of anguish were upsetting but as usual, Mother stayed calm in the face of adversity.

"Now, as I know, there is a list of names in The Fulcrum. Those of you on the list will soon be assigned new tasks. We do not know what these tasks are yet. Praise Gena, they will be good tasks, maybe even duties you enjoy more than the ones you have! So, we all need to stay calm and get on with our day until we know more. Yes?"

"Yes Mother," came the response.

One young woman spoke up "I heard they are taking some of us out of here?"

Mother went red and her eyes widened. "Who told you this?"

The girl looked at her blankly and did not respond.

"Did you hear me?" continued Mother. She walked over and took the girl by the hand and turned to the others. "We will speak later. Get on with your duties please."

While the group were perplexed and anxious, they did seem to be comforted, a little, by Mother's calmness. Mother took the girl by the hand and walked her into the house. Keziah decided to wait outside for a while. She sat down on the bench outside the barn and wallowed in the Autumn sun. There was still some heat in it despite the chill in the breeze. She squeezed her brain in an effort to recall the route to the hermitage, Mother Sarah's bunker. After the red cedar tree landmark she had nothing. Over a year ago she did it, but she had a map then. How could they find it? In light of what was unfolding before their eyes, they needed to bring more food to the cave, and purposely try to find the hermitage. Maybe Mother would allow just her and Charity to go. Where was Charity anyway? She was gone from the dormitory before she woke again. Some mornings she went off with Richard, probably to mind children or spend time with him. She didn't always tell her. She'd show up later with some story, no doubt.

By the afternoon, the whispers said all the people on the list had been brought into the dining hall. Mother confirmed three of her trainees were on the list. Lots of other women she knew were on the list, even some more mature Carers who Mother -knew for along time.

"Please Gena, don't let them take them out of here to sordid places," she said as she sat darning in front of the fire.

"Mother, it's time to get to the cave with more food and finally make a track to the hermitage."

"Maybe. Let's see what Richard says. I will be talking to him later this evening. I don't know if these ten women are still in the plan or included in the lists."

Just then Charity ran in and kneeled before Mother Abi, sobbing.

"What is it Charity?" Mother put away her darning quickly and stroked Charity's head, now lying on her lap as she sobbed.

She looked up at Mother. "I'm on the list."

"What?" Keziah ran over to her and sat on the floor with her arm around Charity.

"We will protect you, Child. Don't worry."

"Did they bring you all into the dining hall and speak to you?" asked Keziah.

"Yes. They put us in different groups and assigned tasks."

"What kind of tasks?"

"Some will go to a factory to work, and some of the men will go to another factory, and then the ten women are going to clean a hotel somewhere and-

She spoke without breathing and Mother Abi put her hands on her shoulder and pushed her a little upright.

"Charity, when?"

"They didn't say, but they said it wasn't tomorrow."

Keziah put her hands to her head. "I can't believe this is happening. What are we going to do? Charity, have you spoke to Richard?"

"Yes he was there the whole time. He will try to get engaged to me, to keep me here."

Mother Abi took a deep breath in and sighed heavily.

"Mother, let Charity and I go first thing in the morning. We won't even go to the factory, just to the cave with some supplies and then to find the hermitage."

"Probably wise. I must go now and speak with Richard. Both of you should wait here. Keep the fire on."

Mother left and they both stared into fire for a minute or two.

"I am one of the ten. The group they are sending to a "hotel". I can't do those things, Keziah," she cried.

"We won't let it happen. Richard won't let it happen. I'm sure of it."

"I saw Father Sy today to. He looks very different. He has lost weight. There's a very strange look in his eyes."

"Where did you see him?"

"They brought him into the dining hall. They had to help him up the steps. He just sat there in silence. It was very disconcerting, Keziah."

"Well, I'm more concerned for your wellbeing and safety than his!"

She smiled, and Keziah continued.

"So, Richard is going to go to them and say he's courting you and wants to get engaged?"

"Exactly."

She didn't smile or look excited like she has been about Richard before.

"Is it what you want?"

"Yeah, why not."

"Why not?"

"Keziah, we're not all fated to go over the wall and live the modern life. If it's not him it would be someone else. Anyway, would I rather marry or go Gena knows where to some weird hotel?"

Of course, she was right. She didn't have any option right now.

"You know, this has to explode. All of it. You'll have a chance to get out of here."

"Do you know how many times I have tried to get out of here?" Charity raised her voice, exasperated. "Do you know how many times? Guess!"

Keziah sighed. "Twice I know of."

"Three times. Twice I have helped others escape and once was supposed to be with you."

"You know I'm sorry it ever happened. I had to run."

"I know. But my life was hell for a year after it. Until Father started to keep me in favour."

"Why do you think he did that? Made you his personal assistant?"

"Because he thinks I'm sly and untrustworthy and I would give him information."

"Did you?"

Charity looked at Keziah. "A bit, yes."

They both laughed.

"I had no choice. I just brought him titbits of information. Nothing of great importance."

"I hope he never hurt you?"

"Nah. A few sloppy kisses good night, but nothing more."

"Oh Charity! That's disgusting."

"You don't need to tell me that." She grimaced and they giggled again, just like they did when they were mischievous teenagers. She didn't truly understand the full magnitude of what had been done to her. Keziah thought of talking to her in a more serious way, but it wasn't the time, and she wasn't an expert. Once outside, Charity will have some heavy things to deal with.

Mother arrived two hours later and sent them up to the room beside hers, with a hot water bottle. She said she'd let Mother Michelle know they were staying in her house. But none of the rules really mattered anymore. Her haggard face told Keziah not to ask about her speaking to Richard. Things were slowly becoming chaotic. As she lay in the bed curled up with Charity, Keziah wondered what tomorrow or the next day would bring. Something huge, no doubt.

Chapter Forty Eight

The next morning Mother woke them in the dark and told them to come downstairs where she had oats and sweet tea waiting for them. She handed them a banana each, which they both ate straight away.

"Now," she said as she brought out the bags and set them down on the table in front of them both. We have two bags for the cave. I've also done a small hand basket each; one for both your lunches, and one in case you meet someone needing food." She eyed them both seriously until the nodded.

"The plan is to avoid the factory and the chances of any guards seeing you. Should you get caught, say you were sent to look for mushrooms and cob nuts After that hard rain the other day, I'm sure there's nothing more."

"What if the children see us and follow us and then a guard sees us?" asked Charity.

"Well, you say you have no idea where these children have come from. If I were you I would get out as fast as you can and arrive at the cave to leave the shoulder bags."

"Mother," started Keziah, "did you speak with Richard last night? Wil Charity be okay?"

Mother Abi now had her back to them as she tended the oven. She didn't answer.

"Mother?" came Charity.

"If Richard can't help you then we will. You've not to worry. End of." Keziah was sick of watching men use excuses to keep women down. Charity needed to heal, to be empowered and liberated. She didn't need to be married.

The fear in her eyes sent a surge of panic through Keziah. She wanted more than anything to take Laura and Mother and Charity and run to the hermitage. They could just hunker down until it's all over.

"Come along girls. Get your warm coats on and hats. Here, put these scarves on too. It's cold out there."

As Charity headed out Keziah lingered at the door. "Mother, I will send a message to Yvonne when I'm out. What do I say?"

"Nothing has changed really; except we know they are moving people about. Tell her. Tell her about the girls. They will be transported in two days' time. On Friday evening. Richard says about 6pm, or after dinner."

"Okay. I'll try not to make it too obvious but..."

"All we can do is try, dear."

She looked at Mother Abi's pale face. "You look tired Mother. Maybe you can go back to bed for a while?"

"Get on with you, before it's daylight!"

Chapter Forty Nine

Although it wasn't raining, bands of mist hung across the dull expanse. They walked closely on the sodden earth to try to stay warm. Once at the cave they immediately unpacked. It was a great relief to be rid of the heavy shoulder bags. Keziah checked the back of the cave and nodded satisfactorily when she saw the other bags of food were still intact. They sat down and had a rest.

"Charity, Can you get your hands on a phone?"

"No. phones."

"Doesn't Richard have one?"

"Yes but he uses it all the time for work. People are always calling him to drive here and there."

"I have an idea, but I need to contact Yvonne."

"What's the idea?"

"To do the same escape route I did before and get Ish to help us out."

"Us?"

"Yes, you and me and Zadie's daughter Laura. I doubt Mother Abi would come but maybe Mother Dorothy would."

"Oh Keziah." She smirked. "Do you really think we could get away with it?"

Keziah couldn't help but feel irritated by her cynicism. "Look, we need you out of here and safe by Friday. We can try our best to communicate with Yvonne via the detectives but I'm very limited. I have no idea if she's on the same page as me."

"What was it to be?"

"Ish and some friends would highjack the bus on Friday. It might still happen, but there are no guarantees."

"How on earth did you try to plan it with Yvonne?"

"Well, by emphasising places and names, but if I could get my hands on a phone, even for five minutes I could call her directly. Even a text would be great."

"Pfft. You're pulling at straws here." Charity of water and shifted to the front of the cave. "Shall we go?"

Keziah didn't move. "I could confirm everything. I'd tell her you might be on the bus. I'd tell her a small group of us will run to the hermitage should things get very bad, and I want Ish to come in and help us out."

Charity shook her head.

Keziah grabbed her by the shoulders. "Charity, do you have any idea what's ahead of you if you go on the bus on Friday? Do you know you will become one their slaves?"

"But Rich-

"Richard what? He hasn't done anything to help us so far. Even he is not sure if he can get you off the list."

"He'll try though."

"Of course. Great. We'll all just sit around and watch as they start enslaving us, beating us, starving us. Is that your plan?"

She sighed. "Okay. Okay. I know. I'm just trying to stay calm."

"You're disassociating, but I need you to be here with me. Be present. I need your help if we are to save ourselves."

Charity nodded. She leaned over and hugged Keziah who received it with open arms.

"We have to find a way, and we will. Keziah hugged her back but persisted.

"Hang on. Father Sy has a mobile. It was on his mantel when I was cleaning his quarters the other week."

Keziah clapped her hands. "We have to get it."

As they crawled to the exit, Keziah spotted something under a large stone just inside the cave. She bent down and pulled it aside. There was an opaque plastic bag.

"What is it? Be careful!"

Keziah took the outer packaging off to find another small, well taped plastic parcel, and underneath it, another. Finally, she got to a cardboard box. She opened it and cried aloud when she saw the phone. She crouched down and let herself fall onto the ground and she opened a small, folded piece of paper.

"Yvonne, Ish. What would I do without you?"

"What? What is going on?"

Keziah sat smiling to herself as she opened the paper.

You got to the cave. Well done! Have you done this before? :P The phone is on silent and there's a charger with it. Text to let us know you've got it. Love, Yvonne

"Yvonne sent me this phone. She stressed *'the cave'* a couple of times but I didn't dare think she'd be so ahead of the game! They have no idea we're storing food here."

Keziah shook her head in disbelief as she tried to get the phone working. How silly she'd been. She should have known Yvonne would not leave her alone in these circumstances.

"Does this mean, if I get on the bus, I'll get out?"

"I think so," Keziah beamed.

"Well then, forget marrying Richard. I'm going on the bus." She clapped jokingly and sat down beside her to watch her work on the phone.

"It took me ages to get used to mine. I forget how to do it all now," Keziah explained.

"You had one to yourself?"

"Yes, Eli and Zadie showed me how to use it, but I couldn't work out half the different things it does. It takes time."

"Hey, if they left the phone in here, then they must know about the people here and the factory."

"I hadn't thought about it. Well, I can just ask them now. No more wondering and hoping!" Keziah beamed as she held the phone in front of her.

She finally managed to send a message to Yvonne, explaining their plan and how they needed to find the hermitage. Within five minutes Yvonne checked with Ish and was back to her with some directions, including landmarks. They agreed she would message back once there.

"Seeing as we're pretty confident of finding it now, shouldn't we bring two of the bags of food?" suggested Charity.

"Good thinking. We've got about twenty more minutes to walk. We can carry them and maybe have time to come back for the others."

"We need to bring some mushrooms back, at least."

"True, it would be great if we can find it today and leave two bags."

All packed up and ready to go they purposely walked widely around the area of the factory, hoping for no contact.

Keziah knew the general direction to head in, towards what they called the frontier, the verge of land running right around the perimeter next to the wall. She headed there the night of her escape, and Ish found her. She had no idea he was coming to meet her. After Yvonne's messages, they knew to go eastwards towards the wall at the other side of the next little woodland, hopefully avoiding the huts and factory, and any contact with the people there, or worse, the guards. It was still early enough in the day though, so they had time to hunt for mushrooms but promised each other they'd only stop if a glut of them presented themselves. Then it would be worth taking some time to collect them.

This particular little woodlands was creepier than the previous. An eeriness she couldn't quite explain occupied the area. The last time she came through here it was night-time, and she was petrified. Today, the woods were silent and dark. They walked through an overgrown pathway into a central area where they stopped to observe signs of life. There was a campfire and logs for seating surrounding it - maybe the men from the huts. There were beer cans though, so maybe the guards. They had cooked something: a rabbit or something small. It's furry skin lay by the side shrivelled and discarded. The meatless carcass abandoned. They both jumped when they heard a rustle behind them. They ran forward until they made a good distance away.

"I think- it was probably just kids or – or – a bird," she panted.

They continued in silence. Keziah led the way, focused on finding the first landmark, a large oak tree with some rocks around the base, on a main pathway. When she came to it, she didn't stop, she remained focused, and they turned left into a smaller brighter woodland area.

She turned to Charity, smiling. "In less than ten minutes we'll be at the bunker."

Now they just had to find the door leading down to it. Yvonne's message said it will be hard to find at first glance, but they should search the scrub. There'll be an old log about two feet long, lying on top of the trapdoor with loose foliage around it. They walked around with sticks, beating the foliage waiting for some loose bush to reveal itself, and it did.

"Here! Keziah, it's here." Charity was whispering so loudly Keziah chuckled to herself.

They moved quickly and silently. They knew to leave it very close to the doorway because it would still hide it from a distance should anyone be walking by. Keziah found a rope handle and pulled the trapdoor up to reveal a tunnel downwards. The first few metal bars were visible. They were attached to a cement reinforcement like a built-in ladder.

Charity laughed and put her hand over her mouth. "What in Gena's...? You go first."

"It's not as deep as it looks. It's just dark."

Keziah climbed halfway down and then reached up to help Charity. It took just five big steps more, before she was down in the dark little room with Charity behind her. Keziah shone the torch around so Charity could get a look at the whole place. The ceiling was low, the walls a dull mud, with shelves enclaved into it. She eventually found the little string and pulled it, to turn on a low orange glow.

"What in Gena's name..."

"Isn't it amazing?"

"So, this is how Ish got you all over the wall? here for a while?" Charity walked around touching the walls in admiration, brushing her hand over the smooth wood of the solid oak table. "Who did this?" she asked as she picked up the little moulded shelves.

"Apparently, Mother Sarah had it built to come to pray and meditate."

Charity sat down on one of the two small wooden benches on either side of a rough wooden table. "Or to escape," she said thoughtfully. She let herself slide down. "We'd sleep on these?"

"Depends on how many of us there are."

"Oh, and there's a stove!"

"We can't use it because the smoke might bring unwanted attention above."

Keziah got on with unpacking the food, putting what she could on the shelves. Underneath the little camping cooker, behind a gingham curtain, there was a bit of space to stack the remaining tins.

She sat down on the other side of the table." So, what else would four or five people need to hide out in here for a day or two?"

"Water, and ," she said as she held a thick shawl up.

"That's a hard . I wonder will Ish come back in to help us?"

"Message Yvonne and ask her."

"There'll be no signal down here."

"Signal?"

"Ah, I'll explain another time, but the phone won't connect here."

"Fine. Oh, and maybe something to occupy the child. Some paper and paints, and the book of Gena."

"Good idea, although let's leave the book of Gena behind."

"There's no point in being so facetious, Keziah."

"Sorry. It's just not something I care about right now. We've enough to remember."

They had a little to eat and decided it was time to head home, this time making a concerted effort to find some mushrooms or something else of value along the way. They climbed up and began concentrating on hiding the door and leaving it the exact way they found it. Once done, they walked quickly, hoping to avoid meeting anyone from the new village. Back they went through the woods with the rabbit carcass and the old fire. They headed back towards the cave. From there, they had no problem getting home. At the other side of the rocky hill at the cave, there was an opening, a meadow. They agreed to run across it fast as they were very visible. At least their heavy shoulder bags were folded up in their baskets now. It gave them speed.

"Hey, laydeeee."

They froze for a second and then turned slowly to see the same little boy, Davit, a distance behind them, waving and smiling. were four more children.

"Just smile and wave but keep on moving, " said Keziah.

"Oh, come on Keziah, Mother gave us food for them in case we met them."

She instantly felt ashamed and beckoned them to come over. They were dirtier than their last meeting.

"Hello," said the little boy, hope in his eyes.

Charity began taking out the food. "You must share, yes?"

The boy nodded his head enthusiastically. "We share."

Each child got a hunk of bread and cheese, a corn biscuit, and some nuts. There was some left over. Keziah looked at Charity knowingly. It would be silly to tell the boy to take it back to the camp. Why not fill their bellies for the day. Charity began dividing the remains up and they sat down around her in a circle, fixated on the food.

"Let's not linger, Charity. We don't want to talk to anyone else."

As Charity got up and fixed herself for the journey ahead, Keziah spoke to the children.

"Now, this is a secret, yes?" She put her finger to her lips the way Mother Abi had the last day. "Don't tell. It's a secret. The food is a special secret."

The little boy translated to the rest of the children, and they all nodded. There was no way of knowing if they understood but it was worth a shot.

"My mamma sore hand," said the boy as he held his hand up. "Fire."

"All mammas and papas sick." He mimicked vomiting.

"How many?" asked Charity as she held fingers up.

"Many, many more," answered the boy.

"Why? What happened?"

The boy made an action with his hands and the sounds of an explosion. "Big bang!"

"We can't go in there right now, Charity."

"I know but I feel awful."

"We've fed them. We'll try to get back, but we need to stick to our plan today. It's important."

Charity looked at the little boy. "We come back tomorrow."

The boy looked disappointed but nodded in agreement. They waved the children away and they went running off in the other direction content with their fill.

On the last leg of the journey, Keziah messaged Yvonne again, explaining they were on their way home, and the only thing the hermitage needed was water, and maybe some more blankets or roll up mattresses. Yvonne asked her to confirm again the definite time the minibus was leaving, so Ish could make plans. She said they would talk about next steps very soon. Keziah explained Charity was supposed to be on the bus, but Richard was also trying to keep her there. Yvonne agreed while Richard was active and communicative, it was probably safer to get on the bus and get ready to run when it was stopped.

"But don't forget that the detectives will expect you to tune in every day as normal."

They charged home full of hope for their futures again. Mother would be happy for sure. By the time they exited the forest into the opening, and before they approached the living quarters, the October sunset displayed hot pinks, orange and blues right across the sky like brush strokes. She would never forget it.

Chapter Fifty

Thursday arrived and Keziah had a knot in her stomach. The next day ten women of The Genus would be taken in a bus under the pretence they'd work in a hotel. Even Richard believed they would be brought to the strip club, where they would be expected to work in a very different capacity. These women were innocent when it came to men and sex. They were in for an extremely traumatic experience if the bus was not intercepted.

Mother Abi agreed with Yvonne that Charity would have better chances getting on the bus. Even if the highjack failed, at least they'd know where she was. Charity was pretty worldly-wise compared to the others. She would try to escape. She would try to find Ish. Richard was saying very little except the had raised it with a senior guard.

"It's not enough. The bus leaves tomorrow," said Mother Abi.

Charity nodded in agreement. "Mother, I see this as an opportunity rather than a kidnap, but it will be different for the others."

"Have you spoken to Richard again, Mother?" Keziah wanted to know if he was giving her different information.

"Yes, but he has to ensure his cover is not ruined."

"But does he agree to open the bus? When I talked to him he was afraid of getting into trouble."

"He'll do it, and he'll bring his friend like you suggested, but he wouldn't promise he would keep it from the police."

"I knew it." Keziah threw her hands up in the air in frustration. She was due to go and talk to Yvonne now under the detectives supervision. What was she to say? She'd play dumb and see if they brought it up.

"Keziah, Richard is on his own mission. He needs to keep himself safe too, so it's understandable."

Charity smacked her lips at Keziah's reaction. "He hasn't refused to let Ish into the bus, so I don't know what you expect of him. He's being pulled in lots of different directions, Keziah!"

"Okay. I suppose so."

She went upstairs to use the pager. While things were quite chaotic nowadays, but she still didn't want anyone to catch wind of what was going on and report her. You just never knew who was to be trusted in here.

Yvonne. Are you there?

Hello Keziah, how are you doing?

Okay, I suppose.

That doesn't sound great.

Well, I'm anxious. They are moving people all over the place and things are a bit chaotic in here.

Detective Frank says to tell you to hold on tight. It won't be long until they go in and raid the place.

Really? What are they raiding for?

All sorts I believe.

Okay. I don't really have much to say today. I am off now to bake with Mother. We eat in Mother's house now most days, so we have to batch-cook for all the Carers needing meals.

Sounds like work.

It is but I'm enjoying it actually.

You'll need to do some baking when you're back in the flat.

I will. How is everyone?

Everyone is fine. They miss you. Eli and Dorcus told me to say hello.

She missed them. She missed her life out there. Sometimes it felt like she'd never get out again.

Keziah?

Yes, Sorry. Send them hugs from me. I look forward to seeing them as soon as possible.

You take care of yourself, darlin' and we'll talk soon, okay?

Yeah. Bye Yvonne.

Oh, wait! Detective Frank wants to know if you are in touch with Richard.

Well, yes, but not for a few days now. He's very busy.

Okay and Frank asks if there are any new movements?

Well, Sy is drugged most of the time. They are changing all the rules and shifting people about. They are using our space and make demands over the intercom all the time. Look, tell him there's nothing new from me. Richard is the one in the know.

After the chat, she went back downstairs and waited for Yvonne's text. She said she would text after the charade of the daily contact with the police. These daily check ins were useless. They were unwilling to share anything of real worth so why should she?

Mother Dorothy sat at the table, sighing, and shaking her head. "I just don't know what to do. I can't allow this."

Mother Abi held her hand tightly. She looked up.

"They are taking some of the children." She told Keziah.

"For what? Why?"

"We don't know. They said they will take them to another community like this, but I don't believe them." Mother Dorothy dropped her head and sobbed aloud.

"Where is Laura now?"

"Having lessons in The Fulcrum."

"Did they say when?"

"Next week some time," whimpered Mother Dorothy.

"Mother," said Keziah pointedly, "It's time we planned a getaway."

Mother Abi shook her head and took a deep breath in.

"Get away?" asked Mother Dorothy.

"Yes. There's a secret place in the woods."

"But how?"

"I have good people on the outside who can help us, Mother Dorothy. Zadie's husband, Ish. Him, and Yvonne the social worker, they and their other people are reliable."

Charity stood at the counter where she was kneading some bread. She inhaled sharply. Mother Dorothy stared downward as if afraid to move. Everyone was in shock, but Keziah had been bracing herself for this moment. She walked into the laundry room and quickly texted Yvonne.

They are starting to move Children. We need to keep Laura safe. Maybe it's time to get to the hermitage.

The reply came quickly. *I'll let Ish know. Let me know when a decision has been made. We are still all set for tomorrow.*

She walked back out and sat down at the table. She took both the Mothers hands and looked at them.

"We have resources, a hiding place, someone to help us over the wall. All of us, and Laura, can go now, any time. Before it's ."

. "I'm not sure I can do that yet, Keziah." She looked down and pulled her hands away to brush something off her apron. "But I think it's time, yes."

Keziah was expecting this but now her mother had said it, she couldn't imagine leaving without her. "I will be so worried about you. Please consider coming with us."

"I just can't get up and leave all these children, or all these young women will need help and direction. No, I'll stay and ride it out. The police will come in soon enough. It will be all over soon enough, Child."

"They might find out you've been involved. They might hurt you." The thoughts of losing Mother Abi again crippled her.

"They have no reason to hurt me. I will just feed and care for the children as I always do." Mother got up and busied herself with something on the kitchen counter.

"I'm so worried about Laura," said Mother Dorothy. How long will it be before they take them all? Why take anyone? Any child or young woman? Only Gena knows the horrible things they have in store for any of our people."

Keziah interrupted. "Mother Dorothy, I can take Laura, but I think you should come with me too."

Mother Dorothy nodded quickly, and Keziah was surprised at her willingness to get out.

"Charity, we have three of us so far. If things don't go according to plan and for some reason you are still here by Saturday Charity, you should come too."

Charity nodded. It was finally happening, and Keziah was ready.

Keziah and Mother stayed by the fire together that evening. She told her of the children in the woods.

"The adults are sick, some of them burned, some of them from what I understand."

"It's the factory. It's them."

"I think they said there was an explosion too."

Mother Abi dropped her head. She looked sad.

Keziah put her arm around her. "I wish you'd come."

"Keziah, I don't want to discuss this again. I am staying. I can help these people as well as my own."

"Sorry. I know."

They hugged and Keziah made her way to the dormitory, staying in the shadows of the hedges and buildings so she wouldn't be spotted walking outside so late, but as she approached a guard on the door stepped forward.

"Where have you been? Everyone should be in their sleeping quarters at this time of the night."

"It's not even nine pm," she answered. "I've been baking in Mother Abi's house. There is a lot more work now because more people eat in the house."

"You need to get written permission the next time."

"What?"

"Keziah, keep your mouth closed and get in here."

It was Mother Michelle, looking cross and ready to pull her by the scruff. Keziah walked past the guard.

Mother Michelle grabbed her at the end of the stairs and spoke through her teeth. "Do not cheek them, you stupid girl. You'll bring trouble on us all."

"Sorry, Mother."

She ran up the stairs and got ready for bed, but she could not sleep. The apprehension of what was about to happen sat in a knot in her stomach.

Chapter Fifty One

The lofty windows in the apartment let the afternoon sunlight to stream directly into the kitchen. Ish, Zadie, Eli and Dorcus stood around the table with a couple of Ish's friends from work. Yvonne was in action mode and decided to wait until later to worry the consequences of her actions. The safety of those woman was the priority now.

"Okay. So, we're clear on the exact location?"

"Don't worry Yvonne. We've got it covered. Everyone in this room knows you've nothing to do with this operation." Ish winked and smiled.

"Well, I need to let Keziah know so she can tell Charity. Let's hope this Richard person is happy to cooperate."

"Sounds like he is though, no?" asked Zadie with concern.

"Apparently so. He's been working with the GCI for over five years. Keziah doesn't like him, but I've been told he's just very involved in his own mission and doesn't want complications."

"Fair enough," said Dorcus, who stood looking at the map biting her nails.

"I can't believe I'm going to see Laura and my mother. I can't believe it." Zadie smiled over to Ish.

Yvonne sighed. "They're going to need so much emotional help and guidance. I can probably get them some funding for accommodation."

"They'll stay here of course!" Zadie scrunched up her nose and tilted her head.

"Where, Zadie? Is this really an option?" Yvonne smiled sweetly. She didn't want to trigger Zadie right now.

"I can stay on the sofa or at my friends for a while," offered Eli. "I can give them my room. They must stay here with Zadie until things are decided."

Ish put his arm around Yvonne. "Zadie and I have been talking about getting a new flat, big enough for Laura, and her mother if she wants. Charity might want to be here with Keziah. We can add two singles to the double room to accommodate the extra head."

"You're all so giving and caring. I'm proud of you. I know it's family we're talking about here, but they're going need intensive counselling, and space. I've arranged a safe house for the women coming out tonight, and from what I can tell we'll have more following very soon. To be fair, we really do need to consider Eli's and Dorcus's daily lives, and the impact of having too many people cramped up in here. Let's think on it, yeah?"

Zadie cleared her throat. "After the initial phase, maybe if we set up another flat close by, everyone else can be here. Then Laura and my mother can have their own beds, their own home with us. I mean – if my mother wants. I hope..."

Yvonne grabbed Zadie and gave her a big hug. "Everything will be okay, love. Your mother understands what she is coming out to, according to our Keziah."

"Knowing Keziah, she has already debriefed her," shouted Eli and they all laughed.

"Big adjustments ahead indeed. We'll have so many new faces and dynamics to manage." Yvonne took a deep breath in and smiled broadly. "By ten pm we'll have ten women here, having some sweet tea and chatting away hopefully!"

"We will!" Ish looked around the table to nodding heads.

Yvonne smiled as she grabbed her bag to leave. "You lot never cease to amaze me!"

She hadn't gone into too much detail about the bizarre happenings over the wall in recent weeks. She didn't want to worry them, especially when they had another job at hand right now. Once this bus thing was over, she could breathe. First thing in the morning she'll be talking with both the police and GCI. What was coming down the line was of huge proportions – people needing care, housing and everything else. It was a logistical nightmare, even if it was to be temporary.

Showing up at the police station every day out other meetings and tasks. Her working days were often hitting ten or more hours. She was also keeping a close eye on the gang. Living through other people's traumatic escape couldn't be easy. Dorcus was very quiet lately and she didn't want her going into herself too much. A few sessions soon might be a good idea. PTSD had a sneaky way of showing up when you least expected it.

Once home, Yvonne messaged Keziah with the time and location. Keziah would tell Charity who would tell Richard. Charity will encourage the other women on the bus to run when they have the chance. She'd warned Keziah that Charity must not do much talking until they were leaving. The plan was absolutely wild and crazy, but also completely doable. She'd watched six young humans do the unthinkable so far, by getting over that wall.

Yvonne sat back on her on her recliner and turned the television on. Her microwave dinner sat on the table beside her going cold. She was so distracted. This whole thing had been a no-go since day one. She knew it was bad news from the beginning. If she had her way she'd make a spectacle of all the departments involved!

The noise of the phone woke her with a start. She panicked and knocked over the phone and her dinner at the same time as she jumped up. She scrambled to answer the thing. It was still ringing on the floor covered in Jalfrezi.

"Hello?"

"It's Ish."

"Are you okay? Is it done?" she asked as she checked her watch.

"All done. We have ten young women in our living room."

"Amazing work, Ish. Well done. Are you okay? Are they okay?"

"Everyone seems to be okay. The guy with the driver really pushed back but we persisted, and the women played along like experts. They are here listening to me and they're eager to meet you."

"I'm on my way."

Chapter Fifty Two

The guards ran around pushing anyone who wasn't moving in the direction of The Fulcrum. Children cried aloud watching the aggression shown onto their carers, who merely asked the guards some questions. A nasal voice dripped over the intercom repeatedly, instructing everyone to make their way to The Fulcrum. People were confused and they ran past the guards in anguish, holding onto the children tightly. Keziah stood inside the door and watched as people were pushed and shouted at. For what? She spotted Richard amongst the guards antagonising people for no reason. Everyone was already doing as they were bid, and heading in the right direction, but these guards were intent on being overly authoritarian, causing stress and worry. People swarmed into the temple and sat down, whispering, and looking around. Keziah chose a seat at the very bottom near the door. The guards, hard-faced and emotionless, pushed people to the ground and into seats. A senior guard stood at the altar looking nervous and emotional.

"People, please sit down and be quiet. It's for your own good."

Keziah sensed he disapproved of what was going on and was somewhat frightened himself.

"We have some very important news. The sooner you all get in and be quiet, the better."

He nodded to someone at the back of The Fulcrum. Keziah turned around quickly to see Richard with a man she had not seen before. He was not of the Genus she was sure of it. A tall, elderly man in a tanned suit made his way slowly to the altar and spoke in the guards ear. He was balding on top, but his thin white hair fell to his shoulders in wisps.

"Firstly, the biggest piece of news is to introduce you to this very important man, Father Norkus."

The man nodded and looked around.

"Now, Father Norkus is here to help us with some sad news."

His small dark eyes and his hard expression chilled Keziah. He was not a good man.

"As you all know, Father Sy has been unwell for some time."

The noise level raised immediately. Keziah guessed the people were expecting the guard to say Sy was dead.

"Unfortunately, our Father no longer has the capacity to lead us on a daily basis. We will continue to pray for him and to care for him."

The guards walked around silencing people.

"Father Norkus has been a friend of Father Sy's for some time. He has been here behind the scenes for months and months, helping us. He would like to address you all now so please give our new leader Father Norkus a warm welcome." The guard stood back and dropped his head. The silence deafened Keziah. The people were scared.

The man stood forward and grinned as he looked out on his audience. "Good people of The Genus, hello to you all. I know this will come as shocking news to you. Sy, or Father Sy, has been unwell for some time. We hoped things would improve but sadly they have not." Those hard eyes scanned the people and his tone changed. "I just want you to know we will continue to care for you; to feed you and organise things as we have been doing for some months."

What on earth is going on here? This guy can just come in and take over all these people as if they were sheep. He must be the man Chairty spoke of who visited Sy with the whisky. She watched the guards walk around waiting for someone to move or talk out of line. It was a tactic, of course, a way to keep people obedient and in fear. This Father Norkus must be Richard's boss, a top guy. He's probably the one who's managing the factory and the stolen car operation.

"Now, there will be some changes." He looked over at the senior guards of The Genus. "These changes are for the good of the people here. For example, we may start up some businesses here on the land, to make more money for supplies. I'm sure you are all aware our supplies are low?"

People nodded and murmured.

"Well, we need to fix the problem. As of today, there is no flour in the stock rooms. None!" He changed his tone back to a gentler caring tone as he continued. "There is nothing for you to be concerned about, but..." He paused. "from time to time you might see some new people in here, working or helping out." He looked around, directly into people's eyes. "From time to time, we may take some of you to work outside The Genus. I am a businessman and have hotels and manufacturing firms all over the region."

Keziah couldn't believe the audacity of this guy. The lies. Mother Abi was up to the front ahead of her. She up turned around and gave her an urgent look.

"We must all work together. We must build an enterprise benefiting us all, yes?"

Silence.

"Let me ask again. Are you ready to do the necessary to keep your people in food, and in the great living conditions you have right now?" He leaned forward and put his hand to his ear.

The masses replied with a mumbling *yes* and he nodded slowly.

"So, you are to continue as you are with the same duties, the same locations for eating etcetera. Some of you will be changing jobs. Those who have been selected already know about that."

Selected. He made it sound like a prize. She looked around at Richard and when he caught her eye she gave him the dirtiest look she could afford and looked away. He must have known all this was coming. Did the GCI know? Did the detectives know?

As the speech ended, Norkus clapped for himself. Some followed suit half-heartedly but the applause trickled to an awkward halt. He handed over to the senior guard in silence and they were instructed to leave in an orderly fashion. The guards weren't as aggressive on the way out, but still stood like soldiers, hard-faced with no emotion and making no eye contact.

Everyone left The Fulcrum in silence, off to their places of duty. There wasn't a whisper between the usual giggly girls or children. It was uncanny. Keziah walked out without looking at anyone and made it look like she walked towards Mother Abi's house. She made a swift left turn and walked the long way around to the back of The Fulcrum and through the pathways leading to Sy's quarters. Climbing the steps, she expected to see a guard at the top by the door, but there was none. Flashes of his ugly venomous face in the dark came to her as she reached the top of the stairs. It wasn't too long ago she took her punishment here. She watched her hand tremble as she knocked the door. There was no response, so she walked in quietly. She knew from Charity, there were three doors to the right of the entrance: a closet, and then a door to fire exit out of the building. The bedroom door was the last, a wooden door with peeling dark varnish. It was slightly ajar. She heard nothing so slowly pushed it wide open. It creaked but Sy lay in the bed with his eyes shut. Keziah stepped into the room and stood looking at him, the one who ruined so many lives with his lies and abuse. She could just jump on him now and box his face over and over again. Her jaw tensed. How weak he looked.

He opened his eyes slowly. "What are you doing here?" he asked in a .

"What have they done to you?"

"Go away."

"Sy, what have they done to you? Have they drugged you? Are they blackmailing you? I need to know!"

He chuckled sickly. "Oh, you were always a pest."

"Maybe I can help. I have contacts in the police."

"Help with what, you stupid bitch. These people don't care about the police. It's over."

What did she want to say to him? Now was her chance.

"You ruined Mother Sarah's vision."

"What do you know of my aunt?" He chortled as if he was being amused by a funny little child.

"I know when The Genus was first conceived, none of your stupid rules applied. I know Mother Sarah really did worship the Goddess. She held women sacred. Women were not baby machines or slaves to her."

"Aunt Sarah was nothing more than a wannabe hippy so don't come at me with your sacred bullshit."

"Deny it then. It's the truth and I've been letting everyone know."

She watched him, the face she was familiar with: nostrils flared and downturned mouth. "What the hell do you want? I'm going to call someone to have you removed."

"I want to know what has happened and who this Norkus is."

"You are in way over your head." He spoke through his teeth.

"Oh, I know. I was sent here to find evidence for some of you petty crimes. Now the GCI is coming for you and for him."

"I'll be dead soon." He looked away, towards the small window.

"Why? What are they doing to you?"

The door opened and they both jumped. Norkus stopped in his tracks and raised his eyebrows.

"Who do we have here?

"It's fine," said Sy nonchalantly, "I called for her. This is one of the escapees. She came back to repent."

"Ah. I see." He looked her up and down. "So, you've been , eh?"

"Yes."

"Yes what?"

"Yes, Father."

He looked at her directly for some time and then turned to Sy who was now sitting up in the bed, in a filthy white t-shirt, his hair longer and matted.

"And are you happy to have atoned? Are you happy to be back?"

"Yes, Father."

"Keziah is a slippery one though." Sy's dark smile sent shivers right through her.

"We'll find a good use for her, no doubt."

"Father Sy, can I go now?"

"Father Sy isn't in charge anymore. You should ask me."

Father Sy looked down. She thought he felt ashamed but quickly realised he'd nodded off.

"Father. Can I be excused?"

"Go, and don't come here again, Keziah."

Keziah ran down the stairs, her heart thumping so much her whole body shook on every step. What had she just witnessed? Sy is defeated. Keziah just didn't get it. Sure, he looked drugged, and he confessed it was 'over' for us, but what did he really mean? What did this Norkus monster do to him? Or what did Sy agree to?

As she recounted it all to Mother Abi and Charity, she realised her mind went completely blank before going to see him. She remembered seeing him at The Fulcrum and then being in his bedroom. Maybe she did it for personal closure of some sort. It would be interesting to speak with Yvonne about it. Maybe she would see her sooner than she imagined.

She messaged Yvonne and told her everything that happened that day. Yvonne was horrified and agreed it looked like they planned to traffic the women. They'd wait until the bus was intercepted, and then threaten Detective Frank or the GCI to go public if they didn't take action. The risk of deaths and serious danger to all involved was growing quickly, all because some head police department wanted a successful haul of intel.

Chapter Fifty Three

Keziah lay on her bed in the dorm outside the blankets, ready to run if needed. She wondered if Charity was on the bus yet. Yvonne said everything was ready on their side. Ish recruited a small team of friends to help. Social Services confirmed secure accommodation, so these women were secure. Frank knew nothing yet. Yvonne would get in there and comfort the women after such a shock. They'll be numb for a while.

"Pssst."

Keziah looked up towards the entrance but saw no one.

"Pssssst. Are you blind?"

She looked to the other side and there was Charity smiling from ear to ear.

"What! What happened?" She rubbed her eyes.

"I'm officially engaged," Charity laughed as she sat down on Keziah's bed.

Keziah sat up and grabbed her hand. "Richard got you out of it?"

"Yes."

"What happened? When did they tell you?"

"They didn't. They just called us all into the dining hall and my name wasn't on the final list. I spoke to Richard afterwards."

"Are you okay? Was Richard happy?"

She shrugged her shoulders. "Who knows with him."

So, he hadn't been nice to her. Why was she not surprised.

"So, I take it there was no romantic gestures. Sod him."

"Yeah whatever. I'll be out of here either way, soon." Charity sniffed and looked around nervously.

"How were the girls? Scared I suppose?"

"Yes they were, but I told a couple to spread the word the highjack was planned to save them from a worse fate."

"Well done."

Keziah wanted to message Yvonne. There was no way of knowing if it had all gone off well or not.

"It should have happened by now," she said as she looked at the clock on the wall. "I think I'm going to sneak down to the toilets and message Yvonne."

Once in a cubicle she typed fast. The last lights would be out soon.

Did everything go well? Is everyone safe? Charity is with me.

The response came back immediately.

"Ten ladies are sitting in your living room having tea, Keziah! Well done to you and Charity. Speak tomorrow."

Keziah did a little dance in the tiny cubicle. This was the start of freedom for everyone.

"Keziah! Watch out. The guards are here. They are searching for something."

It was Charity. Startled, she leaped to her feet and frantically searched for a place to hide the phone. Her heart pounded fiercely in her chest. This Norkus bastard was onto her. Looking around the tiny cubicle she realised the only place to put it was in the cistern. Could she risk it getting wet? She looked up to the small window. It's dark outside. Maybe she could throw it out and collect it when things had settled down. Climbing up onto the cistern, a flash of Abe's bathroom hit her, and she almost fell with the dizziness. She stood still for a second and got on with opening the window as quietly as possible. The phone fell and Keziah waited to hear a reaction. Nothing. The guards' footsteps drew nearer. She could hear Mother Michelle protest as she opened the cubicle door and feigned shock.

"What is happening, Mother?" Keziah held her stomach and looked at Mother Michelle. "I am unwell. Why are the guards here?"

"Who knows?" she said as she shook her head in disgust.

A guard stepped towards Keziah and grabbed her arm. She tried to shrug him off, but he had a tight grip.

"Why are you doing this to me?"

"Father Norkus wants to talk to you."

She heard Charity shout from outside the toilets. "They have ruined the place. They've flipped everyone's mattress and destroyed our few possessions. They are not guards. They are monsters."

Just as Keziah was pulled outside the toilets she saw Richard slap Charity across the face. She fell to the ground holding her cheek and began to cry. There was no way Keziah could hint at her to move the device in Mother Abi's spare bedroom. All she could do is hope Mother Abi heard about this and hid it herself in case they searched her house.

In her bare feet and nightdress, they dragged her over the gravel paths and up the stairs into Sy's quarters. His bedroom door was open, but Norkus was sitting in his armchair in his living room, exactly where Sy sat the night he beat her.

"This must feel like déjà vu to you, Keziah."

"Why have you brought me here?"

"Father Sy tells me you atoned and settled back into The Genus with ease."

"It's true."

"See, I don't believe it for one minute. You're different to the people here, Keziah. You've seen the outside world. You're…" he paused as if reflecting, "…not so innocent anymore, are you?"

"I don't know what you mean! What is going on?" she pleaded with him as he nodded for the guard to let her loose.

As she rubbed her wrists she watched him get out of the chair and walk over to her.

"Where are they?" His face was only millimetres away from hers.

"Who?"

"How did you arrange this?"

"What?"

He slapped her face hard and fast, enough for her to stagger back, but she did not falter. She straightened herself up.

He walked around her. "Oh, you think you are tough?"

"No. I don't. Please tell me what happened? Is Mother Abi safe?"

"You will be closely watched. Very closely watched from here on in. Be careful, Keziah."

"Honestly, please tell me what I'm supposed to have done, Father Norkus. I don't want any trouble. I live my life within the rules."

"It better be so. Now, get out," he roared.

Keziah turned on her heel and walked to the door.

"Remember, you're being watched."

As she ran back down the stairs all she could think about was the devices in Mother Abi's house. She sprinted across the front of The Fulcrum and over to the house. Upon entering all was normal. There appeared to be no upheaval or distress.

"Mother? Have the guards been here?"

"For what, Child? She looked Keziah up and down and ran to her, but Keziah flew up the stairs.

"What's going on *now*?" Mother Abi called after her.

She ran into Mother Abi's room and reached in under the bed for the box, pulling out the bag containing the wire and rushed next door to the spare room where she had hidden the pager. Back on the landing she thought about what she should do with them. There was only one thing she could do. She ran back down the stairs and through them both into the fire. On top she put the biggest log she could find.

"Keziah, calm down, sit down. You're trembling."

"I can't. I have to find the phone. I'll be back soon. I need to make sure Charity is okay."

She could hear Mother calling after her as she ran out the door. She'd explain everything later. The pain in her chest was getting worse as she rushed around without breathing properly. She stopped and bent over to catch her breath. A guard approached her from behind and startled her. She turned but could not see anything because of the glare of the torch directly ion her face.

"What are you doing? Where should you be right now?"

"I'm on the way to the dormitory."

"Under who's authority?"

"Under my authority. What is the problem here, Guard?"

Both turned to see Mother Abi standing with her arms folded as she glared at the guard, waiting for him to answer.

"I- eh – people should be heading to bed for the night, not running from building to building."

"And what would you know of it? Are you part of The Genus? I don't recognise you, and I know every single person of The Genus because I helped to raise them up."

The guard resumed his blank face and turned to Keziah. "Go to the dormitory and settle down for the night."

Keziah ran off in hoping Mother Abi would keep him talking for a few minutes, so she could look along the perimeter of the dormitory building for her phone. She arrived there and found it quickly, lying on the grass just where it dropped from the window above. She shivered as she put it up her nightie sleeve and walked inside, and upstairs to her bed. Most of the women were lying down, all ready to sleep for the night but a small group sat around Charity's bed whispering. Keziah shoved the phone under the mattress quickly. She'd need to find a place for it in the morning.

"Well, what happened?" asked Charity, in front of the other women.

"Charity, I need to sleep. We'll talk tomorrow."

The women scattered and Charity handed her a towel to wipe her feet. "Night."

Things were changing faster and faster, and now Norkus suspected her of being involved in the bus highjack. She needed to get out of here fast.

Chapter Fifty Four

Yvonne stood by the mantel watching the tv, shaking her head as the explosions of fire flew through the air. The flat was packed with the women from the bus, and Ish's friends who were planning to make it over the wall to the bunker. Dorcus was on drink and snacks duty and had some of the more nervous young women over at the kitchen table with her as she worked.

"I just can't believe the GCI haven't gone in and taken them out once and for all!"

"I suppose they have to ensure the safety of their own staff and the innocent people before they go in and obliterate the place," answered Ish who rocked Rachel in his arms.

"Yeah, they say so, but they don't think of innocent people in wars, do they? No, the GCI wants to make sure it gets its claws into the highest ranking of them. They want worthwhile catches."

"True, but if they went in what could they do at this point, Yvonne? More shooting?"

"Oh, I don't know. I'm just thinking of poor Keziah running through the forest with a child in such chaos."

"Keziah can hold her own, and so can my mother and Charity. They're going to be fine." commented Zadie.

Ish walked over and sat down beside her on the sofa. "Yes, of they are."

"It's not the point," said one of the other young women sat on the floor glued to the television, obviously stunned by the events unfolding live in front of her eyes.

"Now there's a girl with perspective," said Yvonne with a smile. The girl looked up to her and returned the smile.

She walked over to the table where Dorcus was encouraging a couple of women to try the toaster. It amazed her how happy most of them appeared to be about being out, despite what was going on! Times were changing and even the innocent knew it was better to be on this side of the wall, rather than the chaotic world on the other. Hopefully it would go in their favour later, during their debriefing.

She walked to the hall and dialled Frank. "Yes. It's me. Any updates?"

"Hi Yvonne. Nothing to report yet."

"I see. They don't seem to be in a rush to get in there and help those who need it."

"I just don't have an update for you from the CGI."

"Well look, I need to tell you Keziah made a run for it and is now in a bunker close to the east wall. We have the exact coordinates."

"I'll let them know."

"That's it? You don't want to know where it is?"

"Yvonne, they are going in there soon to save everyone."

"Fine Frank. I get it. I'll sort it out myself."

She threw the phone on the tiled corridor floor and mumbled something through her clenched teeth.

"Hey" It was Ish standing watching her.

"Sorry, yeah, no updates."

"I wasn't expecting anything. They wouldn't share it with you, anyway, would they?" He smiled calmly and walked towards her with his arms out. "Don't tell me you're blaming yourself again? We did everything to try to convince her not to go back in."

"We didn't know there was going to be a mafia war, did we?" Yvonne accepted the hug gratefully.

"We certainly didn't. But it seems even the mafia didn't know."

She sighed. "I just want her out of there."

"I get it."

"It's relentless. There's no sign of easing off."

"It will."

"When did you become so level-headed and mature?"

"When I made another person and realised I have to care for it too."

He picked up Yvonne's phone, handed it to her, and put his arm around her as they both headed back into the main room.

Chapter Fifty Five

The sheets flapped in the wind as if they were trying with all their might to fly off the line they were pegged to. Mother walked around slowly with a basket, collecting eggs that the chickens laid in the bushes instead of the coop.

"There's a few hens that just refuse to lay inside," she said, as she checked the bush and hedges around them. "Look!" She held up an egg with a smile and Keziah wondered if she was in some kind of detachment mode from all the stress.

"Mother, I need to leave, and I want you to come with me."

"You know I cannot," she replied calmly as she bent down to collect another egg.

The tears built up and she was afraid to blink. If she blinked the floodgates would open. "I understand your reasoning but, we just don't know what will happen next."

"Keziah, you know we will be disbanded. Soon the police will take over and take us to safety. Everything is going to be fine. It is the will of Gena."

"I brought all of this on your home, your life." The hot tears flowed freely down her face.

Mother Abi stood directly in front of her and wiped her tears away. Keziah's head fell onto her mother's shoulder, and she finally let the weeks of tension out. She openly sobbed and let her mother envelope her as she cried for everything; the life she lost and gained again, her new life, Abe. What a mess everything was, and she had no way of knowing what would happen next.

"Now, we have to get some things organised, yes?" She smiled as she patted Keziah's shoulder. "Remember this; I am very proud of you, dear."

Keziah breathed in and out slowly, trying to calm herself and get into the mode she needed to be in, to carry out this escape with three other people, including a child.

They arrived at the porch, at the same time Mother Dorothy and Laura. Mother Dorothy nodded and they all made their way into the kitchen.

"So, tonight? asked Mother Dorothy eagerly.

Keziah nodded. "After dark. It's all confirmed."

It would be tricky in the dark, but Keziah and Charity had recorded landmarks all the way on their last trip out there. Keziah worried for the child. She would need to move fast and in silence.

Ish and his friends would try to get into the hermitage tonight or at least before the dawn light of tomorrow. If not, they should stay put and out of sight. Yvonne expressly advised she should not take the risk of coming back up to use the phone, and Ish confirmed there was ventilation enough for four people for two days.

Remember, things can change when you're down there. We know nothing of the GCI's timelines, and Frank will realise something's up when there's no contact from you.

I suppose Richard will tell him what's going on anyway?
I would think so, but I don't know for sure. Who cares?

Keziah smiled to herself. Yvonne was such an inherently empowering person.

As dusk set in, Keziah and Charity sat at Mother Abi's kitchen table listening to the woman's directions.

"Now, Dorothy just told Laura you were all going on a trip to a little house in the woods for a couple of days. So, no graphic discussions please. Try to remember she is a child, and she does not understand she has a mother outside. Agreed?"

Keziah's mind was flooded with fleeting images: sprinting through dense woods, desperately pulling along the frightened child - Charity tumbling - Mother Dorothy's piercing scream and collapse. A knot tightened in her stomach.

Dorothy arrived with the little girl holding tightly to her, all bound up in a warm coat and scarf and a hat pulled down around her ears. She smiled at Keziah and ran to her.

Keziah opened her arms and took her up to her face. "We are going on an adventure tonight, and we will show you a lovely little house to stay in where we can make tea and food and rest."

Laura looked to the side. "Is Mother Abi coming?"

"Not this time, but we will see her soon."

The child nodded and squirmed, so Keziah let her slide down to the floor. Mother Abi handed her a sweet biscuit which Laura accepted with a smile.

They each swaddled themselves in their heavy coats and big scarves and chunky hats, as Mother Abi put the kitchen light on. Keziah only brought her phone and a torch on a rope around her shoulder. Charity had a small LED torch she'd from Sy's quarters, but it was agreed torch light should be used at a minimum for obvious reasons. Mother Abi gave Mother Dorothy a bag with supplies for Laura, a blanket, water, and some sweet treats.

Charity took the bag instead of Dorothy. "Keziah, you and Mother Dorothy can care for Laura. I'll carry this."

They'd finally arrived at this pivotal moment. Every time she thought about Mother Abi she forced herself to look ahead to a brighter future when everyone was out of this wretched place.

"No goodbyes, please," said Mother Abi as she fussed over the fire. "Focus on getting there tonight. Move fast. I will see you all soon enough. Praise Gena."

The lump in Keziah's throat stung as she tried to stifle her emotions, but she appreciated her mother did not want a fuss, and anyway, she didn't want to upset Laura.

Keziah grabbed Mother Abi, gave her a big squeeze. "Remember Mother, there's still two bags of food in the cave." She put a folded piece of paper into her hand. "I've made a little map with directions to the bunker – just in case."

"Stop worrying. We'll be reunited very soon." She took the paper but was detached. It was time to leave.

"I love you, Mother. Thanks for everything. See you soon."

She walked straight out of the house and the others followed. The black November night enveloped them. By the time they got through the hedge at the end of the yard, Keziah wondered how on earth they'd do it without torches. It felt different now, standing here in the dark. It would be a long night.

Chapter Fifty Six

"I cannot believe you've had the audacity to compromise this mission."

"Oh, stuff you and your mission, Amanda. I *cannot believe* how willing you are to leave vulnerable people in danger!"

Yvonne paced the conference room with both detectives sitting at the table watching her.

"Yvonne, there is a plan. You have to trust the process," pleaded Frank.

"Oh, come on Frank. I know you long enough to know what this is all about! Egos. Getting your name up there with the big guys. Those women were being trafficked for Christ sake!"

"Still, you should have told us."

"Nobody trusts you. Don't you get it?"

Amanda banged her fist on the table suddenly and glared at her. "You don't have authority to go attacking buses carrying armed guards. Jesus! Just who do you think you are?"

Yvonne took a deep breath. This conversation was going nowhere fast. "I didn't do any such thing. Look, these ten girls are now safely housed, and they are all happy to be out of there. they...you know!"

"You didn't have permission, Yvonne!"

"I don't care, Frank."

"You've put the people left in there in danger," Amanda shouted.

"Have you any idea what's going on in there? Apart from recent activities of the Arma Bloods? Forced marriages, forced incest, and god knows what else! Why wouldn't I try to help those poor young women. Two of them are only sixteen."

"It's not the point!"

Yvonne turned to Frank. "Who told you?"

"Richard reported it to GCI."

"Oh Richard. I see. Well, you might not be happy to know, your precious Richard agreed to the plan beforehand."

She was raging he spilled the beans, but it was on the cards.

"Look Yvonne, we're going around in circles here." Amanda sat back on her chair with authority. Her sardonic smile irritated Yvonne so much but she had to keep her cool.

"You know this is out of my hands," she continued. "The case changed. Everything changed and the GCI own this operation now. Big things are happening."

Yvonne ignored her and spoke directly to Frank. "Keziah has no way of contacting you. She might try to run. Will you help her if she does?"

"Oh, you think we'll make commitments based on your requests?" Amanda threw her hands in the air and shook her head before standing up.

"So, if I tell you she has managed to contact me and has taken off, will you get someone in there to scoop her out before all this shit goes down?"

"You know I can't make promises like that."

She heard nothing but weakness in his voice. Pathetic.

"Well, if there's nothing else to discuss here, I'm off to see these young women have warm clothes and food."

Just as she put her hand on the door handle Frank stood up and walked over to her.

"Wait. Yvonne, you have to tell me if Keziah is in touch with you. You were lucky this time, but the next time it could get complicated."

"Is that a threat?"

"Don't be like this."

"It's already complicated, you buffoon!"

As she stormed down the corridor she thought about how many times she had walked out on Frank since all this began. Too many times. Her friendship with him would never be the same. He sold out, lost his scruples. She shuddered as she remembered lying in bed with him all those years ago. He was still in police training, and she was a student, both of them still wet behind the ears. As for Amanda, her sole interest was progressing her career. She obviously had her eye on a place with the GCI. Well good luck to Amanda, but she'd be damned if she'd just sit by, watching a catastrophe unfold without trying to do something!

Once in the car she checked her phone for messages and sure enough there was one from Keziah.

"We're running. Confirmed. Charity, Dorothy, and Laura. It'll be dark and we'll have to keep flashlights to a minimum, but I think we can make it to the hermitage later tonight. I'm scared, Yvonne. If we're caught they'll hurt us, or worse."

Yvonne sat back in her car. This was it. Keziah chose the moment, and she was going for it.

"Okay Darling. I want you to be very careful, if in doubt stay still for a while. Do you hear me?"

"I hear you. I think we just have to get as far into the woods as possible early in the evening. It's important to get past the factory and the new camp site. They are my worries."

"If the unthinkable happens, don't try to save anyone. Run for yourself."

"We leave just after dark."

"I'll call Ish now, pass him your number, and get him in place for the morning."

She started her engine and headed straight for the flat to talk to Ish, Zadie and the gang. She knew she was doing the right thing. Keziah waited until she couldn't wait any more. The consequences were yet unknown, for everyone involved. This was going to be a long, long night.

Chapter Fifty Seven

The clouds parted and revealed a bright yellow moon giving light to their pathway forward. They walked carefully, through the conifer patch, and around the lake. The damp and cold couldn't penetrate the layers of wool they were swaddled in. Mother Abi insisted on them wrapping up to within an inch of their lives. The crunch of the twigs and dry foliage under their feet was unavoidable and it sounded loud in the silence, certainly enough to twitch a guards ear. Keziah told herself to focus on the target and stop worrying as she walked.

"Wait." She heard someone behind whisper.

She turned around to see Dorothy unravel a huge woolly scarf from Laura's neck. "She's too hot," she whispered.

Charity took the scarf and stuffed it into the bag. Laura was looking up towards the moon in awe. Everyone gave a thumbs up and they continued into the next woodland and towards the rocky terrain around the cave.

This was the start of the risky area. The children played in the open meadow between their huts and the rocks. It's where they always met the little boy, Davit, and his friends. They should all be safely asleep at this hour. It must be eight pm already. Although, if their parents are ill, or working, they may very well be still running around. She'd love to take the food left in the cave and give it to the people in the huts, but Mother Abi might need it soon. If she believed in the Goddess, she'd pray right now for all of them left in here. Well, they weren't out of the woods yet, literally.

Charity tipped her on the shoulder and pointed backwards to the next landmark. How did she miss it? At the bottom of a large oak tree sat a piece of wood Keziah placed there herself, on the last walk out here. She walked back, looked at it and then pointed left off the main pathway and towards the campfire they'd discovered the last time they were in the woods. She signed for them to keep low and walk slowly after her. The next landmark they'd placed was just before the campfire. Keziah stopped and crouched down. Dorothy, Charity, and Laura did the same. They watched her for instruction. Keziah had no choice but to whisper very lowly.

"I will go ahead and check if anyone is there. If so, we will need to go around them."

They nodded and Dorothy turned around to Laura and took her in her arms. It was a good opportunity for her to rest her little legs. Keziah crept on her knees in the damp earth until she reached the next stick. It sat at the base of a silver birch tree shining in the moonlight, revealing the most amazing slivers of silver. Left again. As she approached the perimeter of the open space where they'd found the rabbit , she heard low voices, voices of men - some laughter and chat. She dragged herself along by her elbows to a nearer bush so she could watch them. The light of the fire revealed three men sitting on a tree trunk. They directed their words to people opposite them she could not see in the shadows. They didn't seem aggressive or troublesome, but she couldn't tell if they were like the men at the huts or if they were guards, in plain clothes. They wore ragged t-shirts, not the sleek black sweatshirts and jeans of the new guards. Norkus talked of even more new faces appearing. They could be working on something else, but they had been here for at least a week judging by the state of the camp. Keziah wondered where they slept. Whether innocent workers or a new group, they must be careful not to meet them face-on.

One of them got up, still smiling and talking, and walked to the far perimeter of their camp. He pissed with his back to the group facing her, laughing and joking with them. As he turned around, a noise flew up into the air and they all stood up. Afterwards another noise came. It sounded like Laura, shouting or in some kind of stress. She couldn't move now, or they'd hear her rustle back to them. What the hell had happened? Was Laura safe? A couple of the men picked up sticks and walked towards the sound. Keziah began to slither as fast as she could back to Charity, Dorothy, and Laura. She met them face on heading her way. Charity quickly explained Laura got a fright after the bang, but she was okay. Keziah gestured for them to run right past the camp and to the left, while the men were at the other side investigating the noise. They'd have to get out of this area, head towards the wall and around the long way to the opening. The men were shouting and stressed and beating bushes around where they came from. Keziah stood up and took Laura in her arms. The child was wide-eyed. She bent down and kissed her forehead.

"Ready?" she whispered. Laura nodded in response.

Keziah looked at the others. "Now! Run to the wall."

Chapter Fifty Eight

They all ran as fast as they physically could, knowing this could break them. The child bobbed around in Keziah's arms, rigid in fear. This could have them captured and brought back to Norkus for punishment. They couldn't let it happen.

When they reached the wall, they were out of sight and could no longer hear the men. They stopped to catch their breath when another sudden bang left their ears ringing. A whoosh of fire went up in the air, high enough for them to see above the trees at a distance. Laura held her ears and turned around to look for her grandmother. The heat of the fire reached them even though they had made it to the wall. They all stood together, frozen, and watched in shock at a secondary eruption of fire and sparks. No fireworks display could ever match it. Screams of anguish rung in the air and then what sounded like gun shots vibrated all around them. Had the factory exploded? Were people burning, or getting shot? They had to move again. They walked by the wall for some minutes before entering the thicket of the woods again. Laura still held her ears to avoid the abrupt banging. Shouting voices intertwined with pops and screams were now met with sirens. Did this mean they were safe? How would the police know where they were. A helicopter suddenly whirred loudly above them, and Laura finally broke down into hysterics. Suddenly feeling very disoriented, Keziah stumbled back towards the wall for a moment, letting it hold her up. Were the helicopters there to help the people, or to shoot them all?

"Oh Gena, please save us all from this hell," shouted Mother Dorothy, but her voice barely made it over the chaos.

Charity grabbed Keziah and stood in front of her. "We are still going to the hermitage, right? We don't if know anyone is interested in saving us. Who owns the helicopter?" she shouted. "Who is shooting? Are the people in the huts dead? We don't know anything, Keziah!" Her face crumpled and she began to sob.

Keziah turned her around, away from Laura, and walked with her. ", Charity. Don't break on me now." She heard the panic in her own voice. "You're right. We need to get to the hermitage. Yvonne will tell us what's happening."

Behind them, Dorothy caught up. "We have enough food for a few days. It's going to be alright. Gena will protect us."

Another boom reverberated through the forest. They stood facing each other feeling the vibration under their feet. Laura screamed and stuck her head tightly into Dorothy's shoulder.

"Come on," Dorothy pleaded looking at Laura and then Keziah. "Please."

Keziah's mind was a mess of sharp ringing noise and distortion. She stood for a minute trying to get her bearings.

"It's this way. I remember," Charity called out over the noise.

Keziah joined all their hands and let Charity lead. Laura, still sobbing hysterically refused to look up even when Keziah tried to talk her down.

"Leave her. She'll be fine when we get there," called Dorothy.

Finally, they arrived at the opening. Keziah took out her phone as Charity took away the brush on top, carefully placing it as she had been shown before.

"*What's going on? We just made it to the hermitage, but I think the factory is burning down. It's like a war zone in here. Sirens and gunshots and explosions. Laura is not good. I'll check for a response in twenty minutes. We'll get settled here now.*"

They were all inside. Keziah arranged the foliage to hide the trap door. As she closed it and made her way down she heard Charity talking.

"What on earth are you doing here? Where's your Mama?"

Keziah stepped down and turned to see Davit, his little black tear stained face full of anguish. He sat on one of the benches looking at Keziah, with his big brown eyes full of sadness.

"Mama no," he whined to Charity. "Mama gone."

Charity sat down beside him and held him tightly. He let her but stared into space. What did he see? Did he see his mother dying?

"Today? Now?," asked Charity tenderly.

"No, two days." He held up two fingers.

"Surely he hasn't been here for two days?" exclaimed Mother Dorothy.

"The sickness started days ago. I suppose it's possible," said Keziah as she began to take her outdoor clothes off. It was already quite warm in here.

Mother Dorothy sat on the bench holding Laura tightly as she cried into her. "Everything is going to be just fine, Laura. It's over. We are safe. Praise Gena."

Keziah looked at Dorothy. They both knew nothing was over. Although the noise was muffled, it continued on right through the night.

"I'm more concerned about how he found this place and who else knows."

Charity turned to him and tried to find out more. "Mama bring you here?"

He nodded but no one was sure he understood.

She tried again. "This place," she said plainly and pointed here. "You know this place?"

"Yes. My Mamma secret place."

Charity looked up at Keziah who was standing over listening to him.

"Did your Mamma show you here, a secret?"

He looked at her with his sad eyes but didn't respond.

"This place? Who knows?"

Nothing.

"You are a good boy." Keziah smiled at him and sat down on a little box, used for a stool she presumed. "We have food for you, okay?"

"Okay," he replied eagerly.

"But only you. No children. No friends. Secret, yes?"

"Mamma's secret." He nodded like he understood. All they could was hope so.

Laura sat up, curious about the other child in the group.

"We are going on an adventure," she told him sweetly. "You can come too."

He nodded appreciatively.

Mother Dorothy relaxed a little, relieved to see Laura come out of the shock. "I'm going to get you some food. You sit here and I will just be here at the little stove." She kissed Laura's forehead and lifted her down beside her on the bench.

Keziah took out the saucepan. "There's only one. Should we cook some rice and then add some tinned beans?"

"Does anyone even feel like eating?" asked Charity.

"It will give us something to do if nothing else." Mother Dorothy was wise.

They all concurred, and Dorothy went about rinsing the rice while Keziah opened two tins. They had an extra mouth to feed now.

They sat in silence eating slowly. Would this war going on above their heads end in time for them to get out safely? With two children present it was difficult to talk about it with Charity and Dorothy.

"I'm going to peep my head out just to get enough signal to read Yvonne's reply."

Charity glared at her. "Do you think that's a good idea? Remember she warned you not to risk being seen."

"They are all out there otherwise engaged as far as I can see."

"What if someone trying to escape sees you? I think you should get out completely, hide somewhere while you use your phone and then come back. Don't chance anyone realising this place is here."

"She has a good point," offered Dorothy.

Of course, they were right. She should know better.

She climbed up the steps and pushed the trapdoor slightly open so she could make sure no one was around. All was clear but the acrid smoke hit her face instantly. The noise subsided somewhat, but there was still a chopper in the sky with some kind of light that was scanning the whole area. It must be the GCI. Who else would have a helicopter to survey the area like this? She jumped out quickly and ran to a dark area of bushes and trees. She looked for a space with a wide thicket so she would not be noticed should the chopper light land on her, or an escapee passing by spot the light on the phone. She opened the message from Yvonne.

Stay where you are. Ish cannot go in tonight. It's all over the news. A rival gang set the factory on fire, and the police intercepted the feud."

Another gang. They were literally shooting each other and causing injuries to innocent people.

Has an ambulance got in? Is everyone alright? We found a little boy in here. I think his mother has died. We met them before.

Emergency services are at the gate on standby. They'll wait for the go ahead from the GCI. A national broadcaster have helicopters up and the police have told them to land.

Have people died?

Yes, darlin' I'm afraid so. None of The Genus as far as I know. Hunker down for the night. This can't go on much longer, but we certainly can't have Ish climbing over into this mess.

Of course not.

Go now and be safe. Don't be tempted to pop out again. We know where you are. We have your location from your phone. I'm having a call with Frank soon and I'll be telling him exactly where you are, okay?

Okay. Thanks Yvonne.

It's all gonna be fine honey. I will see you tomorrow.

Keziah turned the phone off and crawled towards the trapdoor. She stopped abruptly when she heard steps approaching and people talking between themselves very quietly. She lay flat on her stomach and backed up into a ditch as the voices approached.

"I don't know where the hell this is. He mentioned it once when he was high, and I meant to get more details about it."

"But what did he say, Sir? Did he give any other indications?"

"He never used it himself but was confident it existed. He'd been planning on questioning that little bitch that escaped about it."

"So, an underground hut somewhere past the woods in a clearing, close to the wall."

Keziah held her breath as the steps came closer to where she lay.

"Well, this area fits the bill, but I can't see anything here."

"Put your torch on."

"Sir, if we do, you're done for. They're monitoring us in ariel view."

"." He held his clenched fists in the air. " are going to regret this. Big time."

"I suggest we go to the wall perpendicular to this one and see if there's a side gate out."

"Right, let's go."

Keziah let her breath out, controlled and silently, and waited another few minutes before she dared to even change position. She peeped up. All was clear but she waited. Something exploded in the air right above her and she watched fireballs falling down around her. Everything was too wet to catch flame in the evening dampness thankfully. Finally picking up the courage to move, she crawled as fast as she could, opened the trap door, closed it silently and then let herself fall in. Charity moved to her quickly and knew by her face something had happened.

"Richard and Norkus," she gasped, still in shock.

"What about them?"

"They were looking for this bunker!"

"What?"

Laura looked up with concern. Keziah patted the child and smiled gently. "They've gone now, Laura."

She huddled with the women and explained she head them looking for it. "Apparently Sy mentioned it before but never found it. They had a rough idea where to look."

Charity shook her head in shock. "And Richard was helping him to escape?

Keziah nodded. "They've gone North to try to find another exit."

"Well, so long as they don't come back this way."

"What about your Yvonne? What did she say?" asked Dorothy.

"Ish can't come into this mess obviously, but they have our exact location from the phone and will tell the police where we are."

"Police bad."

They all looked at the little boy.

"No, police help you." Charity ruffled his hair, and he smiled up at her.

"It's all over the TV news. A rival group set the factory on fire. The helicopter up there is owned by a TV news station."

"So," said Charity with a smile, "nothing to do but huddle in and stay put for the night, eh?" The children smiled up at her as she gathered blankets to make a little bed for them.

Chapter Fifty Nine

The booms and thumps and crackles, although muted, continued with no signs of let up. As the children slept restlessly on the benches, the women sat on the floor huddled in blankets and scarves. There was nothing to say, only to wait, to ride it out and try not to think of the worst case scenario. All Keziah could think of was Mother Abi. Yvonne said she didn't think the people of The Genus were in danger, but no one knew for sure. Had the fires or explosives reached the dormitories? They would see the helicopters and the fires from there. They'd still feel the ground vibrating with the explosives and hear the gunshots. Mother Abi must be scared for them, wondering if they to the bunker.

"What time is it now?" asked Charity.

"Five minutes past the last time you asked."

"Surely, it will end soon," said Dorothy. "Either way we'll be in here until Ish or the police get to us."

"Gena knows when."

"Now, Charity. The Goddess is on our side."

Keziah sighed. It was harder than she expected to wait in this small space with other people. Charity was right though, there was no way of knowing just how bad things could get out there. Having seen these wars on the news before, she knew it could last days. She resolved at least they were safe and warm for now. Hopefully Norkus and Richard would be caught before they decided to return. She didn't care by who, the other gang or the police.

She remembered there was a little drafts board on a shelf and pulled it out.

"Let's play. We can have turns. The winner stays in the game?"

Both women looked at her blankly.

She smiled. "Let me explain the rules."

Chapter Sixty

There was no daylight to honour the morning's arrival. They sat quietly waiting. Both children were awake but neither of them spoke or asked for food. They lay on the benches in silence. There'd been no big explosions or gunshots in some time, but every now and then they heard the hiss of fire or a crackling tree. When the children did start to move, Dorothy got up to make them food. Keziah's stomach was heavy and knotted, and she wondered if they were going to get out of this mess at all. They must wait to see if Ish or the police could get to them out but her desire to peep her head out was strong. Yvonne warned her not to, so she'd try to hold it for another while.

Charity pulled paper and crayons out for the children. The little boy was so excited. It must have been a while. What had he been through before he arrived here to The Genus complex? Had he been stuffed in a truck for hours on end? Beaten by his trafficker, seen his loved ones suffer? Even in his hunger, having the freedom of the woods, and other children to roam it with, must have been a luxury to him. Well, until his mother died. She'd found this place. She knew to show him, or to leave him there.

Dorothy handed her a small bowl of tinned fruit in syrup. "Just sup it up. You need something in you."

She accepted it and knocked it back.

Heavy thumps like footsteps came from above. They all stopped what they were doing and look at each other. Laura jumped into Dorothy's arms and buried her head. Keziah thought she could hear some voices she didn't recognise.

"Could it be Ish?" said Charity in hushed tones.

"He knows where this bunker is. He'd be in by now."

Dorothy let her head fall into her hand and began praying in whispers.

"Bad people?" asked the little boy.

"Don't worry. We are safe," smiled Keziah.

"Maybe it's the police," suggested Dorothy.

"The police would have been in by now." Keziah shook her head.

"Keziah!"

Who was it? Who was looking for her?

"Show us where you are. We are here to get you all out," called the voice again.

"Praise Gena," Dorothy cried, and Keziah put her hand over the woman's mouth quickly.

"We don't know who it is," she whispered.

"Keziah. It must be the police," whispered Charity urgently. "Shout back, before they leave. Please!"

She still didn't trust these people, whoever they were. Surely the police would not go around calling out her name like this. And surely Ish would have marked the spot on a map. Something felt off. The thumps were directly above them now and they all huddled in the furthest corner together with blankets over them, holding each other, encouraging each other to stay quiet.

As the trap door opened, Laura screamed, and Dorothy put her hand over her mouth. They stayed as still as they could under the blankets. A body landed inside.

"Keziah. It's Joe. We're here to get you out."

Joe?

Keziah pulled the blanket off her head and flashed a torch at the man who stood before her directly under the entrance. It was Joe, black-faced and with bloodshot eyes. She gasped.

"Joe! What's – what's going on?"

"We have a rescue service at the north gate waiting for you all."

"Where's the police?"

He smiled. "I am the police, remember?"

"You're a law student – a gym instructor." Keziah couldn't decipher what was going on. Why was he here?

"They are above waiting for you all. Everything is okay."

"Where's Ish?" she whispered.

He pursed his lips.

"Where is he?" she demanded.

"They've got him and Yvonne up at the complex. Some men captured them on their way to get you. Armed guards have just arrived up there. They are going to be fine."

Keziah's head dropped. "Why did Yvonne come in?"

"Who knows. Wasn't a smart move, was it?" He smiled as he moved down into the bunker.

This wasn't how she'd imagined it, but was anything in her world as she thought it would be?

"We need to get you out of here. The fires are over. Most people are already out and with emergency services."

Dorothy stood up and pulled Laura up. "I am Dorothy, and this is my granddaughter Laura." She moved towards him holding on to Laura for dear life. Joe called someone above and helped them up the steps.

Charity took Davit and followed. "Come Keziah, it's nearly over."

Her body refused to move. Her arms felt like lead and her head as light as cotton wool. Joe approached her slowly and sat down beside her.

"One hell of a week, right?"

"If anything happens to Yvonne and Ish, it's on me."

"They're sending the big guns in. It's going to be alright." He put his arm around her and gently urged her to move.

Keziah slowly climbed out, and the light of the low morning sun blinded her. She shaded her eyes with her hand to look around. The scorched earth still billowed black smoke. Debris from fallen trees sparked inadvertently and made her jump. This devastated land would remain forever changed, like it's people.

THE END

About the Author

Claire O'Connor is an Irish multi-genre fiction writer. After many years of living away, she recently set up home on the rugged Southwest coast of Ireland with her partner and spoiled dog. When she's not writing she's reading, taking photos on long nature walks, or tending to her veggie garden.

Since she was a little girl, she has been writing stories (including fairy-tale and cartoon fan fiction) and poetry. In 2019, Claire graduated with a BA Honours degree including Creative Writing. Since then, she has contributed short fiction to various anthologies. She enjoys writing short vignettes for fun, and published her first book, an anthology of shorts and poetry in 2020. V is for Vignettes and Verses has recently been relaunched. Claire published Over The Wall in June 2023, the first book in her coming-of-age thriller trilogy of the same name.

Into the Old, the second book is to be released on May 7th of 2024.

Check out Claire's (soon to be revamped) website https://www.claireoconnorauthor.com/

Also By

The Over The Wall Trilogy is a psychological thriller trilogy about Keziah, a 19 year old young woman who escapes the cult she was born into.

From the clutches of the cult she was born into, Keziah emerges seeking true freedom, but will she ever succeed?

Surrounded by an extended family of playful children and nurturing women, Keziah never imagined life would change so drastically. By the age of 16, she is expected to live her life as an adult member of The Genus. By the age of 19, she is expected to marry cult leader Sy, prompting her to plot escape over the wall. When she reaches the outside world, however, what awaits her is not what she thought. Although modern life has challenges, Keziah tries her best to adjust. Despite warnings, she tracks down Abe, a childhood friend and fellow escapee. Why did he go his own way on the side of the wall? No one wants to talk about it. She is determined to find out the truth. Keziah's journey unravels complexities, fuelling determination with each trial.

Find Over The Wall here: https://books2read.com/u/4jYVWj

COMING SOON!

V IS FOR VIGNETTES & VERSES embodies the journey that we can all relate to in some way or another. The journey of becoming.

Delve into a collection of adventures of self-discovery and reflection. While this collection is fictional, much of it is based on the author's personal experiences over a decade of their lives. It represents a time of change, of travel and of new experiences. Each piece is a genre of their own. The stories and microfiction range from historical, to speculative, to political and beyond. There's a time in your life where you must observe, reflect, and finally decide on your own moral compass.

Don't miss out!

Sign up for monthly newsletters and receive free stories and first chapters of Claire's upcoming new releases!

https://claireoconnorauthor.com/contact/